Another Life

Daniel S. Christensen

Minneapolis, MN

Join Our Community

.

For updates on new material, please:

'Like' on Facebook:
www.facebook.com/StudioRemarkable

or

Subscribe to the RSS feed:
www.studioremarkable.com

or

Follow on Twitter:
www.twitter.com/studioremark

Another Life

Prologue:
The Turning Point

♣

It all started because of a near-accident.

At least that was how Chris would remember things. His parents, Richard and Morgan, along with their business partner Ben, had been working on the machine for nearly a decade. Even longer if one considered their time together as graduate students, when the machine was still a vague idea in each of their minds.

Chris's mother Morgan had fallen in love with his father Richard during those heady days while they worked on their doctoral degrees. She still had the same exotic beauty that had caught his eye, but it was her quirky personality that made him fall in love with her. That was what made the relationship last. To be sure, Richard always had his distractions, but Morgan had made a certain art out of snagging some of his attention for herself.

Richard, tall and handsome, made his work his life and his life his work. As much as Morgan might have convinced herself that she had changed – or perhaps 'domesticated' - him over the past decade, that was not entirely correct. Someone as smart as Richard led a complicated life.

Ben, with spiky hair and only a fraction of Richard's polish, worked feverishly at the machine's main control panel. He monitored power levels and adjusted settings as need be. Even though he was conceivably Richard's intellectual equal, Ben had always seemed to be a follower. He had come to the United States as an exchange student, worked hard and won scholarships to the best universities. Like Richard, he had been a star graduate student.

At times, Morgan thought that Ben may have had a crush on her. If that had been the case, then he never showed it in overt ways. They had been colleagues, but never overly close, even after ten years of working together.

It had seemed natural that Richard and Ben would end up as partners, as they complimented one another so well. Neither might have taken the time to understand why, but they needed one another. Richard understood much of the technical side of the project, but also saw things that Ben simply could not. He was the real visionary running their venture. Ben was more the technician, less an idea man and certainly not a businessman. His strength was in the fact that he could grind through the sweat work of the project like no one else.

There had always been a certain potential for jealousy between the pair, but it never seemed to reach the point of being a problem.

As they continued preparations to test their creation, Morgan walked over to Richard and whispered into his ear.

"I can't believe we're about to do this," she said.

"We'll make it count." Richard said.

Ben performed the machine's initial power-up sequence and yelled over the machine's hum to Richard.

"Power-up complete," he said.

The machine's existence was largely a secret. Unfortunately, since it had not come close to working yet, their project had not drawn much more than modest defense department funding.

In theory, the machine could be used to display the image of any location that the machine's user 'focused on.' The machine had two key parts - a helmet that the controller wore and a doorway-sized viewing chamber that showed the desired images. The user experience was similar to watching a scene from a security camera that only existed within the operator's mind.

The control helmet looked like a modified motorcycle helmet. It was not going to win any fashion awards, but it served its purpose.

The machine, via the helmet, used the controller's thoughts as a means of direction. It was limited to showing locations where the controller had physically been in the past, so it could not simply display any random location. Rather, it needed the starting point of the controller's familiarity with a location. One could think of it as a 'psychic GPS.' Once focused, the machine could show what was occurring at a given location in real time.

The viewing chamber looked like an open door frame. It displayed its point-of-view-style images using a built-in holographic projector. The result was that the viewing chamber could generate imagery that looked as realistic as possible.

There was one significant problem though: the machine didn't work. At least not yet. At the time of its first trial, it had still not shown any actual remote images. Of course, there had been glimmers of hope and enough progress to justify continued funding from deep-pocketed United States military budgets. Richard and Morgan had never liked the idea of working for the military, but it seemed a necessary compromise in the name of advancing their science.

Unfortunately, pressure had mounted on Richard, Ben, and Morgan to show results. That pressure meant that the trial that they were embarking upon necessitated taking risks. Morgan looked on with concern as Richard stepped onto the machine's user platform. She walked over to give Richard one last kiss before they began the test.

"It will be okay. Trust me." Richard reassured her.

Morgan nodded, knowing, and said. "You're always so cocky."

"I'm just confident," Richard said with a wink.

Morgan leaned in to kiss Richard. "Love you."

Richard mouthed back "Love you more." His voice was drowned out by the rising hum of the machine. It continued into the next stage of its power-up sequence.

Richard put on the control helmet and began thinking about the location that the machine would use for focusing. Actually operating the machine ended up being somewhat akin to flying a plane as it approached the sound barrier. Certain barriers of resistance seemed insurmountable at first. The 'pilot' wearing the helmet had to be careful to prevent their mind from crumbling.

Morgan walked over to the control panel and stood over Ben. "Re-check the power levels. We don't want anything to go wrong."

"I've got it," Ben calmly replied. "He'll be fine."

"We'll do it this time." Morgan said.

Ben smiled back at her.

The viewing screen flickered as Richard concentrated intently. Images nearly formed out of the holographic ether, but then vaporized. A strain crept onto Richard's face. Morgan noticed it, causing her nervous excitement to shift to concern.

"He's losing it." Morgan yelled to Ben.

Ben was calm, focused.

"Give him another second," he said.

Richard dropped to one knee on the platform and shouted out in pain. Morgan started over to help him, but Richard motioned her away and stood back up. He was still in control.

"Take it up!" Richard shouted.

Ben looked perplexed at the control panel. Richard continued straining. The energy threshold from the machine pounded in on his head. He couldn't understand their delay.

"Power it up!" Richard shouted, even louder.

For the first time, Ben looked scared. Morgan yelled to him. "Don't just sit there Ben!"

Ben was frozen though. What Richard was asking for didn't make any sense. Ben knew that it was madness to increase the machine's power output to an even higher level. Given that Richard was overwhelmed, his request made even less sense.

Fed up with Ben's hesitations, Morgan returned to the control panel and used a series of keystrokes to increase the power output herself. Richard again screamed out in pain.

"He'll kill himself!" Ben pleaded.

Morgan stood, terrified, no longer sure how to proceed. She wondered if she could immediately stop the test or if doing so would only cause more harm. Part of her wanted to trust that Richard knew something that she or Ben didn't.

Images of a home began to appear inside the viewing chamber. They were crude and garbled by static interference, but the images were more stable than before. They didn't disappear. The machine was working.

Satisfied, Richard finally backed off, allowing the images to fade.

"Power down!" he yelled.

As the machine's power-down sequence began, an exhausted Richard again fell to his knees. This time, he pulled off the helmet and looked excitedly into Morgan's eyes.

"I could feel it," Richard said. "It was like a wall in my mind. Instead of backing away, I just needed a boost to get over it."

Richard shouted over to Ben, who was still seated at the control panel. "We did it! We broke through!"

Rather than appearing to be a man who was happy, Ben seemed changed in that instant. They'd broken through all right. The project was about to take another step forward, but it had been in spite of him, not because of it.

Feelings of jealousy that had been kept in check for so long had finally found a way into Ben's heart.

1:
Everyone Hates Chris

Day 1 {7:30am}

♣

It was six years before another day as significant as that of the near-accident. Yes, there were many notable days in-between, but none quite as remarkable as the one that unfolded on this day.

Chris was sixteen and immature, even for that age. He was lanky and always looked a bit ruffled, having never paid much attention to the details of his appearance. He could have been good-looking if he'd tried, but his mind was on other things. His primary motivation had become that of proving himself to his family.

To that end, Chris spent time at his parent's lab whenever he could convince his father to allow him. This was surprisingly frequent, despite the fact that Morgan would be furious if she ever knew that Chris was there.

Over those six years since the project's turning point, Richard and Benjamin had assumed most of the project work. Morgan never again felt comfortable in the lab. Given their breakthrough, the project was generously funded to continue, but it continued without Morgan.

Morgan had grown concerned that working on the project entailed certain inherent risks. If a real accident were to occur, one less fortuitous, then Chris would find himself an orphan. As such, Morgan wanted to stay at home, where she still tinkered on her own projects and fretted about Chris. Richard ultimately agreed to her plan.

As such, Morgan's priorities shifted and the dynamics between the original trio's members shifted. Where they once may have been cordial colleagues or even friends, Morgan and Ben's relationship had slowly acquired a disagreeable tension that surfaced whenever they were together. She wasn't entirely sure why, but after the near-accident, they grew apart.

Richard rarely felt any tension from Ben. He knew that mistakes and conflicts could happen even under the best of circumstances. Working together on a cutting-edge project only made their situation that much more complicated

Furthermore, Richard knew that he needed Ben, at least to some extent. The pair had managed to refine the machine into something that was on the cusp of being truly significant.

What Morgan did sense at some level, but what Richard did not sense at all, was the festering jealousy that had continued to grow within Ben.

Ben's happiness always seemed a step below where he wanted it to be. During the six years since their breakthrough, Ben should have felt as though he was on the verge of changing the world, but he didn't. Intentionally or not, Richard always seemed to steal the spotlight. Ben usually let it slide, but soon that spotlight was to become brighter than usual.

It was relatively early in the morning, but Richard and Ben were already hard at work in the lab. Chris held a camcorder in one hand and tracked with it around the lab's main work area.

"Chris," Richard said. "Stop goofing off with the camera. This is serious."

After a pause to think, Richard added. "Does your mother know that you're here?"

"She knows that I'm on my way to school." Chris replied, dismissively.

"For your sake," Richard said. "I'll hope that's a 'yes.'"

Despite Morgan's disapproval, Richard appreciated that Chris took an interest in his work, but Chris could sometimes be a distraction.

"I thought that I could help you practice the presentation." Chris said.

"We still have prep to do." Richard pointed out, giving Chris only half of his attention.

Chris swung the video camera's lens around and focused it on himself. "Welcome to today's episode of 'Science for laymen, er, lame-men.'"

Richard tried to cut him off, with a simple. "Chris."

"This is Christopher Jennings speaking to you today from the world famous lab of Richard Jennings…"

Behind Chris, Ben dropped a couple of metal tools onto the floor. They made a surprisingly loud noise.

"…and, uh, Ben," Chris continued.

Richard interrupted again. "I don't know if we're that famous."

Chris turned the camera on Richard. "Is this a spy project that you're working on?"

Richard sighed and turned to the camera with a serious expression on his face. He stood up straight and began going through a sort of mock presentation. It was clear that he'd been practicing and that this wasn't the first time he'd run through the routine. He first pointed to the machine's viewing chamber.

"It's not quite anything that exciting, at least not yet," Richard explained. "We've been funded for a number of years now by the Homeland Security department."

Chris continued to interview Richard from off camera.

"So," he said. "This is where all the taxpayer dollars have gone?"

Richard sighed and said. "This project has been ongoing for over fifteen years now, with incremental breakthroughs along the way."

Chris already seemed bored.

"Dad we need to liven this up a little," he suggested. "Can't you just demonstrate it and save the rest?"

"We're dealing with the government Chris. If you want to work on a project like this someday, you'll need to understand how things work, both inside the lab and outside. We have a constantly changing group of military liaisons to keep up to speed while also keeping them happy."

"It sounds boring," Chris snorted. "Why don't you just jump right into showing it to them? You can give them a history lesson later."

Richard didn't know how to reply. He loved Chris, but the two didn't always seem to 'click.' When Richard spent time with Chris, he wanted to instruct him in the 'right' way of doing things, but somehow Chris already seemed to have developed a mind of his own.

"Do we really need the boy here right now Richard?" Ben said with more than a hint of annoyance.

Ben appeared ready to get to their next order of business. Richard looked at Chris.

"Turn off the camera," Richard said. He then turned to Ben. "I said that he could watch the test."

"Is that necessary?" Ben asked, getting upset.

"He'll be leaving in a few minutes anyway," Richard said, before adding quietly to Chris. "Stand in the back, so that your mother doesn't see you around here. She'd kill us both."

Richard picked up the control helmet and put it over his head. It was now much more elegant looking than the version from several years before.

"I'm ready Ben," Richard said while getting into position near the viewing chamber. "Let's go."

As Ben powered up the machine, the process was much smoother than in the past. The humming that the machine generated was not nearly as loud anymore. The process itself had become routine.

"80% power Richard." Ben said calmly. He'd performed the task often enough that what should be mind-blowing results had become second nature.

Holographic energy from inside the viewing chamber crackled and lit up the space. The empty air was soon filled with an image. The projection still contained glitches, but it was much clearer than it had been years before. It might have still been a bit unfocused and still contained some static, but the images displayed in the viewing chamber were clear enough to tell what was occurring in them.

"I'm heading in." Richard said as he guided his way through what seemed to be a lifeless house.

He was confused, as he wasn't seeing what he'd expected.

"Ben!" Richard shouted. "Where's Morgan?"

Ben replied, almost sarcastically. "I don't know Richard, she's your wife."

"I told her that we'd be testing now," Richard said, concerned. "It's 7:30."

"Maybe it's lagging again!" Chris yelled over.

Both Ben and Richard turned to Chris. Ben had a disdainful look on his face. Both men had been thinking about the problem, but Chris had chosen the unfortunate role of voicing their concerns.

Richard yelled to Ben. "Are you testing at the higher power levels again?"

"Just a little," Ben said. "We have to work out this glitch."

Richard was frustrated at Ben's revelation. He knew that something was not quite right with the machine. They'd been avoiding the problem and needed to get over the hump, but now wasn't the time to be troubleshooting it.

"Bring it down," Richard yelled.

"Fine," Ben grumbled while pressing on the buttons of the control panel.

The test was over for now, as Richard was already feeling tired from using the machine at above-normal power levels. Under Ben's instruction, the machine quickly powered down. When it eventually reached a point where it was safe, Richard broke the helmet's connection to himself by removing it from his head. The image in the viewing chamber blinked out.

Richard marched over to the control panel and entered a series of commands into it. Morgan's face appeared on a conventional display screen.

Richard smiled at her and said. "Hi honey."

Morgan's voice came over the display's speaker.

"You're late," she said.

"Are you sure?" Richard hedged.

"Yes," Morgan insisted. "I've been sitting here for fifteen minutes."

"It's the glitch again," Richard shook his head. "I thought we'd pinpointed the problem last week."

"Sorry to hear that," Morgan said before holding up an abnormally large vegetable. "Coming home for lunch?"

Chris suppressed a chuckle. His parents were weird. They were pleasant people, but they were weird.

"I don't know," Richard said. "We're running out of time before the presentation."

"Okay," Morgan said, getting ready to sign off. "Keep me posted."

Richard waved goodbye to his wife and ended the transmission. Ben continued snarling at the control panel in frustration. His temper seemed to get shorter by the second.

"Richard," Ben said. "It still isn't working. We can't maintain the image quality without things going haywire. There's some sort of lag or ghosting."

Richard nodded. "I know. We'll keep the power at normal levels until after the presentation and the image quality will be acceptable."

"It won't be acceptable. It'll be a disaster."

Chris interrupted. "It looked fine to me."

Ben snapped at Chris. "If I had wanted your advice, I would have asked for it Einstein."

Chris was taken aback by Ben's sharp tone, but he was also amused by it.

"Meow," he said in mock reply.

Ben turned back to Richard and continued. "At this point, acceptable isn't going to be good enough for long. You and I both know we're not the only ones under contract."

"We're well ahead of anyone else." Richard said with an edge of pride.

"That may be the case today," Ben countered, "But one breakthrough tomorrow by any of our rivals and we'll be behind without a plan to catch up."

"We already have phase two ready," Richard said.

Chris cut in, asking. "What's phase two?"

Ben ignored the question, instead responding to Richard. "If this doesn't work, that won't work either. Phase two relies on the viewing chamber working first and you know it."

The two men were on the verge of an argument. Richard actually appeared to be losing his calm.

Instead of erupting, the rising tempers were diffused when a buzzing noise filled the room. It was the lab's equivalent of a doorbell.

Ben pulled up the video from a hallway security monitor and turned to Chris. "Your girlfriend's here."

Chris shot back. "She's not my girlfriend."

Day 1 {7:45am}

♣

Chris pulled a large suitcase out from the lab building over to Rachel's waiting car. He then opened the car's rear passenger door and struggled to get the suitcase onto the back seat. It was heavy.

While Chris loaded the suitcase, Rachel sat in the driver's seat, looking back from time to time in wonderment at his exertions.

Rachel was Chris's age, with a tomboy streak. She was the literal girl next door who had grown up with Chris as her best friend. Of course, she'd long had a crush on him, something that seemed obvious to everyone except Chris.

Unlike most people in Chris's life, Rachel believed in him and understood him. She was also, quite possibly, the only person – aside from his parents – who could tolerate being around him.

After Chris had finally secured the suitcase, he shut the rear door and settled into the car's front passenger seat.

Rachel asked. "Bringing something for show-and-tell?"

"Yeah," Chris said, flatly. "It's my science project."

"It was just supposed to be a research paper."

"I know," Chris grinned. "I didn't feel like writing."

Rachel sighed. She'd been around Chris long enough to know that whatever was going to happen later during science class wasn't going to end well. Then again, she also knew that it was too late to stop him.

Chris pulled on his seat belt and began drinking an energy drink for breakfast. At the same time, Rachel shifted her car into gear and merged onto a boulevard nearby the lab.

"You're back on your health food kick?" Rachel observed with more than a bit of judgment in her voice.

"You're my mother now?" Chris responded

"If I were your mother, then I'd kill you for hanging out at the lab."

"Yeah, well, there's stuff going on."

"Like what?"

Chris stared out the window, only partially paying attention to their conversation.

"Some presentation," Chris said. "I don't know why Dad puts up with it."

"How else are they supposed to afford all that equipment?" Rachel responded.

"They could be making a fortune if they weren't working on a government contract. I'm sure that someone out there would fund them."

"Well," Rachel said, trying to sound supportive. "I guess you'll get your shot at that sooner than later."

"Yeah, I will," Chris turned back to Rachel, this time paying more attention. "I'm not going to waste my life working for some stooges in suits."

Rachel tried to turn the conversation in an upbeat direction. "Think that your Dad will let you help out at the lab this summer?"

"I doubt it," Chris said with a hint of disappointment. "If Mom doesn't stop it, Ben will. I can't stand that guy."

"I don't know how your Dad can either," Rachel admitted. "Your Mom always gives him the ice queen look."

Rachel turned her car around a corner. She had to slam a foot onto her brake to avoid crashing into a line of vehicles that had formed ahead of her. They'd arrived outside of the school parking lot and would have to wait their turn to enter it. Chris sat restlessly.

"We should have gotten here a few minutes earlier," Chris said. "I'm not going to have time to set up before class."

"And whose fault is that?" Rachel asked. She wasn't going to roll over and take the blame for his lack of preparedness.

"I wish I could have just driven myself in," Chris said, only making the situation worse.

Rachel was furious. She had made a special trip when she'd picked up Chris at the lab, yet her generosity hadn't seemed to matter to him.

"You could have," she said. "If you hadn't lost your license."

Chris slipped back into his own thoughts.

"That car idea would have worked," he said.

"Yeah," Rachel said. "And maybe you should have checked first to see if it was illegal to have a turbocharged blower thing or whatever it was in your car."

A loud car horn honked behind them, interrupting their conversation. Rachel checked her rear-view mirror to see who was behind them.

"Speaking of an ice queen," Rachel announced.

The car horn honked again. It was from a red sports car driven by Tyler, the school's sport's star. He had the classic sneer that everyone loved to hate, unless you were part of the popular clique that adored him. He was privileged and, while not dumb, spent most of his time in a weight room.

Seated next to Tyler was his girlfriend Jessica, the school beauty. She had long, dark hair and seemed more mature than Tyler. As such, she was disinterested in what appeared to be a typical temper tantrum coming from him.

A keep observer might have noticed that Jessica was the sort of person who was merely tolerating high school, rather than actively enjoying her popular status or star boyfriend.

In response to the horn honks, Rachel inched her car ahead. Chris perked up in his seat when he noticed that Jessica was sitting behind them.

"I don't understand what she sees in him." Rachel said dismissively.

"I know what he sees in her." Chris replied, trying to get a look at Jessica through his passenger side mirror.

"She's not interested in you," Rachel tried to discourage him. "You realize that, right?"

"Maybe not right now."

"Maybe never," Rachel said, clearly not a fan of Jessica. Rachel was already annoyed and Chris was only making it worse.

"Look at her," Chris remarked. "She looks bored."

Rachel observed, sarcastically. "And you're Mr. Excitement?"

Chris mocked acting offended. "I should have you know that if she knew me, I mean, actually knew me, then she wouldn't be wasting her time on him."

Rachel moved the car ahead again. "Uh-huh."

Tyler honked one more time. This time, he let it linger for several seconds.

"Where does the jerk think I can go?" Rachel said, losing her temper.

Chris reached into the back seat for his backpack. "Hang on, let me try something out."

"Try what?" Rachel was confused.

"Something I've been waiting to use. Never knew when it might come in handy."

Chris produced a small device that looked like a car's keyless entry remote. He pointed the device back at Tyler's car. An instant later, Tyler's car alarm went crazy.

"Universal remote," Chris said with a smirk.

Despite Tyler's attempts to disable it, his car alarm continued to go berserk. The loud noises and flashing caused other students to join in on the noisemaking. Honks were heard from the long line of cars behind Tyler. He struggled to get his car's alarm under control.

Jessica sat embarrassed, shaking her head in disgust. She got out of Tyler's car and walked toward the school on foot, leaving Tyler behind to deal with the chaos.

Rachel pulled her car forward as the line of vehicles ahead of them loosened up.

"My hero," Rachel said, smiling at Chris. He didn't notice or pay her any attention.

Instead, Chris watched as Jessica walked over a small hill and disappeared.

Day 1 {9:00am}

♣

Chris arrived at science class with his suitcase in tow, rolling it to the rear of the room. Once he found a place to work, he opened it up and began fiddling with the contents.

Two bookish looking girls, both seated nearby, took notice of Chris's actions.

One leaned over to the other and said. "Couldn't he get a date this weekend?"

"No," the other girl replied. "He needed to work on whatever that is instead."

"Showoff," the first girl said, shaking her head.

The teacher, Mr. Barns, read off mundane school announcements from the front of the classroom. He wore school athletic paraphernalia, a reminder to everyone that he was a coach, as well as a teacher. His enthusiasm jumped up when he reached the final announcement item.

"Don't forget about tomorrow's big pep rally," Barns said. He looked to Tyler, who was seated in the rear of the room, opposite where Chris was working. "We need everyone there cheering our guys on to state, right Tyler?"

"Coach," Tyler boasted. "Those boys over at Westby will be scared to face our softball girls after the beat-down we'll be putting on them,"

A couple of girls who were seated nearby Tyler, clearly softball players, bristled at the remark.

"Pig," one of the softball girls said.

Just the same, many of the kids in the room hollered out with their approval. Barns let them linger before waving them to quiet down.

"Save a little for tomorrow," Barns said.

Barns noticed Chris in the back of the room, still rummaging through his suitcase.

"Mr. Jennings," he said. "Do you have something that you'd like to share with the class?"

Chris stepped up and smiled theatrically.

"As a matter of fact," he said. "I do."

Chris reached down into the suitcase and tapped at a sort of remote control device. The torso of a crude robot sprang up.

Several teens in the classroom gasped. Everyone stood and gathered around Chris. He loved the spotlight.

"Can you say hello?" Chris asked the robot.

The robot replied in a female voice that featured a French accent. "Hello Christopher. I'm here for you."

Several of the teens giggled. The robot continued on, saying, "How may I serve you master?"

The laughter in the room escalated, and Chris wasn't sure what to do since the robot kept repeating the phrase over and over. Clearly, the robot was not functioning as Chris had programmed it to operate.

Chris wrestled with the robot's controls for a few seconds, before finally pulling out a wire to turn it off. The robot powered down with a strange whine. He smiled at his classmates and said. "It must be a bad transistor or something."

"Hey Jennings," Tyler catcalled from the other side of the room. "Maybe you should have taken your girlfriend out on a date instead of making one."

Rachel scowled at Tyler and Chris was still too flustered to come up with one of his usual retorts. As Chris was taking his seat, Barns stopped him.

"I'll need your paper Mr. Jennings."

Chris acted surprised.

"But I did this project instead," he insisted. "I spent more time on this than I would have a paper."

Barns pushed back. "The assignment was for a research paper Mr. Jennings, not a project."

Chris sat down, dumbfounded. Barns disregarded him.

"And let's not forget that we have a test tomorrow. This will be worth nearly one-third of your final grade, so you'd best not brush it off. In fact, I'd hope that you've already been studying."

Rachel leaned over to Chris and whispered to him. "You had to do that, didn't you?"

Chris shuffled through some notes, ignoring her.

Rachel continued. "I have some other stuff to work on tonight, so I was hoping we could study for the test a little later."

Chris brushed off her request. "I'm busy later."

"Why?" Rachel said angrily, before thinking. "What are you up to?"

2:
Seeing The Unexpected

Day 1 {7:00pm}

♣

The sun was setting as Chris walked up to the lab entrance. The lab, located in an office park suite separate from other buildings, sat amid dead silence. Chris had walked over to it from his home and, at this hour, the parking lot appeared empty for the day. When Chris reached the lab's front door, he entered a series of key pad entries. A thumbprint scanner glowed. Chris pressed his finger onto the scanner to provide identification. After a moment, his identity was confirmed and the building's door opened to allow him inside.

Chris walked down the lab's entry hallway and into the lab's main working area. As he walked, he wondered if his father was aware that he'd created his own lab access account. Chris assumed that Richard was smart enough to know. Maybe Richard was impressed by Chris's rogue initiative? Perhaps Ben noticed too and objected, but Richard had defended him? It was hard to say, but Chris enjoyed the fantasy.

Regardless, Chris strode down the entry hallway and was inside the lab itself a few seconds later. The machine stood silent in the middle of the room, its control panel and related electronic hardware taking up a majority of the room's space.

Chris walked around the lab with a purpose. After checking the viewing chamber, he flipped various switches back on the control panel and powered up the machine. It was obviously not the first time he'd been inside the lab alone.

As the hum from the machine increased, Chris grabbed the helmet. He couldn't operate the power controls while using the helmet, so he had to bring the power up first and then slide on the helmet apparatus. With his free hand, Chris pressed several buttons on the control panel. He stopped after pulling up a security camera's display. The parking lot outside remained empty, so Chris moved his focus back to monitoring the machine.

Operating the machine alone wasn't a particularly wise idea, since Chris had no assistant to monitor the control panel for problems. Nor did he have someone assisting him with raising and lowering the machine's always-dangerous power output.

Of course, Chris had little choice if he wanted to use the machine. No one who understood how the machine worked was going to help him.

After a few more seconds of powering up, the viewing chamber crackled to life. As it had during the earlier test, it was filled with raw energy. Everything appeared ready for Chris to begin.

Chris put the helmet onto his head and closed his eyes. The helmet might have been refined, but it was still bulky and cumbersome to wear. He seemed calm at first until he felt the bombarding waves of energy from the helmet. His eyelids flashed opened, and panic knifed through him.

Unlike Richard, Chris was not as effortless at controlling the machine. That was a matter of experience, and Chris had little experience 'piloting' the machine. Strain filled his face, but he seemed to work through it. Finally, the random energy inside the viewing chamber crackled into an image.

The images that appeared were just what Chris was hoping to see, and also confirmed that Chris was a bit of a peeping Tom.

Inside the viewing chamber was the image of Jessica's room, as seen through her window. The image, displayed in a first-person perspective, grew larger as Chris navigated the landscape in his mind. Through the window into her room, a figure that appeared to be Jessica was seen arguing with someone who he assumed to be Tyler.

Neither the quality of the picture nor the sound helped matters. The audio from their location was patchy and the image kept getting invaded by waves of static pixels.

All that Chris could understand was a male voice telling Jessica. "I can't be getting distracted before the game."

Chris kept thinking that something wasn't working right. He went to the control panel to lower the power level and the image on the screen disappeared. He knew that he needed to fix something, but he wasn't entirely sure what to do next. Then he remembered that early that morning, Ben had been adjusting the power levels. He thought that perhaps he'd simply not selected a high enough level of power output.

Chris pressed a few buttons on the control panel and the machine's hum grew slightly louder. He powered it up higher this time. Putting the helmet back on, he went through the same routine as before, concentrating until an image appeared inside the viewing chamber.

This time, Jessica's room looked slightly different. Things didn't exactly match what Chris had just seen. Items in her room were not in the same location and Jessica appeared to have changed clothes.

Chris didn't immediately notice those discrepancies though. Rather, he was distracted by what appeared to be Jessica kissing Tyler. Only, the guy holding Jessica in his arms didn't look like Tyler and his hairstyle was entirely different. Chris peered in closer, just as Jessica pulled back from the kiss.

"I'm so lucky to be with you Chris," she said.

Chris was taken aback by her words, at first unsure that he'd heard her correctly.

Before Chris could observe anything more, a security alarm sounded inside the lab. It was so loud that it even overpowered the machine's hum. Chris began powering down the machine and quickly put the helmet back into its holder.

Chris went over the machine's control panel, where he then turned off the security alarm. He pulled up the view from an exterior security camera on one of the control panel's monitors. To his horror, he noticed Ben walking toward the office entrance with a food container in hand.

Chris rushed to finish powering down the machine. Its hum fell sharply to nothingness. Chris knew that he only had seconds before Ben would be inside. It was time for him to plot an escape.

Ben made his way through the building's front doorway and down the hallway that led up to the lab. By this time, Chris had hidden in a crouched position right next to the lab's main entry door.

The lab door opened and Ben strode through it. He didn't notice Chris slip out behind him, bolting through the still-open lab doors. The doors closed an instant after Chris had cleared them and Ben only paid tacit attention to noise that he thought he might have heard inside the hallway.

Ben walked over to the control panel and placed his dinner on a counter. After no more than a few seconds of sorting through his meal, he pulled up the same security camera image that Chris had looked at earlier. It showed a large, black luxury sedan pulling into the parking lot. Ben didn't appear overly surprised by the visitor and left his food to go greet them.

After arriving outside, Ben noticed that the driver of the parked car had opened his window. Ben walked over to speak to him. The man behind the wheel was a slick-talker named Jai Lei. Rather than exchanging pleasantries, Ben made clear that he was annoyed by Jai's sudden presence.

"I didn't think you were coming," Ben said. "You're late. I went and got my own dinner"

Jai tried to keep a positive demeanor between the men.

"Sorry friend" he carefully replied. "I do apologize Ben. I suppose I am late. I had some opportunities pop up."

Ben wasn't impressed with his excuse.

"Same old Jai, is it?" Ben wondered. "Always hustling? Trying to find the best new angle?"

"Actually," Jai replied. "This opportunity is one that might interest you."

Ben seemed skeptical.

"Is that what this is about," he asked. "A job offer?"

"Maybe," Jai motioned Ben over to the car's passenger seat. "Let's find somewhere to talk."

Day 1 {7:30pm}

♣

Jai and Ben were seated at a wobbly table inside an Asian restaurant. It was the sort of place that one might have been hesitant to eat at based on the outward appearance, but surprised by the delicious authentic cuisine.

Jai started the conversation, while Ben picked at a plate of sesame chicken.

"Maybe you could fill me in a little about what you and Richard are working on?" Jai asked.

"There's not much to say," Ben said, coyly.

"How's his wife doing?" Jai pressed. 'What was her name again? Monique?"

"Morgan," Ben said, doing little to hide his disgust. "She hates me."

"Why's that?"

"It's nothing."

"It doesn't sound like 'nothing.'"

Ben was quiet. The tone of the conversation had thrown him off. This probing wasn't how he'd expected the meeting with Jai to start. He was often nosey when they got together, but not usually so pushy.

"I thought that we were just going to catch up?" Ben said.

"That's what we're doing Ben," Jai laughed. "I haven't seen either Richard or Morgan since engineering school. If you and I didn't get together from time to time, I wouldn't know what anyone was up to. It's a pleasure to check in on what you and Richard have been up to since we left the university."

"I can't really talk about it," Ben said, truthfully. "Maybe if there were non-disclosure agreements."

"Come on Ben," Jai insisted. "High profile guys like you and Richard can't exactly hide. I hear things. You're not the only guys working on remote viewing you know."

Ben paused. Jai was right. Ben's project with Richard wasn't entirely a secret. There were rumors amongst some of their peers. People had a way of piecing things together. Ben himself had hinted at the nature of the work in the past when he and Jai had gotten together.

"Things are going okay," he admitted. "We're ahead of the rest of them."

Jai smiled. "Good, I'd have expected nothing less from you two. But, are you going to stay ahead?"

Ben's face betrayed his concern. It was subtle, but it was enough that Jai took note.

"We'll be fine," Ben said, wondering what Jai might be up to. He decided to switch topics. "What have you been working on that's so important?"

Jai continued to flash a smile that seemed to be permanently affixed to his face.

"Me?" Jai asked. "Oh, I've been working for the government. The 'old' government, I mean, and some unusual investors. In fact, I'm a celebrity back home."

"Really?" Ben replied.

Jai knew that he had Ben curious, but he didn't elaborate. Instead, he switched back to his earlier line of questioning.

"You have a presentation coming up next week?" Jai pressed.

"How do you know about that?" Ben shot back, clearly surprised.

Jai didn't bother explaining. "When they visit, are they treating you like Richard's partner or one of the hired help?"

Ben was both suspicious and insulted by the inference.

"Jai," he said. "This has been an odd conversation. You can't be digging around like this or I'll have to report it. We're under the watch of the U.S. government."

"Oh, I know." Jai replied, not seeming to care. "It's not a particularly close watch, so don't worry. I wish that I could flatter you more, but they aren't convinced that any of the remote viewing projects – either yours or those from the other groups - will pan out. It's too much science fiction right now."

Ben looked annoyed and said nothing further. Of course, everything that Jai had said was true. Ben knew it. In many ways, Ben and Richard were an afterthought, a hedge. Two geniuses working in obscurity, their budget a relatively meager amount.

"That is," Jai continued. "Unless you've had a breakthrough that we don't know about?"

Ben's pride was hurt enough by this point that he didn't realize that he was playing right into Jai's probing hand.

"I think that they might be surprised." Ben said, quickly catching himself after he spoke.

"Oh really?" Jai mused, sensing that Ben suddenly wanted to retreat. "And, despite that, are Richard and Morgan still taking you for granted?"

Before Ben could answer, Jai's cell phone rang. He reached for it, looked at the number and turned to Ben. "I need to get going."

Jai stood to depart. He wanted to leave Ben with something to consider.

"Call me if you decide you want to work for someone who really appreciates your abilities," Jai said. "There are other options for a better life."

Day 1 {7:30pm}

♣

Chris came home and nearly tripped over his suitcase after walking inside his room. He'd dropped it off there after school and still needed to unpack the robot inside.

It took a few minutes for him to get the robot torso reassembled atop a chair next to his desk. As he turned on its power, he grabbed for a screwdriver and wrench to fiddle with its circuits again.

A screechy voice cried out from it this time. "Chris. Chris."

Chris jumped back, surprised. He caught himself. The voice hadn't come from the robot. Instead, it was from his pet parakeet, Tiny.

Tiny had been Chris's roommate for a number of years and lived in a cage next to his desk. The bird didn't get nearly the attention that it used to, so it constantly reminded Chris of that fact.

"Chris. Chris," Tiny kept repeating until Chris gave him a pinch of bird seed. After it had gobbled the seed down, the bird appeared to be momentarily content.

Chris sat his tools on the floor and went to a corner of his room where he allowed himself to fall into a lounge chair. He looked defeated and, in many ways, this was the real Chris.

Despite his bluster, Chris knew that things weren't working out nearly as well as he'd hoped. His ideas to impress his classmates, to get Jessica's attention, or to get his father to notice him all seemed to fall short.

"Chris, I need a hand down here."

It was Morgan's voice, floating through the open window behind Chris's head.

There would be no time for self-pity. At least not this evening.

"Just a minute!" Chris yelled down in reply.

Chris headed outside. In his mind, he was still unable to shake what he thought he'd heard Jessica say through the viewing chamber in the lab. How could she be glad to be with him? How could that have been what she'd said?

Surely, Chris thought, she couldn't have meant his name. She must have been talking about Tyler. Yet, he couldn't entirely ignore what he thought he'd heard. At least, he didn't want to ignore it.

As soon as Chris appeared outside, Morgan waved him over to a small greenhouse that she had in the backyard. The greenhouse was full of odd creations. These were some of the things that she'd worked on in lieu of her time at the lab. It was obvious that Morgan was not the typical homemaker.

In one corner of the greenhouse were giant watermelons, while in another corner sat large pea pods. Morgan had spent the past several years learning to cross-breed different plants. They were the fruits of her labor, as she liked to state as a bad joke.

Somewhere in her ambitions, Morgan thought that she could feed the hungry of the world. However, like many of her ideas, this one seemed to be working out better in theory than in practice.

Chris watched Morgan weed around one of the giant pea plants. When she looked up at him, he was immediately worried that Morgan hadn't actually asked him down for help. It was a setup.

"Anything you want to tell me about this morning?"

Chris hedged. "My robot wasn't working right in class."

"Anything else?"

Chris knew that he was busted.

"You know that I want to help out," he said, defensively. "I want to do something."

"It didn't take too long for me to get suspicious after I noticed Rachel leaving for school without you," Morgan said. "Your father told me that you were at the lab with him this morning."

Chris grimaced. He thought he'd covered his bases, but obviously he'd left open a hole or two. He knew that the lecture was coming next.

"I worry about you, you know," Morgan began. "You and your father are the most important people in my life. I don't want something to happen to you."

"Things are fine Mom," Chris said. "Nothing is going to happen. It isn't the same as it was years ago. The kinks with the machine are worked out now."

Morgan knew that her son was being naive, but she wasn't entirely sure how to convince him of that fact.

"Chris," she said, trying a different tactic. "You'll have plenty of time to spend in a lab. The whole rest of your life. You've only got a couple of years left in school before you'll start college. That'll fly by too."

Morgan paused. The gravity of the words hit her as they came out of her mouth. Until that instant, she'd not reflected on how fast Chris had been growing up.

Given Chris's frustrations earlier in the day, her talk of patience wasn't what he wanted to hear.

"I don't need to spend my time hanging out with those losers," he insisted. "The most important thing to them right now is the next big game."

Morgan sympathized, but felt as though Chris was missing the point.

"Your father and I both know that you're special," she said. "But we wanted you to be a kid for a while."

"I wish that it was more fun."

Morgan wasn't utterly clueless about her son's life. She was only idealistic to a point.

"After things are done with the presentation and your father is less busy," she said. "Maybe we could talk about some ways to get you more involved."

"Really?" Chris said, clearly surprised at the suggestion.

"I don't mean hanging out at the lab Chris. I mean spending time going over concepts with you. The building blocks."

Chris was dashed a little, but he knew that it was a battle he wouldn't win all at once.

"Fine," Chris said. "But you and Dad need to know what I'm capable of."

"We do Chris."

"I don't think so," Chris said. "Then why does Dad always want to spend his time working with Ben? That guy's a clown Mom."

Morgan had heard his complaints before and, deep down, she didn't necessarily disagree.

She took the high road though and said. "Was Ben acting his usual angry self this morning?"

Chris nodded in confirmation and added. "I just don't understand why Dad keeps working with him."

"I've told you before that it's your father's decision. Ben is a brilliant man and that's not something to question. Your father seems to think that he needs him, at least for now. Maybe things will change in the future, if more funding gets approved."

"I hope so," Chris said.

"Be glad that neither of us has to work with him," Morgan suggested.

"He gives me the creeps."

"Just between you and me," Morgan confided, "me too."

"I just don't get how you guys all could stand working together for so long."

"He wasn't always like he is now," Morgan confessed. "It's only been in the past few years that Ben has been hard to be around."

"Whatever," Chris scoffed. "I don't remember Ben being all that nice when I was a kid."

"He wasn't that bad back when we were all in grad school," Morgan trailed off, remembering what seemed like a long time ago. "He was actually pleasant to be around. Social, funny."

"He always seemed a little distant to me," Chris said.

"He was a likeable guy when I first met him, but that light inside him somehow went out. I even used to think he had a bit of a crush on me, but I didn't pay it much attention."

Chris was horrified at the thought. "Geez Mom, thanks. Now I have one more reason to hate him."

"Well, it was nothing," said Morgan, reassuring him. "Your father was always the only one for me."

"Did you really need me to help with anything?" Chris said, turning to leave the greenhouse. "I've got to get going, big test tomorrow."

Morgan smiled and shook her head. "I just wanted to talk."

Before Chris left, Morgan seemed to remember something and rummaged through several of the large plants. After a moment, she found what she had in mind

"Try this," Morgan said as she held up a large strawberry. It was the size of a grapefruit. Chris looked skeptical.

"You worry about me being safe at the lab," Chris said, motioning to the produce growing around them. "But you don't worry about us eating all this stuff?"

"Just try it, it'll be fine," Morgan paused. "Not like last time."

"Yeah," Chris said, remembering. "Not like last time."

"Bring them over with you to Rachel's." Morgan suggested with a mischievous look on her face. "She said that you two were studying together later."

"When were you talking to her?" Chris asked, as he reluctantly took the fruit.

"Rachel came by looking for you," Morgan said, staring skeptically at Chris. "She said that's why you were late getting home, that you needed a book. I trust that you found what you needed?"

Chris looked guilty but said. "Yes." He knew that he'd have to thank Rachel for covering while he was at the lab.

Chris tried to leave before Morgan could question him further, but she made one more remark.

"I like her Chris," she said, ignoring the groan from Chris that followed. "Your father likes her too."

Rachel was startled by a knock at her door. She peered over to discover Chris poking his head inside.

"Hey loser," she said. "We should have been studying two hours ago."

She then looked at Chris quizzically as he carried a giant strawberry into her room. He put the strawberry down on a corner of her desk.

"Don't let it ruin your dinner," Chris said.

Rachel wasn't impressed. "Your Mom tried to give me one earlier."

"Hey, thanks for covering for me."

"What else are friends for?" Rachel said with a hint of frustration. "Maybe next time you'll keep your commitments."

"Maybe," Chris said, without a hint of apology.

"So what happened down there?" Rachel asked. "You got caught?"

"No," Chris said, "Ben came back though. I don't know what he's doing working late. I powered down the machine and snuck out. It was weird."

"You should have assumed he might be there. I thought that he and your Dad had a presentation or something coming up?"

"They do," Chris said, thinking back. "But someone else pulled in right as I was leaving."

"Your Dad?"

"No," Chris said. "It was a flashy car. I don't know who it was.

Chris hesitated before telling Rachel what was actually on his mind.

"When I was using the machine," he said. "I saw something really weird."

"What? Like a monster?" Rachel dug at him. "Jessica without her make-up on?"

"I saw Jessica kissing someone."

"Yeah, Tyler. And it serves you right."

"No, there was something weird going on." Chris said. "It was like it was me with her."

Rachel laughed at Chris. This seemed like a new pathetic low for him.

"Uh-huh," she said sarcastically. "It sounds to me like delusional wishful thinking, Chris."

"I know it doesn't really make sense," Chris said, knowing that she didn't believe him. "I'm just telling you what I thought I saw."

Rachel was frustrated that Chris insisted on dragging out what seemed to be a fantasy about Jessica. She hated to see Chris wasting his time pining for someone whom Rachel thought was a stuck-up witch. Unfortunately, now he seemed to have actually convinced himself that he had a chance with Jessica.

"Just forget about it. It's crazy enough that something like that viewer even kind of works." Rachel said. "Part of me hopes your Dad keeps having problems with it, because we don't need that in the world."

"Why would you say that?" Chris said, annoyed by her discouragement. "You want my Dad to lose the lab?"

"No," Rachel tried to backpedal, realizing she'd gone too far. "But do you really want the government to be able to leer in on anyone at any time?"

Chris grew uncomfortable with her implication. He finally said. "You're not supposed to be telling anyone that you know."

Rachel knew that she was getting herself in trouble. Chris was never supposed to tell her anything about the project. It was a bad enough security breach that Chris knew about the project.

It made Rachel feel special that he'd shared the secret with her, even if it had likely been more about him bragging than anything. It still showed a certain level of trust in her.

"I know," she said. "Calm down. I didn't mean anything. What are you planning on doing?"

"I have to go back down there," Chris said as though his reasoning was plainly obvious.

"What?" Rachel exclaimed in disbelief. "What if Ben is still there?"

"Then I'll wait," Chris said, his excitement bubbling over. "I need to check things out again though. I'm telling you, I saw something."

"What about our test?" Rachel said.

Chris sighed. "You know that I could pass it half-asleep."

"What about me then?" Rachel asked, looking into Chris's eyes for something. "You said we'd study together."

"I'll be back in an hour or so."

Rachel shook her head, not believing him. "Promise?"

"Promise."

Chris left Rachel's room as abruptly as he'd entered it. She knew that she should study on her own, but she became distracted thinking about Chris's overzealous behavior and some of the bizarre things he had shared with her while he had been there.

To get her mind onto something else, Rachel examined the giant strawberry that was still sitting on her desk. It had been next to a hot desk lamp and started to make a deflating noise, falling flat into a little pile onto itself. Rachel jerked back, half-scared of it.

A second later, the deflated strawberry made a strange noise that sounded almost like a burp.

Gas inside it had built up, causing an explosion. Pieces of the strawberry flew all over Rachel's room, leaving red streaks and smears down the walls. Strawberry residue also clung to the furniture.

Rachel sat silently with bits of strawberry stuck to her face, smudging her glasses. She sat silently, wondering how the day could get any worse.

Day 1 {9:00pm}

♣

It was dark outside by the time Chris snuck across the lab's parking lot. Neither Ben's car nor Jai's luxury sedan was parked in the lot. Chris went through the same routine at the front door as before, getting himself past the security checks and into the lab itself.

When Chris flipped on the lab's lights, he felt an eerie still inside.

That tension wasn't the only thing on Chris's mind. He felt some guilt about again disobeying his mother's wishes. Rachel seemed to be mad at him too. He'd promised Rachel that he would study with her and he was going to try to get back in time to do that.

First though, Chris needed to find out what was going on with the machine. Perhaps there was actually something wrong with it? Maybe he could catch a glitch and impress his father. He reasoned that Richard might take notice of his finding and want him to help on other things.

Yet, as Chris prepped the machine, his main motive remained wanting to know if he had actually heard what he thought he'd heard. He had replayed the moment over and over in his mind, only growing more certain than ever that he hadn't made it all up. He was more certain than ever that Jessica had been talking about him in the image and he wanted to know why.

After Chris pulled the control helmet onto his head, he increased the machine's power up to similar levels as before.

At first, the strain of having the power output at such a level was almost too much to bear. Chris kept feeling as though his mind was butting up against a wall. Finally, he was able to focus enough that he seemed to climb over that barrier in his mind. As he did, the viewing chamber came to life with a clear image.

Like before, the machine's viewing chamber showed an almost three-dimensional scene outside of Jessica's bedroom window. Chris was disappointed to see that she was seated alone at her desk. There was no one else inside the room at that late hour. Tyler, or whomever Chris had seen earlier, had since left.

Chris didn't want to stop for the evening just yet. He took a few moments to look around inside Jessica's room. He had never actually been inside it, of course, but he'd ridden by her home on his bike. While passing, he'd usually hoped to catch a glimpse of her. Now he'd been granted that wish and more.

Given the decorations in Jessica's room and the condition of the outside of her home, Chris knew that Jessica didn't come from a wealthy family. Her parents had a working class background that she tried to hide, but there wasn't much that she could hide about where she lived.

While Jessica envied the material things that cluttered the rooms of some of her friends, she got by with her modest possessions. Jessica knew that it was her natural beauty and not the ordinary clothes that she wore that made her stand out to people. That realization didn't necessarily discourage her though. In fact, quite the opposite. She knew that she should take advantage of whatever she could use to get ahead in the world. She was more calculating and more of a strategist, than her peers suspected.

Chris noticed different posters hanging on Jessica's wall – all of teen heartthrobs of the moment, all living lives more spectacular than her own. He then turned his attention to Jessica herself as she typed away at an antiquated computer. The old machine fit in as a hand-me-down. It was functional, but nothing fancy – an assessment that fit most of Jessica's surroundings.

The telephone sitting on Jessica's desk rang. She was quick to answer it.

"Hi Chris," Jessica said with a smile. "I miss you."

Chris was stunned. With one statement, Jessica had instantly dismissed any lingering doubts regarding what he'd witnessed earlier. Chris's mind raced to explain how she was somehow talking to him on a telephone. He grew so excited that he actually lost his concentration and the viewing chamber's image vanished.

Suddenly cutting a mental connection with the machine was not a graceful way to deactivate it and Chris fell to the ground in pain. In his mind, it felt like he was tumbling down a hill and he had to concentrate hard to make it stop.

It took considerable effort, but Chris was able to regain control. As he reestablished his mental footing, he had to work his way back over the energy barriers that the machine had created in his mind. As he did so, the image in Jessica's room stabilized again inside the viewing chamber.

Jessica was still speaking with someone on her phone, "Maybe you could sneak over later?"

There was a pause while the person on the other end of the line replied.

"Chris," Jessica continued. "You know how my parents are. They just want to make sure I'm not letting my grades slide. They know how crazy I am about you."

The image in the viewing chamber flickered, but Chris was able to hold back his emotions this time. He still wasn't sure if what he was seeing was real, but he wanted it to be.

Chris looked right into Jessica's eyes, knowing that she couldn't see him. He wished as he'd never wished for anything before that he could be with her.

Inside the viewing chamber, the image showed Jessica looking confused.

"Hello?" Jessica asked into the phone, annoyed. "Chris?"

A moment later, Chris collapsed onto the lab floor. After a few seconds, the machine went into an automatic shutdown mode. As it cycled down, the humming from the machine decreased. The lab lights remained shining, illuminating Chris's motionless body.

3:
Switcheroo

Day 2 {7:00am}

☺ ↔ ☻

At first, Chris saw a blinding tube of light that formed a sort of tunnel that he felt like he was traveling down. Eventually that tunnel led into darkness.

When Chris woke up, it was morning. He found himself still in bed. He stirred, waking up calmly at first. As he recovered his senses, he panicked.

Chris looked around hurriedly, disoriented, until he realized that he was in his room.

Chris tried to get out of bed too quickly and stumbled onto the floor. He paused for a moment, feeling as though he might throw up. He managed to quell his churning stomach, but he felt awful and noticed that he was sweating profusely.

He rubbed his forehead while muttering to himself. "It was just a dream."

The morning light was still dim. Chris's room remained mostly dark. Out of habit, Chris tried to turn on his desk lamp, but couldn't find the switch. He felt around to no avail, finally giving up and flipping the room's main light switch on instead. After rubbing his eyes and letting his vision adjust, Chris surveyed his room.

It looked totally different. Almost every feature of the room had changed from the prior evening.

Shelves previously filled with books were now full of trophies and other sports memorabilia. Mementos from Chris's youth that were familiar were still scattered about on certain shelves and stands, but there was little of that on display anymore. Instead of geeky posters of science in-jokes, the walls featured framed shots of athletes in action.

"Is this some joke?" Chris said aloud in shock He looked around the room, wondering how someone could have so thoroughly pulled off such a prank while he was asleep.

Chris dug through his drawers, dismissing most of what he found as not belonging to him. He got annoyed, wondering where most of his stuff had gone. If a joke were being played on Chris, it didn't strike him as being particularly funny. Chris worried that some of his equipment might have been damaged while setting up the prank.

Looking around the room even further, Chris noticed that Tiny the parakeet was still there. After walking over to his cage, Chris tried to goad the parakeet. "Chris? Chris."

Nothing worked. Tiny just hovered in the back his cage and, more than anything, seemed afraid of Chris.

Chris tried to log into the computer on his desk, but his password didn't work. It became obvious to Chris whatever was happening was bigger than a simple prank.

As Chris walked around the room, he caught a reflection in his closet mirror and jumped back. He was surprised by his own reflection and went wide-eyed when he stepped back into the mirror. His body was slightly more muscular and certainly more toned.

"Whoa," Chris said, staring at himself. "I'm ripped."

Things like that didn't just happen overnight. The realization dawned on Chris that something must have gone wrong with the machine. He'd done something to his body and had short-term amnesia. Certainly he'd somehow gotten back to his room and then slept through the night, but he wasn't sure what had occurred that previous night.

Chris worried that his parents might notice that he'd suddenly gotten in shape overnight. They'd probably know that something had gone wrong. He'd be in more trouble than he'd ever been in his life. He wondered if he could reverse it or if he even needed to reverse it. He thought that he might be able to hide it.

His mind now racing, Chris still couldn't explain the apparent make-over prank that had been carried out in his room. It must have happened when he was at the lab. He'd come home and not noticed it. Yet, that seemed like an odd coincidence.

Surely, he thought to himself, his parents would have had to have been involved.

Chris looked at a clock and noticed that it was already 7:15am. He knew that Rachel would soon be in front of his house, waiting to give him a ride to school. He had to figure out a way to hide his appearance until later. If he had a little more time, perhaps he could figure out how to explain everything to his family.

Racing to get ready to leave, Chris opened his closet door and shook his head at what he found inside.

"What did they do with my clothes?" Chris asked himself.

There was nothing on the clothing racks that he recognized. Whoever had pulled the prank had been thorough.

Confused, Chris held up the stylish clothes that he found and, with few other options, selected a set to wear. As he put them on, he was surprised to find that the clothes actually fit his frame quite well.

"Not bad," Chris thought, "I finally caught one break this morning."

From the perch of his windows, Chris saw Rachel's car pull out of her driveway. She was leaving without him.

"Hey!" Chris shouted down to Rachel. "Wait!"

Chris ran downstairs, breezing through the quiet house. He didn't have time to notice any of the significant changes that he otherwise might have observed throughout the home's hallways.

Instead, Chris quickly slid on his shoes and ran outside. He was a few steps too late though. Rachel's car whizzed right past Chris's house. She didn't even bother to turn and look as she accelerated past Chris.

Confused and annoyed, Chris stood in the middle of the street, waving to Rachel. His efforts didn't matter though, since her car was already turning at a stop sign farther down the block.

"She's furious with me," Chris thought, remembering his promise to Rachel that they'd still study after he came back from the lab. Obviously, that hadn't happened. Instead, it would be one more thing for Chris to try to fix.

In the meantime, Chris needed to find a way to school. He ran down a mental checklist of options and came up short. If he called his parents, they'd be angry. Chris thought about walking to school, but then he'd be late.

Just as Chris's options seemed exhausted, he heard the school bus rumble around the corner. Figuring that it would be better than nothing, Chris flagged the bus down. The driver noticed him, slowed, and opened the door.

When Chris stepped onto the bus, he towered in the isle over the mostly-younger riders. All of the students on the crowded bus looked up from their seats in awe.

Chris immediately felt awkward – even the bus driver gave him a curious look. Finally, Chris quietly said, "Hi."

The students on the bus erupted in a cheer. Their reaction confused Chris, who simply waved and waited for them to calm down. Having rarely ever ridden the bus, he assumed that it was a joke that the kids on the bus did to everyone his age.

Chris ended up taking a seat near the middle of the bus, next to a heavy-set elementary schooler. The kid appeared overjoyed to have the empty spot next to him selected by Chris. In fact, the kid seemed too excited and nervous to speak.

Chris tried to make the best of the situation. He leaned in close to the kid and said, "You okay?"

The kid nearly exploded as he pushed himself to speak.

"Good luck with the game Chris!" he said.

Chris wondered if the kid had mistaken him for someone else. Considering the other things that Chris already had on his mind, he decided to let this latest confusing situation go. Chris nodded to the kid, smiled and turned his attention back to figuring out how to untangle whatever had happened at the lab.

Day 2 {7:00am}

♣

    While it was not immediately apparent to Chris, he was no longer in what we would refer to as 'the real world.' Rather, back in the real world, someone whom everyone thought was Chris had regained consciousness in the lab.

    He felt as though he was in a dream and was having a difficult time distinguishing what was reality. The lab's surroundings were unfamiliar to him, as it was a place he'd never visited before in his life. He remembered being in his room the prior evening, talking on the phone with Jessica and, beyond that, his memory was a blank. Chris thought about it more, recalling that his head had suddenly ached and that he'd ended up falling asleep. Since he'd woken up on the lab floor, it was perfectly natural for him to assume that he was still dreaming.

    If this other Chris had immediately realized that he was most-certainly not dreaming, he might have been a bit more excitable regarding what occurred next.

    Ben had discovered Chris right away that morning, as the noises made by Ben when he entered the lab were what actually awoke the other Chris. Ben immediately noticed him lying on the floor and, in a fury, quickly walked over to assess the situation.

    Chris spoke first. "Where am I?"

    Ben didn't realize the extent of Chris's confusion and paid the question little attention. Instead, he barked. "You'd better not have destroyed anything."

    Ben angrily picked up the machine's helmet from the floor. He was terrified that it might be damaged and, not surprisingly, seemed much more concerned about the condition of the helmet than the condition of Chris.

    "What happened?" Chris asked.

"You're lucky that you didn't damage any equipment," Ben said. "Were you trying to use the machine? Is that it?"

"Ben," Chris said, confused. "What are you talking about? Where am I?"

"You're an overzealous punk aren't you?" Ben said, oblivious to Chris's confusion. "You think that you can come here whenever you want to. I can assure you that after I have a word with Richard about this, you'll not be setting one foot in this lab again."

The lab's warning buzzer sounded, prompting Ben to check a security camera on the control panel's monitor. He saw Rachel waiting outside.

"Your girlfriend is here to get you," Ben said.

"Jessica?" Chris replied. It was still evident in his voice that he was not grasping that this Ben wasn't the Ben who he knew.

Ben said nothing in response. Instead, he focused on getting Chris to his feet and out of the lab. Chris didn't exactly resist, stumbling as they went along.

"What's your problem?" Chris asked. "Why are you talking about my Dad and being a jerk? I thought that we were friends?"

"You must have me confused with someone else." Ben sneered, assuming that this other Chris was toying with him. "I'm not playing your games."

Ben led Chris down the hallway, to the lab building's entrance. Rachel was about to ring the buzzer again when the pair appeared outside. Ben was not happy to see her, even if she might be there to take Chris off of his hands.

"Why are you here too?" Ben asked Rachel, sternly adding, "Were you part of this?"

Rachel immediately shot back. "Part of what, jerkwad?"

Ben was taken aback by Rachel's insult, "It shouldn't surprise me that his friends are as childish as him."

Rachel walked with Chris back to her car. Ben lingered outside long enough to issue one final remark.

"He fell asleep in the lab," Ben said. "I'll be making sure that his father knows."

"Why don't you go back into your cave?" Rachel said.

Ben gave an icy look and turned to leave.

"Where's Jessica?" Chris asked Rachel.

"Probably at school," Rachel said, "Where we should be."

Chris stood outside Rachel's car while she got inside and unlocked the passenger door.

"Get in!" Rachel shouted from her car. "Are you drunk?"

Chris still didn't know if he should get inside the car or not. He truly had no idea where he was at, since he couldn't understand why Rachel would be picking him up for school.

"No," Chris said. "I just want to know what's going on."

After sitting inside the car for a moment, Rachel realized that Chris wasn't getting inside. She slid over and looked up at Chris through the passenger window.

"Did you want to do something else to tick off the caveman?" Rachel said.

Chris reluctantly reached for the door handle.

Chris rode down the street inside Rachel's car feeling like a pinball in a bad dream. He still had no idea where he was at and, although he hadn't caught everything that Ben had said, what he had caught was downright weird. He couldn't understand why Ben had been so rude. Also, he wondered about the reference that Ben had made to his father.

Lost in these thoughts, Chris sat silent in the passenger seat as Rachel drove them to school. Rachel tried unsuccessfully to engage him.

"So you're ready for that test that we were going to study together for last night?" Rachel asked. "Before you blew me off."

She was obviously still annoyed that she'd been forgotten.

"What test?" Chris asked.

"Uh huh," Rachel said sarcastically. "You know that I can't be constantly making up excuses for you, right? Your Mom was wondering where you were this morning. I told her that you'd said you might get an early ride, but she didn't seem to be buying it. Now Ben is going to bust you and me."

Chris still didn't seem to be paying much attention to Rachel.

"So did you see anything else at the lab?" Rachel inquired. "You said something about you and Jessica last night."

"Yeah, where is she?" Chris was confused and annoyed.

"That's what I'm asking you," Rachel shot back, impatient. "You're being such an idiot."

Chris looked down at his clothes and had no idea where he'd gotten them. They were different from any clothes that he'd owned. He felt sloppy and his clothes smelled as though he'd been wearing them for a few days.

"Whose clothes are these?" Chris wondered matter-of-fact. "They smell awful."

Rachel was surprised by the seemingly-random statement, but she was focused on the traffic around them and only paying partial attention to Chris.

"You just noticed now, huh?" Rachel snorted. "I've been saying that for years."

"I'm being serious."

"Yeah, I am too," Rachel said. "Maybe you knocked your head good in there."

As had been the case the prior day, Rachel slowed for the stop-and-go jam of cars outside of the school parking lot. As if on cue, Tyler pulled up behind them in his sports car. Rachel noticed him immediately.

"Oh great," Rachel said.

Tyler didn't seem as eager to honk his horn that morning though. It wasn't worth the hassle to him after the prior morning's incident. Just in case, Rachel thought of the device that Chris had used to on Tyler's car.

"Do you have that clicker thing along?"

Chris had no idea what she was talking about, "A what?"

"You know, that key chain to make a car go nuts."

"Why would I have that?" Chris asked, oblivious to the potential drama that still might unfold.

"Because," Rachel said. "Tyler's behind us with Jessica."

Chris looked around excitedly. "Jessica and Tyler? Where?"

He seemed relieved to see the couple in Tyler's car. Within seconds, he'd opened the door to Rachel's car and had walked over to Tyler's car. Rachel watched him go, dumbfounded.

Chris yelled to the couple. "Hey guys, where have you been all morning?"

Neither said anything in reply. Chris noticed that Tyler had his arm around Jessica.

"What's going on?" Chris asked.

When they realized that he wasn't going away, both Tyler and Jessica gave Chris an annoyed look.

Tyler yelled to Chris, "Hey lab rat, why don't you go hang out with your robot. If she isn't working out, you've always got your pal to fall back on."

Tyler motioned to Rachel, just as she was getting out of her car. Rachel scowled at him but didn't say anything in reply. She was intimidated by Tyler and didn't want to pick a fight. Students in cars behind Tyler began to honk their horns.

"Get in the car Chris!" Rachel yelled.

"Yeah loser," Tyler laughed. "Listen to your girlfriend."

Tyler didn't bother to wait for Rachel to move her car. He turned his steering wheel, gunned his car's accelerator, and moved his vehicle rapidly past her. When he reached the end of the block, he cut off another student before pulling into the parking lot entrance.

Chris stood watching, shocked. Students in cars in line behind Rachel's vehicle continued to honk their horns.

"Get back in the car!" Rachel yelled again.

Chris obeyed this time and Rachel soon had her car rolling again. As they approached the parking lot entrance, Chris turned to Rachel.

"What's going on?" Chris asked. "Is this some joke?"

Rachel was at the end of her fuse. "You're the one acting all weird this morning. Weird even for you, so maybe you can tell me who the joke is on?"

Chris sat quietly again, dumbfounded and clueless.

"I'm having a dream right?" Chris concluded. "This has to be a dream?"

Rachel wasn't sure what to say. She wondered if something might be genuinely wrong with Chris. She thought back to when she had picked him up at the lab that morning. It occurred to her that potentially something more had happened to Chris than simply getting caught by Ben.

After a long, awkward pause, Rachel said, "I think that you should go see the nurse."

Chris chuckled. He thought that he'd finally figured it all out.

"Tyler put you up to this didn't he?" Chris said. "He's always pulling crazy pranks. I bet that this is his biggest one yet.

Rachel didn't say anything, instead growing worried about how she should handle him.

"So," Chris said with genuine curiosity in his voice. "What's next?"

Day 2 {8:00am}

☺ ↔ ☻

In the 'other' world, the real Chris tried to keep a low profile when stepping off of the school bus. He wasn't one to care what others thought about him, but he didn't need to deal with his latest indignity if he could avoid it. Unfortunately, he hadn't gotten far when he heard an unwelcome voice from behind.

"Dude, what were you doing on the bus?" Tyler asked.

Like everyone else whom Chris would later encounter, this Tyler wasn't quite who Chris thought he was. Not that Chris knew that yet.

Tyler stood behind Chris with a small group of baseball players. They all wore matching letterman's jackets.

"Don't you have something better to do jock strap?" Chris asked.

Tyler's jaw dropped, obviously taken aback by Chris's combative tone.

"Dude," Tyler said. "I'm sorry. I was just giving you a hard time."

Chris tried to ignore them and walked the opposite direction down the sidewalk. Chris's behavior only confused Tyler more.

"Where are you going man?" Tyler shouted.

Chris continued to ignore Tyler and stepped into a stream of students heading into the high school. Chris was determined to avoid getting caught up in an embarrassing incident. He didn't need his seemingly rotten luck to continue.

Unfortunately, it was only a second later when two baseball players grabbed him by the arm.

"Buddy," one of them said with a smile. "Coach is going to be here any minute."

Chris jerked free of their grips.

"Let go of me," Chris snapped.

Tyler walked over close enough to step in and join the other ballplayers.

"Whoa man," he said. "What has gotten into you?"

Before Chris could answer, a voice boomed behind them.

"Everyone here?" Barns said as he walked up to the athletes. He immediately noticed Chris. "Jennings, why aren't you wearing your jacket?"

Chris was dumbfounded. His day continued to get weirder by the minute.

"Because I'm not on the team," Chris said, condescendingly.

Tyler and the other ballplayers chuckled. Barns looked annoyed; he was a disciplined man who didn't tolerate insubordination from anyone on his team. He took Chris aside.

"I'd expect you not to take that tone with me young man," Barns said sternly. "Is there something wrong Chris?"

"I don't think so," Chris said. "I just wanted to get to class."

An announcement came over the public address loudspeaker that drowned out their conversation.

"Please join us in the gymnasium for a pep rally," a voice said. "First period will start twenty minutes late today."

After the message concluded, Barns continued to evaluate Chris. He thought that something seemed off about him.

"Something happen with that girlfriend of yours Chris?" Barns asked. "You know that you can talk to me about anything, right?"

"What?" Chris asked, confused. He just wanted to get away from Barns. "Shouldn't we get inside?"

Barns relented, knowing that they needed to get moving.

"Don't be making a habit out of this," he said. "It makes us look sloppy."

Barns turned to address the ballplayers.

"You heard the announcement guys," he said. "Let's get in there."

Barns, Tyler, and the other athletes all headed toward the school's gymnasium. Chris followed them inside, trying to blend in amid the stream of students already headed in that direction.

The gymnasium was meticulously decorated, ready for a pep rally to begin. The ballplayers all took seats in a line of chairs at the center of the hardwood basketball court. One chair still remained empty.

Chris had taken a seat in the bleachers, assuming that he could use the time to start thinking out his problems. Unfortunately, no sooner than he had sat down though, he received a tap on the shoulder. Looking back, Chris saw that Barns was standing behind him, looking like an angry drill sergeant.

"We're over there Jennings," Barns said, pointing to the athletes seated at the center of the gymnasium.

"I'm not going up there." Chris responded. He had no intention of playing along with what seemed to be a setup.

"Stop fooling around Chris," Barns said. "This isn't funny anymore."

The last of the students took their seats while hundreds of teens all waited for the rally to begin. Amid a quiet roar of conversation, someone began chanting "Chris! Chris! Chris!"

The chant continued over and over until more students joined the chorus, genuinely cheering for Chris. Out of embarrassment, Chris allowed Barns to lead him to mid-court and the empty seat. That seemed to calm the crowd down.

Barns took to a nearby podium, grabbing the microphone and readying his address to the student assembly. His already-intense demeanor shot up a level.

"Many of you know that Westby has long been a thorn in my side," Barns said, growing more theatrical with each word that came out of his mouth. "This school has had to endure their taunts and their insults since I was a player here."

Barns paused. The gymnasium grew quiet enough that one could have heard a proverbial pin drop. Barns continued to hold his pause, using every trick in his book to build up the enthusiasm of the masses.

"This year is different though," Barns continued. "We're heading into battle with the finest group of young men that I've ever had the privilege to coach."

The voices in the crowd started to chant again. "Chris! Chris! Chris!" The students were soon in a frenzy.

For his part, Chris had sat at the end of the line of athletes hoping that this latest embarrassment would simply end soon. Unfortunately, it only got worse.

Barns tried to continue speaking, but it was futile, given the volume of the chanting. He reluctantly motioned for Chris to come over to the podium. Chris had no intention of standing up, but the crowd insisted. Barns was leery of Chris's earlier behavior and worried about what he might say, but the students demanded a few words from their chosen hero.

As Chris took the microphone from Barns, the chanting reached a crescendo before quieting down. Normally, Chris would have enjoyed grabbing the spotlight, but these circumstances were ridiculous.

"I want to thank everyone for your enthusiasm today." Chris said. "I wish the team the best of luck. And I hope that you all remember a quote that I like to keep in mind: 'Every one of us is gifted, but some people never open their package.'"

As Chris paused, the students sat in silence, confused by what they'd just heard. Finally, some started to chuckle and, eventually, raucous cheers broke out.

Barns stood by, still dumbfounded.

Chris concluded by saying. "Thank you." But his voice was drowned out by the crowd's cheers.

Day 2 {8:00am}

♣

Back in the real world, the other Chris walked toward the high school building with Rachel. She was still intent on taking him to see the nurse. Ahead of them, much like in the other world, the other students herded together to file into the gymnasium.

Rachel sighed. "It's that stupid pep rally."

In the distance, Chris could see the baseball players heading towards the gymnasium entrance.

"Hey," Chris said. "The guys are up there."

Rachel noticed that Chris had started walking towards them and tried to stop him.

"Get over here!" she yelled. "I thought we were going to see the nurse?"

Chris looked back at Rachel like she'd just made up the entire notion.

"It's okay," he said to her. "You don't need to keep up the act."

Chris kicked himself for not assuming that his friends would pull an elaborate prank on him before the rally. In his mind, the timing was perfect.

Amid the crush of students trying to get inside the building, Chris couldn't quite catch up with the ball players. Rachel managed to keep behind Chris while everyone squeezed inside the gymnasium. As expected, the gym was meticulously decorated. This time though, when the baseball team members took their seats, there was not an empty chair left over.

As the last of the students arranged themselves in the gym's bleachers, Chris walked towards the ballplayers.

Rachel gasped and yelled to Chris. "What are you doing?"

But it was too late. Chris had already stepped out onto the court.

Tyler and the other ball players were confused to see Chris approaching them. Before Chris could say anything, Barns stopped him.

"Just what do you think you're doing Jennings?" Barns asked.

"Coach," Chris said. "I'm taking a seat with the rest of the guys."

"Find one in the bleachers," Barns said, about to snap. "We need to get started."

Chris looked at Tyler and winked.

"Man," Chris said. "You guys are really going all out, aren't you?"

Tyler sat burning in his seat. He practically growled at Chris.

"Go sit down Jennings," Tyler said. "You're embarrassing yourself."

Instead of heading back to the bleachers though, Chris looked around for a microphone. Unfortunately for him, Barns held the only microphone securely in hand. With nothing else available, Chris turned to the waiting student body and began to chant.

"Beat Westby! Beat Westby!" Chris repeated, over and over.

The students' idle chatter stopped as they looked on with amusement at Chris's antics. Instead of joining in his chants though, they all laughed at him.

Chris turned forlorn when he realized that his peers in the crowd were not with him. He turned back to Tyler, who shook his head.

Barns came up behind Chris and said. "Take a seat before the administration wants to have a talk with you."

"But," Chris said. "I didn't do anything wrong…"

His voice trailed off as the laughs continued and he reluctantly took a seat in the bleachers.

Day 2 {9:00am}

☺ ↔ ☻

Events continued to unfold much better in the other world for the real Chris, to the point where he had momentarily put aside in his mind how weird it should have all seemed. In fact, he was nearly late to science class, due to all of the high-fives and admirers who stopped him in the hallway after the pep rally.

Chris had remained skeptical of the sudden popularity that he was experiencing. Yet, as the morning continued, he'd started to enjoy it. While he still couldn't explain what was going on, he figured that maybe he was finally receiving his due.

Most of Chris's fellow students had taken their seats for science class by the time he wandered into the room. Barns was already walking around the room, passing out exams. Most of the other students smiled at Chris as he took his seat.

Chris settled into his usual desk in the back of the room, next to Rachel. It was the first time he'd seen her since she'd sped past his home.

Chris leaned over to Rachel. "Why didn't you pick me up this morning?"

Rachel looked at Chris as though he was a complete stranger.

"Excuse me?" Rachel asked.

"You drove right by," Chris said, indicating motion with his hands. "I had to take the bus."

Rachel wasn't sure how to reply.

"Why would I pick you up?" Rachel said.

"Dude, get over here!" Tyler interrupted before Chris could answer her. "Stop fooling around!"

Chris saw that Tyler was indicating that he should move to a nearby empty desk, but he gave Tyler an annoyed look and ignored the request. Rachel might have been acting strange, but Chris wasn't about to become Tyler's new best pal.

Barns reached Chris's desk and got his attention when he slid Chris an exam. Chris looked mildly concerned, but Barns leaned in to reassure him.

"Don't worry about it," Barns whispered.

Chris gave Barns a crooked smile, not sure if he should trust him or not.

Day 2 {9:00am}

♣

The other Chris experienced a much different reception while walking to science class in the real world. He noticed students turn away from him as he passed them in the hallway. Some of the students appeared to be whispering to one another, presumably about him. It was strange behavior, given that he'd expected to be treated like a celebrity. For a joke that he remained sure the guys on the baseball team had planned, it sure was elaborate.

Chris arrived at science class and headed straight for an open seat next to Tyler. Tyler seemed amused when Chris sat down near him.

"Dude," Tyler chuckled, ready to rip into Chris. "What are you doing?" It was almost becoming too easy for Tyler.

Chris leaned over to Tyler.

"I just want you to know that I'm on to you guys," he said. "But, you know, this whole thing has been pretty funny."

Tyler sat back and smirked, clueless as to what Chris might have been referring to. He wondered if Chris had been taking drugs.

"You finally have a little too much of the catnip Jennings?" Tyler said. "Or was it something a little stronger this time?

Chris laughed in response. He couldn't believe how well Tyler was playing this 'character.'

Tyler continued. "You're talking like a crazy man."

Mr. Barns came over and handed Tyler and Chris their exams. Barns whispered something to Tyler and continued walking down the aisle. Before he had gone more than a couple of feet, Chris stopped him.

"Hey coach?" Chris said, motioning Barns to come closer.

"Now what Mr. Jennings?" Barns asked, obviously annoyed. He'd had enough of Chris that morning.

Chris kept motioning Barns closer until he relented and leaned in.

"You've got me covered," Chris whispered. "Right?"

"Exactly what do you mean Mr. Jennings?" Barns replied, obviously surprised by the suggestion.

Chris looked down at his test and then back at Barns.

"You know," he said.

"I don't think that I do Mr. Jennings."

Barns snatched the test away from Chris. His voice grew loud enough for all of the other students to hear him.

"Are you suggesting that I should help you out with your exam?" Barns said, letting the accusation linger.

Chris's face turned red. He looked around like a young child who had just gotten caught stealing.

Barns grew more furious as he realized that this was his chance to put Chris in his place. He was going to take full advantage of it. Barns stepped over to his desk and dialed a number on his telephone. A secretary's voice answered on the other side.

"Yes, this is Coach Barns. Chris Jennings is on his way down to discuss his interest in cheating on one of my exams. Please make sure that he speaks with Principal Thofson."

Barns turned his attention back to Chris.

"Mr. Jennings," he said. "We're going for a walk."

Chris gathered up his belongings and walked out of the room. His day was only getting weirder and weirder.

Day 2 {10:00am}

☺ ↔ ☻

The real Chris left his science class after the period bell rang. He had finished the exam with little effort, despite Barns's earlier promise of a helping hand. He figured that, as good of a day as it was turning out to be, he shouldn't take chances. In light of everything that had happened over the past few hours, Chris realized that maybe things weren't as dire as they'd seemed earlier that morning.

Sure, Rachel still appeared to be mad at him. She didn't even look his direction during the exam and left at the bell before he could catch up with her. He couldn't blame her for being upset with him though, since he had promised to be home in time to study with her

Overall, Chris couldn't help but feel like people were finally coming around to him. He was being appreciated.

Of course, Chris was still leery that something fishy might be afoot, but those concerns had begun to fade away. Obviously someone had done something to his room and he still had no idea how he'd gotten home from the lab the prior night. And there was the matter of the machine likely having done something to his body.

Yet, those problems seemed less pressing to Chris now that he was suddenly the most popular guy at school. When Chris walked through the hallway to his next class, smiles and stares continued from students whom he didn't even recognize. It didn't seem as though life could get much better.

And then Jessica walked up to Chris and gave him a kiss. Chris went wide-eyed in shock, but let the kiss linger for a moment. He assumed that he was going to be in trouble over it, but, in the moment, he didn't care.

When their kiss ended, Jessica looked Chris in the eyes. He could tell that she was excited to see him, but he had no idea why. So far as Chris could tell, there wasn't a punch line about to be delivered.

"And just where have you been Mr. Superstar?" Jessica said, playfully. "I've been missing you all morning. You were excellent at the pep rally."

"Ah," Chris said. "You don't think that Tyler and his goons might be around, do you?"

"Why would I care?"

That was not at all the answer that Chris was expecting, but he wasn't about to argue with Jessica. Perhaps she'd broken up with Tyler. Who knew? It had already been an unusual day, so why not that too?

"Oh, okay," Chris said. "I was just wondering."

Chris kept staring at Jessica. His greatest wish had finally come true, yet he had no idea what to do next.

"Are you okay?" Jessica asked. "You seem kind of spacey."

"Ah, no, I'm fine," Chris said. "You're fine. It's good."

Jessica laughed.

"So, like, what happened to your clothes?" Jessica crinkled her nose while checking Chris over. "You look like maybe you slept in them."

Chris glanced down at himself and realized that he'd not bothered to straighten his clothes after getting dressed so hurriedly earlier that morning.

"No," Chris replied. "I was kind of in a hurry getting to school."

"Yeah, I was wondering about that," Jessica said. She had a hint of annoyance in her voice. "I stopped by your house, but no one was home."

"Oh really?" Chris was dumbfounded that she'd stopped at his house.

"Yeah, I assumed you'd call or something if you were heading in early."

"I'm sorry," Chris stammered. The conversation grew increasingly odd and he had a hard time keeping up. "I came in a little early, um, on the bus."

"What?" Jessica said, looking like she couldn't process his statement.

"You know, the pep rally and the test and…"

Chris's voice trailed off. He realized that he was trying to lie in order to cover up an oversight that he'd not even realized he'd made. Life was getting complicated. Of course, he didn't want to jeopardize Jessica's newfound attention, so he would have probably agreed to apologize for just about anything at that point.

Unfortunately for Chris, Jessica didn't appear as though she was buying his excuses. She might let the miscommunication go this time, but she wasn't going to forget about it.

"Next time," Jessica scolded Chris. "Call me, okay? I was worried."

Chris, in his nervousness, awkwardly attempted damage control.

"Hey, I'm sorry," he said. "I'll, ah, make sure to keep you in my, um, loop."

Jessica needed to get to class and let him off the hook.

"Anyway," Jessica said. "I'll see you after practice. Don't forget about me tonight."

"What practice?" Chris said.

"Baseball, duh," Jessica said. "Coach Barns will probably have you tired as a limp noodle by the time I see you."

Jessica leaned in and gave Chris a kiss again. He held her tighter this time.

After a few seconds, Jessica broke the kiss. She smiled as she stepped away.

"I'm going to be late tiger," Jessica said. "I'll see you later."

Chris smiled back and caught himself nearly waving good-bye. He might have been clueless around Jessica, but he thought that he could become accustomed to her attention.

Chris was still flying high from Jessica's kiss as he walked to his next class. Even if the day's events all turned out to be a practical joke, he'd still have gotten a chance to kiss her – twice.

As excited as Chris was, those emotions all felt bottled up inside. He didn't have anyone to share it with, until he noticed Rachel ahead of him in the hallway. Chris caught up with her, startling her in the process.

"You're not going to believe what just happened." Chris's arms stretched wide while he spoke.

Rachel was already annoyed with Chris from his earlier behavior in science class. His remarks to her only added fuel to that fire.

"What now?" Rachel asked.

Chris blurted it out, nearly yelling. "Jessica just kissed me."

Rachel didn't care about the news.

"Ok," Rachel said, trying to move past Chris. "Can you leave me alone so that I can get to class?"

Chris doesn't understand why Rachel kept ignoring him.

"What is wrong with you?" he asked. "I thought that you'd be excited for me."

"She's your girlfriend," Rachel said, talking to Chris as though he was two years old. "Isn't that what you two do?"

"No," Chris continued, talking faster. "You don't understand."

"Shouldn't you be with your jock friends right now?" Rachel muttered.

"What?" Chris said, not letting up or truly understanding her. "I wanted to tell you. I thought that you'd be excited for me."

Rachel had none of it.

"Look," she said. "I don't know if this is some cry for help, but you're really creeping me out."

"I wanted to tell you though," Chris replied, hurt by her words. Chris knew that Rachel was obviously not fooling around. "You're my best friend."

Rachel calmed down enough to deliver a verbal gut punch.

"Yeah," she said. "I was your friend. And you were a show-off and I liked that. I understood it when everyone else didn't. It always had to be about you, but usually you included me too. I knew that after the accident things had to change, but I didn't expect that our friendship was going to die then too."

Chris was stupefied.

"Accident?" he asked, confused. "Nothing's changed."

"If this is you finally coming around to apologizing," Rachel said, choosing her words carefully. "That's fine. Better late than never, I guess."

"Apologizing for what?"

"Being too cool for me," Rachel let the words come out, but immediately wanted to take them back. She was embarrassed for saying too much and knew that prolonging their discussion would just make it worse.

"Look," Rachel said. "We both know that when we were growing up, I was the only person who put up with your crap."

At first, Chris didn't know how to respond. It was as though he was talking to a different person. He stepped back and let Rachel walk away.

After she'd gotten a few feet, Chris said faintly. "But you still put up with my crap."

Day 2 {10:00am}

♣

The real world's Barns escorted the other Chris down the hallway to the principal's office. Along the way, Chris gave Barns frequent looks, assuming that the coach might break what he thought was an act. His demeanor didn't change though and, after walking a few yards, they headed through a doorway into the principal's office.

A rosy-cheeked secretary smiled blissfully as the pair entered. Barns motioned Chris into a waiting area and then took a moment to check in with the secretary. Before Barns left the office, he turned back to Chris.

"I don't know what's gotten into you today Jennings." he said.

The office door slammed behind Barns. Chris sat for a few seconds before the secretary called to him.

"He's ready for you," she announced, not even bothering to look up at Chris. The mood in the office was incredibly impersonal.

Chris headed into Principal Thofson's office. He couldn't help but think that whatever prank was being played on him had started to go too far. It was one thing to get some laughs at his expense, but involving the administration made him feel uncomfortable.

Chris especially wondered what Barns had been thinking. Joking about their little 'arrangements' on his exams was treading dangerously close to exposing some of the secrets to the coach's success. It wasn't that Chris wasn't smart and couldn't pass the tests, but he had other priorities to keep in mind.

Principal Thofson looked up at Chris from a large desk. Thofson was middle-aged, a little thick around the waist, and mostly bald. He was the type of man who didn't like being distracted and he considered discipline cases to be distracting.

"Take a seat," he said, referring to a single chair in front of his desk.

Thofson was clearly not pleased with having to spend time reprimanding Chris.

"I had already made a note to speak with you about your antics this morning during the pep rally," Thofson said. "Now I find myself having to meet with you about trying to coerce one of our most upstanding teachers into cheating for you.

Thofson paused, as if to take it all in for himself.

He continued. "This has certainly been a banner day for you Chris."

Chris wasted little time in offering a response.

"There's really been a misunderstanding here," he said, hoping to talk his way out of the situation.

Thofson wasn't open to even considering the excuse. "You clearly have no idea how much trouble you're in, do you?"

"Look," Chris said. "I know that the guys on the team have been playing some jokes. It's funny, I get it. But I think that they might have gone too far this time."

Thofson was puzzled by the suggestion. "What on earth are you talking about?"

Chris leaned forward. "I just want to know that everything is fine for the game against Westby, right?"

"Why wouldn't it be?" Thofson looked at Chris for a long second, wondering if he had a plan to spoil the game too. "It's nothing that you need to worry about."

Chris misunderstood Thofson's remark and assumed it to be a direct response to his question. He seemed relieved.

"I was just wondering," he said.

"You should know that this will be going on your permanent record," Thofson said, laying down the law. "I can't keep giving you breaks. We've had enough issues in the past with your behavior Chris. This is one instance that we can't let slide."

Chris sat back, not sure if he should even take seriously what Thofson had just said.

Thofson, of course, was gravely serious and had a hint of sadness on his face. He wasn't at the school simply to collect a paycheck, so it seemed a waste when he watched as students didn't live up to their full potential.

"This really disappoints me," Thofson concluded. "With a little discipline and focus on priorities, things at this school might be a lot different for you."

Day 2 {3:00pm}

☺ ↔ ☻

After the afternoon's classes in the other world were completed, Chris wondered what he should do next. On the one hand, he'd let the day's events distract him from covering his tracks at home regarding his use of the machine. On the other hand, Jessica had indicated that she'd be waiting for him after school. He didn't want to miss that opportunity.

Besides, with Rachel acting so weird towards him, Chris wasn't entirely sure how he'd get home. He certainly didn't want to end up on the bus again, not if Jessica might finally be interested in him. Of course, her strange mention of baseball practice, coupled with the earlier odd behavior by Barns still floated around in the back of Chris's mind.

Chris was still thinking about trying to find Jessica when Tyler came up behind him, trailed by several of the baseball players, the same guys who'd been with him earlier at the pep rally.

"Buddy," Tyler said, slapping Chris on the back harder than was necessary. "We figured you'd already be out hitting."

Chris flinched. There was no way that he was going to head to baseball practice with them. It was obvious that they were trying to embarrass him. Chris was about to excuse himself when he heard Jessica yell from behind them.

"Wait up guys," she said. "I'm heading out to practice with the girls."

Chris had no idea how to react, fearing that Tyler might somehow be upset by Jessica's earlier advances. Before Chris could react though, Jessica stepped up and kissed him. With Tyler watching nearby, Chris seemed hesitant and didn't let it linger this time.

As soon as he broke the kiss, Chris immediately looked to Tyler for a reaction, but he didn't act as though anything was out of the ordinary. Chris expected at least a hint of something. Anything. But that wasn't the case.

"Nice to see you again too," Chris said to Jessica, sheepishly.

"I wanted to take care of my special guy before practice." Jessica concluded, smiling at Chris one more time before walking away.

"I have to meet the girls," Jessica said, adding a cute little wave to her good-bye.

Tyler smiled and again patted Chris on the back.

"I don't know what she sees in you buddy," he said.

It was the second time that day that Chris felt as though he was being, literally, swept along by circumstances that he didn't understand. As he had done before at the pep rally, Chris thought that it was best to let the immediate events play out.

As much as he wanted to enjoy these new circumstances in his life, it was increasingly obvious to Chris that something odd was going on. Every hunch that he kept having seemed to be quickly proven wrong and Chris wasn't sure what to do next in order to get to the bottom of things.

Even if an elaborate joke had been playing out, Chris knew that Tyler was a jealous type. As such, it seemed unlikely that he would allow his girlfriend – or even a recently-ex-girlfriend – to kiss Chris in front of him and his cronies.

For a fleeting moment, Chris wondered if he had somehow changed his reality, but that idea was too weighty for his mind to wrap itself around.

Chris followed the ballplayers down to the men's locker room, his mind racing with other theories, but he didn't come up with anything that seemed realistic. Chris only grew more curious when he found that he had an assigned locker.

The ballplayers all quickly dressed, but Chris was busy digging through his supposed locker. He examined the uniform hanging inside and noticed his name stitched on the back.

Figuring that it was time to disappear, Chris started to wander out of the locker room. Tyler noticed him leaving and stepped up to stop him.

"You're not trying to cut out are you?" Tyler asked, intimidation in his voice.

"No," Chris responded, sheepishly.

"Good, because you might be a stud, but we're all going to need practice with Westby coming up."

Chris wanted out of the immediate situation, but Tyler's tone made him wonder if 'escape' was even an option. He didn't want to get beat up by the entire baseball team.

Chris let the other players head out to the practice field ahead of him. He eventually came outside, still wearing his regular clothes, hoping to find Jessica. He'd wondered if maybe he couldn't talk her into an early ride home.

Instead, he first noticed the ball players, who were gathered on a set of bleachers. Barns was addressing them.

"I know that normally we talk about one game at a time," Barns started. "But I'm sure that you have all had Westby in the backs of your minds since last season."

A number of catcalls ensued from several players.

As Barns spoke, Chris looked around but still didn't see Jessica or any of her friends out practicing yet. He also looked for signs of Barns or one of the players letting on that they were pranking him, but he noticed nothing.

After Barns's pep talk concluded, the players moved on to start their loose warm-ups. Barns came over to Chris.

"Running late Jennings?" Barns asked.

"No," Chris replied.

"Then why aren't you in uniform yet?" Barns pressed.

As had become the norm by now, Chris figured he'd play along. "It got ripped and I couldn't find an extra."

Barns looked at Chris like he was an idiot and said. "Have one of the trainers run and find you something. Get changed right now."

Barns walked away, leaving Chris standing next to a pile of equipment. Chris looked around for somewhere to wander off to where he could hide.

Before Chris made any moves though, Tyler yelled over to him. "Ready to take some real batting practice champ?"

Tyler handed Chris a bat and stepped into pitching position a number of yards away. As if on cue, another player crouched behind Chris, ready to catch.

Chris assumed that whatever was about to unfold wasn't going to end well for him and he started to walk away, but Tyler threw a fastball that nearly hit him.

"At least give me a few throws," Tyler said. "I'm still warming up."

Chris didn't want to get beaned and figured that if he went through the requisite humiliation, he'd be able to leave the situation. Chris held the bat up and let a few pitches go by. When he eventually started taking swings, he missed at every attempt.

Chris's swings were simply too slow to make contact with pitch after pitch from Tyler. Eventually, Tyler slowed his pitches to an easier level and Chris made contact, if only to chip at the ball. He had the strength, but not the speed.

Barns turned to watch the batting practice. He noticed that Chris had trouble making contact with Tyler's pitches. Concerned, he left fielding exercises that he'd been monitoring and came over to see what was going on.

Barns barked at Chris. "Your stance is a disaster Jennings. Get your legs apart and hold the bat right."

With the spotlight suddenly shifted to him, Chris felt even more uncomfortable than before. Tyler threw several additional pitches to Chris, but his changes in stance didn't matter – Chris's swings were simply too slow and off-the-mark.

When it was all over, Chris looked over his shoulder and noticed Jessica staring at him. She'd begun practicing nearby with the dance team, but they'd stopped amid the commotion caused by Barns. The other dance team members were gathered around her. Chris could see a hint of concern, or perhaps disappointment, in her face.

Barns noticed Chris looking over at Jessica, so he leaned in close to Chris.

"Something on your mind with the girl?" he asked, reiterating an earlier theory that he'd had regarding Chris's strange behavior.

"No, I'm just not feeling myself today," Chris said. "This has been a crazy day."

"It'd better be something that you can get over quick," Barns said, considering what he should tell Chris to do next. He decided to try letting him off easy for now. "Go home and rest. Get your head straight Chris. You're making quite the spectacle here and I don't want you affecting the other guys."

Day 2 {3:00pm}

♣

The other Chris, still angry from having to endure the earlier lecture in Principal Thofson's office, thought that he was late when heading outside to baseball practice in the real world. Adding to his frustration was the fact that he'd been unable to find his gym locker. Of course, he'd assumed that the ballplayers were still messing around with him and hiding his equipment was yet another facet of their 'prank.'

That said, Chris was starting to realize that things weren't adding up with his assumption that he was living out a practical joke. That theory didn't explain why he felt sluggish or why he felt so much weaker. He knew that he'd let himself relax a little bit since the team had clinched their conference title, but he couldn't see how he would have suddenly lost a noticeable amount of muscle after just a couple of days. Chris was an athlete and those things simply didn't happen that quickly. Unless he was gravely ill and that fear had started to surface in the back of his mind.

Furthermore, Chris hadn't seen Jessica since their brief encounter that morning. He'd seen her riding with Tyler, which made him assume that his friends were up to something. A prank might have been amusing to Chris if they hadn't pulled it the week of the game against Westby. Because of that, he couldn't understand why the guys had picked a day right before a big game to execute such an elaborate deception.

Chris was friends with the guys on the team, but he didn't otherwise have a great deal of trust in them. They were high school jocks and, as such, they had a way of being opportunistic when the chance arose. The other Chris thought of himself as undeniably a baseball star and the team's leader, yet he'd long wondered when one or more of his teammates might push for more attention.

Thus, as Chris approached the other ballplayers in mid-practice, he wasn't surprised when Tyler continued to show him attitude. In fact, Chris wasn't entirely sure if that disrespect had been part of an act or if it were real.

"You're really trying for an epic day aren't you loser?" Tyler said.

"Cut it out man," Chris shot back, frustration coming through in his voice. "This was funny for a while, but now it's a distraction. You guys need to drop it."

Tyler grabbed a baseball and threw it toward Chris, and he caught the ball with his bare hand, not even flinching. He looked like a natural as he flung it right back at Tyler, who caught the hard throw in his glove.

Barns immediately noticed the exchange and gave Chris a curious look. He walked over to Tyler, cutting in before there could be any altercation.

"What's going on here?" Barns asked the young men.

Tyler pointed at Chris and said. "Jennings is interrupting our practice."

"I just want to get in my swings Coach," Chris said.

Barns was curious enough by Chris's catch and throw to grant the request. "Let him take a couple of swings."

Tyler looked stunned by the order.

"Why Coach?" he protested. "He's not supposed to be out here."

Barns thought that Chris had been acting odd all day, but Barns was not one to pass up an opportunity to recruit solid talent.

"You can always use throwing practice," Barns said to Tyler. "Get to it."

Tyler seemed annoyed by having to throw to Chris, but he obeyed Barns's request. Barns handed Chris a bat. Chris carried it with him into the batter's box without any instruction.

Tyler's first pitch was fast and cut inside, almost hitting Chris. Chris thought about ending things right there by taking a charge at Tyler, but Barns quickly spoke up.

"Knock it off with the funny stuff," Barns snapped at Tyler.

Tyler responded by throwing another pitch that was closer to the strike zone and Chris had no problem making contact. He didn't have the power that he was accustomed to, but he still managed to knock the ball into a solid grounder.

Tyler was annoyed that he'd even allowed the hit and the next time he threw a trickier pitch. Chris made contact again, this time hitting it high into the air. Tyler responded by throwing another pitch and another. Both times, Chris made contact.

Barns stood to the side grinning, growing impressed with Chris after each hit. Finally, Tyler couldn't take it anymore.

"Don't we need to get going on practice coach?" Tyler asked, half-defeated.

"Take some laps guys and we'll get started," Barns announced to the groan of the ball players.

As the other players ran off, Barns happily thought that he might have randomly had a diamond in the rough drop into his lap. He was warmer to Chris than he'd been earlier.

"Don't mind them, Chris," Barns said. "Hey, I'm sorry about what happened earlier this afternoon."

Chris thought that it was about time that Barns admitted he'd made a mistake by sending him to the principal's office.

"I know that the guys are all in on the joke," Chris replied. "I'm not stupid."

Barns ignored what he thought to be an odd remark, busily thinking about getting Chris involved with the team.

"Look," Barns said. "I've got to talk with the athletic director, but that should be a formality. Why don't you stop in and see me before school tomorrow."

Chris was confused, assuming that the charade had ended.

"Why don't you want me practicing?" he asked. "We don't have time to waste."

Barns knew that he wouldn't be able to get the team to accept Chris without laying some groundwork first. Tyler's behavior alone had shown him that involving Chris at all with the team at this point would be a risk. Just the same, Barns couldn't deny that there seemed to be incredible raw talent inside Chris. It was too good to pass up.

"No, no," Barns said, definitively. "Get ready and we'll talk tomorrow."

Barns turned away from Chris to re-start the practice. Chris was about to protest further, but he spotted Jessica's car pull up along a street that ran near the school. He assumed that she might be waiting for him.

"Jessica!" Chris yelled.

Jessica was too far away to hear Chris and didn't acknowledge him. A few moments passed before several of her friends came out of the high school building and got into her car. Chris watched as Jessica's car then pulled away.

Chris was upset, but didn't have long to think before he heard a voice behind him.

"I've been looking for you for the past hour," Rachel said. "I called your Mom. She said you weren't home and hadn't checked in either."

Chris turned around to find Rachel looking at him with her hands on her hips. She was clearly angry at him, yet he couldn't figure out what was wrong with her. She had done nothing but snap at him every time she saw him and he could tell that now she was still mad after apparently tracking him down.

"Oh," Rachel continued. "And exactly what was your plan for that test? Getting taken down to the principal's office was real slick."

"I'm getting tired of this you know," Chris snapped.

He was about to accuse her of being nosy, but then realized that he didn't have many options left for getting home. He didn't have his phone on him and Jessica appeared to be long gone. He resolved himself to taking Barns' advice and simply going home to rest.

"Look," Chris said. "I'm just not feeling like myself today. Maybe you could just drop me off at home?"

"Sure," Rachel said, still worried about Chris's bizarre behavior. "That's fine."

After taking a few steps towards Rachel's car, Chris went for broke.

"I want you to level with me," Chris said. "This is some joke, right? The guys are doing this?"

Rachel looked disappointed at the question. It only made her grow even more worried.

"What has gotten into you today?" Rachel said. "You're all spacey and acting like everyone is playing a prank on you. You never went to see the nurse did you?"

Chris tensed up. If Rachel knew about what had been occurring, she wasn't giving up any information. And Chris didn't want to see a doctor. He reasoned that the day's events must have been the combination of a prank and a few misunderstandings mixed in with Rachel's suddenly-needy behavior. He hoped that when he arrived at home, he could clear everything up.

After Chris was dropped off, he went straight to his room. Having woken up in the lab earlier that morning, he'd not yet been home and was stunned to find his room arranged altogether different than normal. It made him think that his teammate's prank had clearly known no bounds. His trophies and posters were gone, replaced by some sort of geeky collection of signs.

The changes made Chris feel even more defeated. The day's string of events simply wouldn't end. He plopped down into the chair in his room, thinking that he was sitting against a pile of blanket and pillows, but that wasn't the case.

The robot torso sprung up and it startled Chris. He jumped away from the failed science project as though it was a snake about to strike.

The robot said in its monotone voice. "Hello master, welcome home."

After Chris didn't reply, the robot shut down.

"What the heck is going on?" Chris sighed to himself.

Chris went to his closet to change clothes and was disappointed to find that his wardrobe appeared to have been looted. His clothes had been replaced with items that matched the ill-advised outfit that he'd discovered himself wearing that morning.

For the first time since that morning, Chris started to think about just how truly odd those early events had been. It seemed a bit extreme in hindsight that he'd somehow woken up wearing someone else's clothing. And he'd simply explained Ben's behavior and the mysterious lab as part of the prank, but now he realized how unusual it had hall been.

With so much having happened throughout the course of the day, Chris felt as though he'd been dealing with one surprise after another. He'd not had much time to stop and think extremely hard about it all.

Chris's mind continued to swim as he tried to put the different pieces together. He kept searching for an anchor of sorts. He hoped that finally speaking with Jessica might put him at ease. He knew that she was smart and thought that they could talk through the situation and put it together.

Chris realized that he didn't have his cell phone on him. That was another seemingly lost item to track down. He instead called Jessica's phone on the home phone, but she didn't pick up. His call was sent to her voice mail.

"Hey, it's me," Chris left a message. "The guys and coach have been fooling around all day. I'm sorry that I've missed you. Give me a call when you get this. I need to hear your voice."

Chris thought about taking a nap, but couldn't get Jessica out of his mind. He assumed that Jessica had been in on the 'joke' too, but he thought that, more than anyone, she'd be the first to open up to him regarding what had been going on. Jessica's house was merely a long walk from Chris's home, so he decided to go there on foot.

As Chris walked downstairs, his home's front door opened. Morgan stepped inside, surprising Chris.

"Mom," Chris said. "You're home?"

Morgan looked around in a bit of confusion.

"I hope so!" Morgan said. "Am I supposed to be somewhere?"

"I just thought that you might be at the lab," Chris said.

"Why would I be there?" Morgan wondered.

Chris realized that it wasn't worth arguing over and changed the topic.

"Did you let the guys mess with my room?" Chris asked. "I want my stuff back."

"What do you mean?"

"My room," Chris said. "It's totally different. Someone's playing a joke on me."

Morgan had no idea what Chris was talking about. She followed him upstairs and found his room appearing how she thought it normally looked.

"What's wrong?" she asked.

Chris looked at Morgan as though she were crazy, but then realized that she would have had to be in on the prank for anyone to pull it off.

"Never mind," Chris said. "I need to get going."

"Maybe you need to get some rest instead?" Morgan said. Her motherly antennae now up, it didn't seem like she'd easily let Chris leave.

"I'm heading over to Jessica's," Chris said.

"What?" Morgan said, still confused. "Why are you going to see her? We're about to have dinner."

"Because she's my girlfriend," Chris said, a touch of sarcasm in his voice. "Don't worry, I'll just grab something to eat quick."

Morgan didn't like either the tone or the information.

"That's news to me," Morgan said. "When did this start?"

"It's been a while now Mom," Chris said, while gathering up food to take along. "I'll be back before too late."

Morgan didn't know what to say. She knew who Jessica was and she didn't regard her highly. But if Chris had been dating Jessica, then Morgan needed more about the situation before raising her concerns. And if her son didn't want to tell her anything, Morgan knew where she could find that information.

The other Chris walked quickly down the street, towards Jessica's home. He'd barely left the house when Morgan headed next door to Rachel's home. Morgan noticed Rachel sitting by her window, perhaps eavesdropping. This was something that Morgan knew that Rachel did from time to time. Rachel spotted Morgan approaching her already-open window.

"Rachel," Morgan said from outside. "Did you spend much time with Chris today?"

Rachel didn't want to rat out Chris for being at the lab overnight, but she couldn't keep her concerns quiet either.

"I gave him a ride," Rachel replied. "And then dropped him off this evening. I think that he had a pretty eventful day."

"Why's that?"

"He kept thinking that some guys on the baseball team were playing a joke on him."

Morgan thought back to the 'joke' that Chris had referenced regarding his room.

"What kind of joke?" Morgan asked.

"I'm not sure," Rachel said. "He usually likes to be the center of attention, but today he wasn't acting quite like himself. I just assumed that maybe he was tired from last night or our test and everything."

"Maybe," Morgan considered. "Do you know anything about him suddenly dating Jessica?"

"What?" Rachel asked, clearly surprised.

"Apparently they're dating." Morgan said, not quite believing herself. "He's on his way to her house right now."

"That's probably not a good idea," Rachel said.

The neighborhood around Jessica's house was quiet, although the area clearly rated a few steps below where Chris lived. It seemed safe enough, but the homes were in more of a state of disrepair.

Chris approached Jessica's front door and repeatedly rang the doorbell. He waited. When no one answered, he decided to check Jessica's room.

While stepping across the lawn toward her bedroom window, Chris was shocked at what he saw through the open blinds.

Tyler was kissing Jessica.

Furious by the sight, Chris ran up to Jessica's window and banged on it.

"What's going on?" Chris yelled, barely able to believe what he had witnessed.

Jessica and Tyler were both startled by Chris's action. Jessica literally jumped back from the window, while Tyler angrily moved closer to Chris.

"Get out of here you freak!" Jessica screamed.

Chris kept pounding at the wooden window frame, rattling the glass pane enough to nearly break it. After a few seconds, Chris finally stopped raging and stepped back a few feet. The sight of Jessica with Tyler was a nightmare come to life for him. His head felt as though it was spinning.

Tyler opened Jessica's window and swiftly climbed through to the lawn outside, ready to confront Chris.

"Dude," Tyler laughed. "You're out of control today, aren't you?"

"We're friends man," Chris pleaded. "How could you do this?"

Tyler paid the remark no attention.

"Beat it Jennings," he said, getting ready to take a swing at Chris.

"And you," Chris turned his attention to Jessica. "I care for you and this is how you treat me? Cheating with this scumbag?"

That was all it took for Chris to get punched. Tyler's fist landed hard against Chris's cheek. As he barreled backward, Chris thought that he'd perhaps lost a tooth.

In the blink of an eye though, Chris punched back. On contact, he could feel his strength falling short. His punches landed, but they didn't have the same impact that he'd hoped.

As the exchange continued, Chris soon fell to the ground in pain. He could taste blood dripping from his nose and knew that it was probably broken. Battered, Chris scrambled to avoid a kick from Tyler.

Eventually, Tyler let Chris stumble off of Jessica's lawn. Tyler didn't pursue him. Instead, he straightened his rumpled clothing. He was not much worse for the wear. Jessica watched from her window as Chris disappeared in retreat down the street.

"He sounded as though he'd lost his mind," Jessica said.

"Wouldn't surprise me," Tyler replied in his know-it-all tone. "Guys like him always turn out to be crazies."

Chris staggered home, occasionally wiping the blood from his nose until it finally stopped. It took him twenty minutes to arrive. When he did, he discovered lights on downstairs. He knew that he looked like a mess and couldn't simply walk inside bloodied, so he climbed up the back of the garage to its roof. It was his usual secret way into his room and, from the garage roof, he could easily sneak back inside through his window.

Once Chris was back in his room, he quickly fell asleep on his bed. He didn't bother to take off his clothes or clean himself off. The day had been the worst of his life. He wanted for it to be over.

Downstairs, Morgan welcomed Richard home from a long day at the lab. She could tell when he was stressed, but with the presentation coming up, she didn't have to be very observant at all to notice that he was moody from being under pressure.

"Did you guys figure anything out today?" Morgan asked.

"Not really," Richard shook his head. "Ben and I checked the data from the last test, but we're still not finding any problems. He seems distracted and that isn't helping."

"I'm not surprised that Ben would let you down when he was being counted on the most."

"Honey," Richard sighed. "That's not helping either."

Morgan fidgeted, distracted. She debated with herself about what to say next.

"I probably shouldn't be bringing this up until after the presentation," Morgan said, piquing Richard's interest. "But I'm worried about Chris."

Richard didn't seem overly surprised with her concern.

"Ben mentioned something about Chris being at the lab this morning," he said. "I guess that he was there before Ben arrived to work. Rachel picked him up for school, but Ben said that he'd seemed in a daze."

Morgan was upset that Rachel hadn't been quite honest with her. She worried for Chris's safety if he had been doing something unsupervised at the lab.

"How would he have gotten in there?" Morgan asked. "I thought that you guys had security all over the building."

"We do," Richard smirked. "But he's our son and rather clever, in case you hadn't noticed."

"Well," Morgan said. "He was acting like a space cadet to me when I saw him this evening, so I spoke with Rachel about him."

"What'd she say?"

"He apparently did some odd things at school today," Morgan said. "Interrupted a pep rally. Pretended he was on the baseball team or something."

"That's typical for him," Richard said, seeming unconcerned. "Isn't it?"

Morgan wasn't amused.

"Honey," she said. "Be serious. I wouldn't bring this up if I didn't think that it was something out of the ordinary. He also told me that he was dating that girl from school, Jessica."

"Really?" Richard seemed genuinely surprised.

"Yes," Morgan continued. "He headed over to her parent's house earlier tonight. Rachel said that it was the first she'd heard about it."

"Where's he at right now?" Richard asked.

Morgan motioned upstairs.

"I heard him come in just before you got home," she said.

Richard and Morgan went upstairs to the hallway outside of Chris's room. They could hear Chris snoring on the other side of the closed door.

"He's sleeping," Morgan said.

"Should we wake him?" Richard asked.

"No," Morgan said. "Let him rest. We'll talk in the morning."

Day 2 {4:30pm}

☺ ↔ ☻

Not long after the real Chris had been dismissed from baseball practice in the other world, Jessica was given permission to leave her practice early too, so that she could take him home.

As Chris rode in the passenger seat of her car, he quickly realized that he wasn't even sure what to say to Jessica. The truth was that he'd pined for her for so long that he'd never actually considered what they might have in common. His nervousness around her only made thinking of things to say that much harder.

Luckily for Chris, Jessica wasn't shy.

"You don't really have to go home do you?" Jessica asked.

"What do you mean?" Chris reacted as though it were a trick question.

"I mean, did you want to come over to my place instead?"

Despite everything that was on his mind, Chris couldn't help but like the idea that he might hang out with Jessica at her house.

"Oh," Chris stammered. "That'd be great. What did you want to do?"

"I'm going to take care of my guy," Jessica said.

"I could handle that," Chris admitted.

"Well, don't get too comfortable or you won't land that scholarship playing ball," Jessica continued, playfully. "Did you need anything at your parent's house?"

Chris noticed that the car was nearing his neighborhood. He wasn't sure if Jessica had just asked him a leading question or if he had overlooked something.

In the end, he didn't try to guess. "Did I forget something?"

"Well, if you're going to miss practice, you might want to watch the scout recording of Westby again."

"Sure," Chris said, still pretending that he was somehow a baseball player. "Right."

Unfortunately, Jessica's statement only reminded Chris that what was happening wasn't real. His mind got back on track as she slowed her car to a halt outside of his house. He wanted to enjoy whatever was going on with Jessica, but he knew that he needed to figure out what had happened the night before.

While Chris was concentrating, Jessica leaned in for a kiss. "I love it when you have that look on your face," she said.

"What look?" Chris asked, again thrown off.

"You just look so cute when you're thinking hard," she said with a wink. "Now hurry up and get that recording."

After walking into the house, Chris strode quickly up to his room. As he'd feared, it was still filled with things that he didn't recognize. He paused to think about what to do next and became resolved to the fact that he'd need to admit to his parents what was going on. They'd be horrified to previously unprecedented levels, but it appeared that he was in too deep and needed help.

Before he could do anything next, Chris heard a commotion down the hallway, just outside of his room.

"Mom?" he asked.

Chris didn't hear a reply. After several seconds, he stuck his head out into the hallway. He didn't see anything, but someone was clearly in the upstairs bathroom.

"Mom?" Chris repeated the question.

"Chris is that you?" a voice asked.

The voice came from the other side of the upstairs bathroom door. Chris didn't immediately recognize it and stepped out into the hallway. He was walking towards the bathroom door, just as it opened.

To Chris's shock, Ben stood in the doorway, looking much better-groomed than the real-world's Ben. As he strode into the hallway, Chris still recognized him and was stunned.

"What're you doing here?" Chris shouted, nervously.

Ben gave no indication that anything was unusual.

"Is something wrong?" Ben said.

"Get out of here you freak!" Chris yelled.

Chris backed away from Ben, taking one step too many. Before Chris could catch himself, he fell backwards down the stairs, sliding all the way to the first floor on his back.

When Chris reached the lower landing, he knocked his head against the floor. The blow rendered him momentarily unconscious.

Ben rushed down the stairs to help Chris. An instant later, Morgan walked through the front door and was horrified by the scene.

"What happened?" she asked, dropping down to Chris's side.

"He fell backwards," Ben said.

"What if there's bleeding?" Morgan pleaded. "Call 911!"

Ben ran out of the room to make the call, while Morgan took his place at Chris's side.

Chris slowly regained consciousness. Morgan tried to calm Chris down.

"It's okay," she said. "You hit your head, so you need to stay awake for me."

"I don't feel right." Chris said.

Chris turned and caught a glimpse of Ben on the phone. That sighting only caused him to get excited all again.

"What's he doing here?" Chris asked, mustering the strength to point at Ben.

Morgan continued to try to project a calm voice of reason.

"It's just your stepfather Chris," Morgan said. "It's okay."

"No it's not okay!" Chris exclaimed. "Where's Dad!"

Chris blacked out again when Ben re-entered the room. He only heard fleeting bits of conversation between Ben and Morgan.

"Paramedics are on the way," Ben said.

"He thinks that Richard is still alive," Morgan told Ben.

"I thought he was fine," Ben said. "We've really been getting along lately."

"He hit his head and is liable to say anything," Morgan replied. "I don't think it was you."

After a few minutes of being barely conscious, Chris heard an ambulance pull up outside. At the same time that the paramedics were rushing inside, Jessica wandered into the entryway. Her presence only added to the commotion.

"What happened?" Jessica shrieked.

As Chris was being carried out on a stretcher, Morgan took Jessica aside.

"Chris fell," Morgan said.

"I want to go along to the hospital," Jessica pleaded.

Morgan was curt with Jessica. She clearly didn't like the girl very much.

"Just go home for now and I'll call you later," Morgan said. "They'll only let family be with him."

As the paramedics loaded Chris into the waiting ambulance, he wasn't entirely sure what had just happened, but he knew that the machine must have had something to do with it.

It was late at the hospital when a doctor walked into the small patient area near the emergency room. Chris, Morgan, and Ben sat together, expecting him.

Chris was still rubbing his head and had a splitting headache from the fall. He wished that his head would stop hurting, since he wanted nothing now but to figure out what was going on with his life.

In hopes of learning more about what had changed, he'd kept quiet while waiting and avoided raising concerns regarding Ben during their time at the hospital. Chris could tell that everything seemed normal to Ben and Morgan and, until he could untangle his predicament, he didn't want everyone to think that he was crazy.

"The good news is that we didn't find any bleeding in his head." the doctor said.

Morgan immediately looked relieved and wiped away a few tears. It had been stressful for her as they'd waited with Chris.

"What's the bad news?" Ben asked.

"He'll probably have a splitting headache for a while," the doctor replied. "He did suffer a concussion, so he'll need the rest."

"You're feeling better though?" Morgan asked Chris. "Not imagining things anymore?"

Chris continued to play along, assuming that the sooner he could get home and out of watchful eyes, the faster he could start figuring out what had happened.

"Yes, I'm not sure what got into me." Chris said before he flashed Ben a wry smile. "I just want to take it easy and rest."

"Are you sure it's safe for him to sleep?" Morgan asked. Concussions could lead to a coma in some cases, so I worry about letting him sleep.

"He should be fine, just check on him every couple of hours." the doctor said.

It wasn't long after Chris arrived home that he snuck out of his room. In fact, as soon as Morgan had left Chris in his room to rest, he'd cracked open his bedroom window and then climbed out onto the garage roof. After a shim down the back of the garage, he was on the ground and running.

Chris had formulated a plan to get to the machine, but he knew that he wouldn't have much time. Leaving his room was a risk unto itself, since his mother would frequently check on him. As a precaution, he'd stuffed his bed to make it appear as though he was sleeping. Unfortunately, he knew that the low-tech ruse might only work if she peeked in from the door. At best, he assumed that he had less than two hours in which to find answers.

It was after dark as Chris ran through a series of residential streets. It took a while, but he eventually arrived in the lab's familiar office park. He was relieved to discover the parking lot clear of cars.

Getting into the lab itself proved to be a problem. Chris's usual method at the security keypad didn't work. He began thinking of other ways to get inside, but stopped after noticing a sign near the entrance. The lab wasn't the lab anymore or so a sign seemed to claim.

Chris was confused by markings indicating that a software consulting business occupied the space. He rubbed his forehead in frustration. Nothing was right in this world. He couldn't even find the machine.

Chris spent a few minutes running around the office park, trying to see if the lab entrance had somehow changed, but he came up empty handed. Giving up, he decided to head back home. He spent the entire journey worried that he'd be caught missing, which would only arouse further suspicions.

It was Chris's only positive break of the evening when he arrived back in bed a few minutes before Morgan came in to check on him. She'd woken him up, not realizing that he'd never fallen asleep.

"You're all sweaty Chris," Morgan said.

Chris hadn't bothered to change and was still cooling down from sprinting back to his room. He adjusted a blanket on his bed.

"I must have had too many blankets on," Chris suggested.

After Morgan was convinced that he was doing okay, she left the room and left Chris to his thoughts.

Above all, Chris was focused on finding the machine, hoping that it could still be used to turn everything in his life back to normal. To his dismay, he'd quickly gone from thinking that his life had finally taken off to feeling like a prisoner, trapped in a warped new reality.

4:
Caught Up

Day 3 {7:00am}

♣

The other Chris slept without interruption all night in the real world and woke up starving. His senses were likely stimulated by the smell of food being prepared downstairs. The smell struck him as unusual though, since it indicated that an elaborate breakfast was being readied. In the other world, Morgan was usually on her way to work by the time he was getting ready for school.

As Chris stood up, he looked down at himself and realized that he'd not bothered to change his clothes before falling asleep. His shirt had dried blood on it and, when he glanced into a mirror, Chris noticed blood caked under his nose. His body ached from the beating that he'd taken at Tyler's hands.

After showering and changing clothes, Chris headed downstairs. While descending the staircase, he thought about how he hoped that his mother wouldn't notice the swelling around his nose. Unfortunately, it would be hard to miss. He would have to come up with an excuse.

Chris found Morgan happily preparing the morning's breakfast offerings. She'd already placed a massive cantaloupe in the middle of the table that immediately caught Chris's attention.

"Mom," Chris asked while motioning to the cantaloupe. "Where the heck did you get that?"

"From my garden," Morgan said. "They don't sell those in the store you know!"

Chris was befuddled. "What?"

Morgan added with a smile. "At least they don't sell them yet."

Chris took a seat at the table and kept his head down, thinking that doing so might help Morgan not notice his face.

"You'd better hurry with breakfast," Morgan said. "Rachel will be by any minute."

Morgan stopped her work and looked over at Chris. She could immediately tell that his face looked swollen and rushed over to the table. She put her hand on his face.

"What happened?" Morgan asked.

"It's nothing." Chris responded, trying to downplay her concerns. "Tyler and I just had a misunderstanding."

"What kind of misunderstanding?"

A moment later, Richard was heard making his way down from an upstairs bedroom.

"Honey!" Morgan raised her voice and called up to him. "Chris hurt himself last night."

"What happened?" Richard asked.

Richard entered the dining room reading off of a tablet computer. He didn't look up at Chris until reaching the table.

"Dad?" Chris asked. His voice was heavy with disbelief.

"Are you sure you're okay?" Richard wondered. "Your mother said that things were a little off for you yesterday?"

Richard took a seat at the dining table and Chris sat, shocked at the sight of him. Chris's mind raced, not believing that it could be possible. Until this point, he had still believed that the weird events of the prior day were all an elaborate joke or something crueler.

But Chris was certain that seeing Richard was something that could not be faked. This was because, so far as the other Chris had ever known, his father had been dead for six years. Chris's mind couldn't process this new reality any longer. He passed out. His limp body slumped off of his chair and onto the floor.

"Chris!" Morgan screamed, running over to his side as he toppled down.

Richard crouched next to Chris, supporting his head while trying to help him regain consciousness. Chris quickly came back around, but remained in a mental haze.

"I don't feel well," Chris said.

After a few seconds, Chris was able to get back up into the chair. At least to Richard and Morgan, the panic of the moment seemed to lessen.

"Let's get him to the hospital," Richard said.

"But what about your meetings?" Morgan asked, looking at a clock. "You said that they're sending someone over to review the presentation logistics. They're probably already on the way."

Richard looked at his watch, unsure what to do.

"I'll take him in," Morgan told Richard. "It'll be okay."

A car horn honked from the street outside the house.

"Rachel's here," Morgan said, looking out the window.

Richard rubbed Chris's back and said. "You get checked out and stay home until you're feeling better."

Chris mumbled in agreement, still disoriented.

Richard rose and said to Morgan. "Call me from the hospital. I'll want to know what they have to say right away."

Morgan nodded. She knew about the deadlines and pressure that Richard was under. Because of that, she looked forward to the latest milestone being passed, so that their lives could calm down. More pressing though, she was worried about Chris. He hadn't quite seemed like her son over the past day or so.

Rachel laid out a long horn honk as Richard stepped out the door.

Richard added. "I'll tell Rachel that Chris is staying home."

The doctor who had examined Chris knew for sure that he had a broken nose in need of icing, but he couldn't confirm that much of anything else was wrong.

After Chris more-fully regained his senses, he convinced himself that he'd simply hallucinated the sight of his father being alive.

"The blood tests will take a few days to run," the doctor said. "But we didn't find anything out of the ordinary during our initial exam."

Morgan was understandably worried about determining why Chris had passed out. She hoped that it was just a fainting spell, as opposed to a larger problem.

"He seemed really disoriented," Morgan said.

"Most of the cases that come in like this are related to stress," The doctor said. "You'd be surprised. A significant event might occur in someone's life or things pile up, so they have an episode."

The doctor turned to Chris, who had largely sat silent during the entire visit. Chris didn't want to raise any flags, hoping that whatever was causing everything around him to be off-kilter might go away. So far as he knew, he still had the big game coming up. He didn't want people worried into thinking he shouldn't play.

"Is anything unusual going on at school?" The doctor asked.

"Not really," Chris said. "I have a big game coming up. I wasn't hitting really well yesterday at practice, so coach sent me home."

Morgan looked extremely confused by the remark. Her Chris had never showed so much as an inkling of interest in baseball.

"When did you start playing baseball?" Morgan questioned.

"Um," Chris started to answer. He was paranoid about how everything he was saying seemed to make him sound crazy. He knew that he had to be careful with his words. "It's been a while Mom."

Morgan was flabbergasted. "Well, this is certainly news to me."

Chris shut down again, assuming that he'd said something wrong. He didn't want another comment to blow up into a big concern.

The doctor cut in. "I'm not suggesting anything just yet, but if we don't find anything in the tests, I could refer you to a psychologist here in the building who might be able to help."

Morgan thought about his offer for a moment. She hoped that there would be a straightforward explanation.

"Let's see what we find out from the tests," she said and then turned to Chris. "It sounds as though there might be some things going on that I'm not aware of."

It was late-morning when Chris and Morgan arrived home from the hospital visit. During the entire car ride, Chris had remained worried that he'd lost his mind. What he'd thought had been an elaborate joke was obviously nothing of the sort. After eliminating that explanation from the equation, his only remaining reasoning for all of the weird things that had recently occurred in his world was that he'd gone crazy.

Morgan had been hesitant about letting Chris go to school that afternoon, but she ultimately relented. He'd kept the conversation with her to a minimum, but otherwise seemed okay and eager to get back to his normal routine. Morgan dropped him off at school and pulled away assuming that he'd be heading into class.

However, Chris didn't go to class. His mind kept swimming. He couldn't let go of the lingering thought that somehow his father was alive and that maybe he wasn't crazy. As such, he spent the day walking to where he thought his mother and step-father's lab was located. When he arrived at the location though, it was vacant. In fact, the facility looked like it hadn't been used for months.

That discovery was a breaking point for the other Chris. The bit of hope that he'd momentarily conjured up in order to maintain his sanity faded away.

Chris knew that he should seek help, but he also knew that anyone who he talked to would immediately want him to be medicated or treated in some way. That worried him, even if a quiet voice in the back of his mind began to wonder if it were the right thing to do.

Broken down, Chris returned to school, hoping to find Rachel. His problems had gotten much more complicated than worrying about baseball practice or Jessica's behavior. He also didn't want to get beat up again. As it was, Rachel had been the only one helping him out over the past day who hadn't asked too many questions.

Rachel was surprised when she noticed Chris approach her car. She had just gotten out of school and was ready to head home.

She yelled over to him. "What the heck are you doing here?"

"I was at the hospital," Chris said. "But everything was okay."

Rachel looked closer at Chris and noticed his swollen nose.

"You look awful," Rachel said.

"I'm fine."

"You don't look like you're fine."

"I passed out or something."

"Why were you at the hospital then?" Rachel asked. "You look like you got beat up."

"My Mom freaked out." Chris said. "It's nothing."

"Uh-huh."

"Look," Chris said, not interested in arguing. "Do you think you could take me back to the lab?"

Chris knew that Ben must have a lab somewhere, since he'd woken up in one the prior morning. If Richard actually were alive, even if it was not the correct lab, Chris hoped that he'd be there.

Of course, Rachel had had enough of the lab after her confrontation with Ben the prior morning and wasn't overly-excited about heading back.

"Are you sure that's a great idea?" she asked.

"It'll just be a minute," Chris said, hoping that everything could still somehow be explained.

Day 3 {11:00am}

☺ ↔ ☻

    The real Chris had stayed up much of the night, having been doted over every couple of hours by the other Morgan. As morning neared its end though, much like the other Chris had done, he was able to convince Morgan to let him head to school. She insisted that he not take part in baseball practice later that afternoon, but that was an easy enough promise for Chris to make.

    Of course, Chris had no intention of actually going to school. Morgan drove him to the school building and, not long after she'd dropped him off, he snuck off the grounds. He had renewed hopes of locating the lab.

    Unfortunately, it was a several-mile walk on foot to the lab's office park. Upon arriving, Chris's efforts only led to more frustration when he again came up empty handed. Most of the offices in the area were still recognizably in place, but the lab itself was nowhere to be found.

    Chris had told Morgan that he'd get a ride home later from Jessica. That hadn't actually been his plan, but he'd wanted to give himself as much time as possible to locate the lab. With the lab search at a dead end, Chris headed back to the school, wondering if he couldn't get a helping hand from Jessica.

    With his long-distance walking, Chris didn't arrive back at the school until after classes had ended for the day. He assumed that Jessica would be at dance team practice, so he headed behind the school to find her.

    When Chris arrived at the school's athletic area, baseball practice was already well underway. At roughly the same time that Chris spotted Jessica, Tyler called over to him.

"Where were you man?" Tyler asked as he approached Chris. "You're letting us all down."

Tyler seemed genuinely upset, aggressively tapping a bat in his palm that he'd carried with him. Chris tried to brush him off.

"I was in the hospital last night," Chris said. "So lay off, okay?"

"You look fine to me man," Tyler observed.

Barns spotted Chris and came over in the middle of the discussion.

"Look what turned up coach," Tyler said.

"The school nurse said that you'd been to the hospital," Barns said to Chris, genuinely concerned. "Everything okay?"

"Yeah," Chris said. "I had an accident. They think maybe a concussion."

Tyler let his bat drop against the ground. Barns shot him an annoyed look.

"Settle down Tyler," Barns said, before turning back to Chris. "Look Chris, I can't force you to play out here, but we're going to need all of our top guys putting in their best effort before the game."

Chris played along, to a point.

"Yeah," Chris said. "I'll see about tomorrow. The doctor said I shouldn't be at practice today."

"Tomorrow's the game Chris," Barns warned. "Don't let us down."

Barns walked away with Tyler, but Tyler turned back to flash Chris a disgusted look. Chris couldn't care less about the baseball game, as he wanted to avoid distractions. If he were supposed to be a star baseball player, it worried Chris that Tyler seemed to resent his inability to play.

Jessica approached Chris a moment later. She'd witnessed the discussion with Barns and had held back from interrupting.

"Where've you been all day?" Jessica asked.

"You know my Mom," Chris covered. "She wasn't going to let me come to school."

"How'd you get here then?"

"Well," Chris grinned, realizing he was not lying extremely well. "I talked her into finally letting me come."

The remark only confused Jessica.

"But you said that you can't practice," she pointed out.

"I know," Chris said with a smile. "I wanted to see you."

Jessica wasn't dumb though and knew that something didn't make sense about Chris's story. She should have been flattered, but he'd been acting weird even prior to falling down the stairs. In many ways, it seemed to Jessica like Chris was suddenly an altogether different person.

Jessica gave Chris a skeptical look.

"We're almost done with practice," she said. "Meet me at my car in a few minutes."

Jessica assumed that Chris was coming over to her house, but he had other plans in mind. In order to look less suspicious, he didn't bring those plans up right away. Instead, he let Jessica vent about her day.

"I tried to visit, but your Mom said that you had to rest," Jessica said. "She hates me. You know that, right?"

Despite everything else going on, Chris had picked up on that fact. He was intent on keeping Jessica happy though and lied to her.

"I don't know," Chris said. "She's probably just stressed out about me. You know how she worries."

Jessica sniffed at Chris. He'd assumed that he could use the car ride to learn some information, so he needed to start guiding the conversation in that direction. If the machine had somehow changed his reality, Chris knew that he was going to need to be a detective to piece those differences together.

"So," Chris said, "Uh, how about Ben? You like him?"

Jessica perked up. "Yeah, he's cool."

"Really?" Chris asked.

Chris was so surprised by her reply that he almost blew his 'cover.' It was clear that he was not cut out for a career as a secret agent.

Jessica's brow crinkled as she misread Chris's reaction.

"Why?" she asked in reply. "What'd he say? He doesn't like me either?"

"No, no," Chris backpedalled. "I'm sure he likes you just fine. He's just been a jerk from time to time to me."

"That's not what you said last week," Jessica said.

Chris realized that he seemed to be incapable of missing potential landmines when it came to these sorts of conversations. He'd not done much better when trying to fish around for information from Morgan. Sensing trouble, he changed the subject.

"Hey," Chris said. "I just realized that I need to stop at the lab to pick up some stuff for my Mom."

"What?" Jessica exclaimed, clearly taken by surprise.

"Sorry," Chris apologized. "Do you mind?"

"I guess not." Jessica was confused, but turned the car around. "Why do you need to go there? You never go there?"

"I think that my Mom misplaced some medication that they gave me for headaches," Chris said. "And I might need something for my project in science class."

Jessica was only further confused.

"What project?" she asked. "We have something coming up in there?"

Chris was running out of explanations.

"Some extra credit for Barns," Chris said. "Need to do some make-ups."

Jessica remained skeptical, but let it slide.

"Okay," she said. "I just wish you'd said something earlier. Now we'll to have to totally backtrack."

"Sorry," Chris repeated and then let a moment of silence pass before he continued. "You know, I was trying to remember how long they've been in a new location?"

"I thought you told me that it was a few years ago," Jessica said. "After the accident."

Her reference to an 'accident' made Chris think back to the machine's breakthrough a few years prior. Chris thought hard about what that might mean. He wondered if there was a connection that he was missing.

Jessica didn't give Chris much time before she interrupted his thinking.

"Does your Mom know that we're coming over?" Jessica inquired. "I thought that she didn't like you being around the lab since your Dad passed away?"

Chris shrugged.

"They're probably gone for the day," Chris said, gambling that that was true. He supposed that it didn't hurt to try.

Besides, Jessica had just confirmed that, at least in this version of reality, his father was dead. That meant that things were, indeed, much worse than he'd originally feared.

Jessica's car pulled into a decidedly less-sophisticated office park than the one that Chris was familiar with. Chris looked around but didn't recognize the area at all. So far as technical firms were concerned, this was the low-rent district.

Chris and Jessica walked up to the building's front entrance, but Chris wasn't immediately sure how to gain access. The building's entry console was decidedly low-tech. Chris pushed on an old intercom button. A moment later, Ben's voice came loudly through.

"Hello?" Ben said. "Can I help you?"

"It's me, Chris," Chris replied. "Can I come in?"

"Sure."

A buzzer sounded and the lab door popped open. Chris and Jessica headed inside. It wasn't hard to find the lab itself, since the building had no sprawling hallways or cavernous interiors. The lab was relatively small in comparison to what Chris was accustomed to in the real world.

Ben waved at Chris from the center of the room. He stood behind a circular table that contained flickering holographic images.

"Feeling better?" Ben asked as Chris approached.

"Yeah," Chris said. "I'm not sure what happened, but I'm fine now."

Morgan rushed over from the opposite side of the room.

"I told you to head home after school," she protested.

"I know," Chris said. "But I wanted to see what you guys were up to."

Morgan seemed surprised.

"Well," Morgan said. "That's a rarity, isn't it?"

Jessica spoke up to Morgan. "Hi."

Morgan gave Jessica an icy smile and responded. "Nice to see you Jessica."

Chris ignored the obvious tension between the two and walked over to where Ben was working. Along the way, he picked up a small cube that had a large red button on the top. Before he pressed the button, Ben stopped him.

Be careful with that," Ben said. "We're still working out the kinks."

"What is it?" Chris asked. "A flashlight?"

"It's a flashlight alright," Ben responded. "A high-intensity flash generator. It'd put us both out cold if we looked at it when it went off."

Morgan interjected. "Ben knows that firsthand."

Ben shrugged. "Like I said, we're still working out the kinks."

Ben had been tinkering at a control panel that looked similar to the one used by the machine. However, now it was being used to run a holographic display. The display appeared to be showing converted images from old films.

"You're working on 3-D movies?" Chris wondered aloud.

Ben piped in. "Didn't your Mom mention our new contract?"

"No."

"A couple of film companies down in Los Angeles are sponsoring a proof of concept."

"Really?"

The idea seemed out-of-place to Chris.

"Yeah," Ben said. "It took a bit of doing, but we dusted off some of the old equipment and we're planning on repurposing what we can."

Ben motioned over to a pile of electronic machinery in the rear of the lab. Chris gasped and immediately recognized an earlier version of the machine's viewing chamber. The control helmet, albeit an early model of it, sat nearby.

"That's the machine," Chris said matter-of-fact.

"Yep," Ben informed him, a hint of melancholy in his voice. "Your mother has always wanted to sell it for parts."

Morgan came up behind Chris and interjected herself into the conversation.

"I just want us all to move on," she said.

"I know," Ben replied. "I hope that this new project lets us dust some of that off and get a little value out of it."

"Chris," Morgan said. "Jessica mentioned that you came by to find something?"

"Oh, yeah," Chris said, thinking for a moment. "Did the doctors give us any pills for my headache?"

Morgan immediately looked concerned and asked. "I thought that you said that you felt fine?"

"I do feel fine," Chris insisted, trying to play innocent. "Just in case."

Jessica cut into the exchange.

"I was hoping that maybe we could get some time to study," she said.

Chris was surprised by Jessica's appeal and wondered if she might be trying to find excuses to leave the lab. Of course, after having spotted the machine and being filled with a desire to investigate, Chris didn't want to leave just yet. He was running out of excuses though and resolved himself to returning on his own.

"I'll see you guys later then," Chris said, leaving with Jessica.

"Take it easy Chris," Ben said, cheerfully. "You've had an eventful day."

On his way out of the lab, Chris took note of the control panel immediately inside the main entryway. It was primitive. Chris spent a moment punching away at it on an administrative screen, oblivious that Jessica was growing impatient while waiting for him.

"What are you doing?" Jessica asked.

"Just looking at how the security is set up," Chris replied. "It's pretty light."

"Why does it matter?"

"We wouldn't want anyone breaking in," Chris said, looking up at Jessica with a sly grin. "Now would we?"

Day 3 {4:00pm}

♣

When Rachel and the other Chris arrived at the real world's lab, only Ben's car sat outside.

"Great," Rachel observed. "Ben's here."

"Good," Chris said.

The reaction confused Rachel and she simply said. "Glad you've got him under control.

Rachel and Chris walked over to the lab door. Chris examined the control panel next to the door but didn't push any of the buttons. He wasn't sure what to do.

"I thought you had a pass code to get in?" Rachel said.

Chris gave her a dumb stare. He had no idea what the code might be.

"Maybe we should knock or something," Chris offered.

"Funny," Rachel said, clearly impatient.

Chris looked around for some sort of buzzer or intercom, but he didn't see anything obvious.

"Stop fooling around," Rachel said. "You really think that Ben's just going to let us in?"

"Why not?" Chris asked. A moment later, he found the most likely button to 'ring' and pressed it. Nothing happened at first, but his action at least seemed to satisfy Rachel.

"You're still acting really weird you know," Rachel said. "It's getting annoying."

After waiting a few more seconds, Ben opened the lab door looking as angry as ever.

"I don't understand why you kids keep coming around here," Ben said sternly.

Rachel cut in before Chris could say anything.

"Well, it's not for your hospitality," she retorted with a snort. "That's for sure."

"Hey Ben," Chris started. "I was hoping we could maybe come in and hang out for a little while.

Rachel looked at Chris as though he was a complete idiot. Ben assumed that he was being mocked. He hated it when he felt that his time was being wasted.

"We're in the middle of highly-intense testing, so we don't need your distractions," Ben said, adding. "When Richard gets back here I'll be reporting this disturbance to him."

Ben abruptly shut the lab door and stormed away. Chris immediately banged on the door, hoping to get his attention again. After another few seconds, Ben reopened the door.

"What part of what I just told you didn't you understand?" Ben asked. "I thought that you were so smart that it would have been clear."

Chris blurted out. "Where did you say my Dad was at?"

"I don't know," Ben said. "Maybe you could try at home, since that's where you should be right now anyway."

Ben again shut the door, but Chris let him go this time.

"Wow," Rachel said, taken aback by the entire exchange. "That was smooth."

"I'm not sure why he seemed so upset." Chris said, clearly still not understanding Ben's behavior.

Rachel and Chris walked back to her car.

"He's so creepy," Rachel said.

"He's fine," Chris said, defending Ben. "Something must have been on his mind I guess."

"What're you talking about?" Rachel said. "You're pals with him? He didn't seem like he was your friend just now."

Chris didn't respond. The pair got into Rachel's car and headed toward Chris's house.

Ben returned to the lab confused by Chris's behavior. He couldn't understand why the teen had tried to be polite to him. Of course, Ben didn't realize that the other Chris wasn't the Chris whom he'd long known.

In recent years, Chris had been a thorn in Ben's side. He resented Chris's presence and saw him as an annoyance to be sure, if not also a distraction to Richard. And a distracted Richard meant a slower-moving project.

Ben returned to work, troubleshooting the machine. At one point, he checked the parking lot security camera and thought that he'd spotted Rachel's car returning. When the car came into sight though, he realized that it was Jai Lei's sedan pulling into the lab's parking lot. Ben made his way back to the front entrance and greeted Jai.

"This is a surprise." Ben said.

"I apologize," Jai said. "I should have given you more notice."

Ben seemed unconcerned, almost eager to see Jai.

"Not a problem," he said. "It's always good to see a friendly face."

"Indeed," Jai said, pleasantly surprised by the warm reception. "Is Richard around?"

"No, he won't be back until later."

Jai motioned over to his sedan.

"Good," Jai said. "I'm sorry to be in a rush about this, but my employers insisted. I'd like to take you out for dinner again, are you free?"

After Rachel had dropped Chris off at home, she continued to worry about him. His behavior had still not seemed right. When Rachel noticed Morgan working outside in the yard, she thought that it would be worthwhile to speak with her again.

Rachel parked her car in her parent's driveway and then approached the section of the fence where Morgan was gardening. Rachel was concerned about being eavesdropped on and made sure that Chris couldn't see her from his room when she spoke to Morgan.

"Hi Mrs. J," Rachel said.

"Hi Rachel," Morgan said in a cheerful tone. "What's up?"

It was an open secret that Morgan wished Chris would notice Rachel's romantic interest in him. Morgan was happy that Rachel was friends with Chris, but she secretly hoped that it might eventually blossom into something more.

Morgan feared that Chris and Rachel might drift apart after high school ended. She knew that Chris had a hard time making friends and Rachel certainly was exceptional, given her ability to handle all of Chris's quirks. It didn't hurt that she was quite intelligent too.

"I just wanted to check in about Chris again," Rachel said, trying not to concern Morgan.

Morgan knew that Rachel didn't stop by without a reason though and asked. "What's wrong? He wasn't feeling faint again, was he?"

"No," Rachel said. "But he keeps acting odd."

Rachel thought for a moment before deciding that it was best to betray a little of Chris's confidence.

"Don't tell him that I told you," Rachel said. "But we stopped by the lab tonight."

Morgan became angry for a moment before catching herself. Not aware that this Chris wasn't her son, she was disappointed that she'd clearly not gotten through to him as she'd hoped.

Rachel continued. "Ben is probably already complaining to Mr. Jennings. He didn't let us inside and was seriously freaking out."

"I can't say that I'm surprised," Morgan said. "Chris knows that he shouldn't be down there."

Rachel tried to soften the situation, not wanting to get Chris into trouble.

"That's not it though," she said, pausing to get her thoughts straight. "I can usually figure out what Chris is up to, but he's done things over the past couple of days that have really confused me."

At first, Morgan wasn't overly surprised.

"He tries a lot of things to get Richard's attention," she offered.

"I know," Rachel said. "Maybe that's part of it, but it doesn't seem like the only thing this time."

"Is it something to do with Jessica?" Morgan asked. "That whole business about dating her?"

Rachel bristled at the question. The suggestion still rubbed her the wrong way.

"If they were," Rachel said. "It must not have lasted long. He didn't say anything about her today."

Morgan and Rachel both sat at mental dead ends for a moment.

Rachel broke the silence, saying. "He's just not been himself lately. I'm not sure what it is, but something is 'off.'"

Morgan nodded in agreement.

"Don't worry," she said. "Richard and I have noticed the same things too. We're going to speak with him once Richard gets home."

"Maybe he's chemically imbalanced or something," Rachel offered. "I was reading online about it and…"

Morgan cut Rachel off and explained. "The doctor ordered some tests, so we'll find out soon if there's a physical explanation. I did want to ask you something though. Is Chris hanging out with any new people? People we should be concerned about?"

Rachel knew what she might be implying.

"I don't think so," she said, but then admitted. "I haven't seen enough of him over the past couple of days to know for sure."

During their car ride, Ben and Jai exchanged pleasantries, but discussed little regarding why Jai was interested in meeting again. They returned to the same restaurant that they'd dined at during their previous encounter. Ben couldn't help but notice that Jai seemed more business-like during this meal. His demeanor raised Ben's suspicions and Ben wasn't sure if he might be nervous or excited by whatever was going on.

Finally, Ben asked. "What's with the surprise visit? You wanted to wait until we were here to discuss things. Now we're here."

Jai smiled and started. "Things are speeding up a bit with my employers. They had been sitting on the sidelines for the past few years, but some things have emerged that have begun to force their hand."

"What kinds of things?"

"International politics. Espionage. You know, the things that can't be spoken about in much detail."

"What does that have to do with me?"

"It has everything to do with you and your creation," Jai said, chuckling an odd laugh. "I know you're working on something that can change the world."

Ben knew that the machine didn't work entirely as Jai likely hoped or assumed. For that reason, Ben didn't want to find himself caught misrepresenting its functionality, but Ben also didn't want Jai to lose interest.

"Maybe," Ben said. "But it isn't perfected yet."

Jai interrupted, seemingly ignoring Ben's admission. "I know that things have not been going well between you and Richard for a long time now."

Ben was silent. As with their earlier conversation, he wasn't going to dispute Jai on that point.

"After your presentation," Jai continued. "You'll get your next level of funding, right?"

"Probably," Ben admitted, knowing that the project sponsors would still be encouraged by their progress.

"Do you think that Richard will want to continue keeping you around?"

Ben had considered that prospect already, that Richard would push him out of the project, and it worried him. Jai seemed to know exactly what to say in order to get his point across.

"What did you have in mind?" Ben asked.

"My employer would like to make you an offer," Jai said, growing more serious.

"What kind of offer?"

"The kind where you wouldn't have to worry anymore about money," Jai replied, selling it. "Where you'd be calling all the shots, free from distractions. Where you're a hero, not a helper."

Ben hung on the words while Jai paused for dramatic effect.

"The opportunity to be appreciated for being a genius," Jai added. "Rather than having to tolerate being in another's shadow."

Ben took it all in for a moment. It would be his wildest dreams come true."

"Surely," Ben said. "You want more than just me in making this deal?"

"Ben," Jai said. "We want you to work with us because you're a genius. You're the creator of what is to be one of the greatest landmarks in scientific history."

Ben knew that Jai was speaking in hyperbole, but his ego continued to like what he heard. And hey, when the machine did work perfectly, Jai might not be too far off of the mark.

Jai continued. "All that we're asking is that you build it for us, rather than the United States government."

Ben didn't act surprised or upset by the request. He'd half-expected it and would consider it. Everything about it made him actually begin to feel a certain release from the problems of his current life. He already started to feel all of the petty rivalries and conflicts fade away.

"They wouldn't let me just walk away you know," Ben said. "Certainly not to work for a, er, rival."

"You'd be well protected," Jai insisted.

"They're powerful." Ben observed.

"So are we," Jai said, his words hanging in the air, cold and confident.

After a moment's consideration, Ben said. "Maybe we should start talking about more of the details."

Jai smiled, knowing that Ben was now his.

"Excellent," Jai said.

Richard was about to head inside to the lab just as Jai's sedan pulled out of the parking lot. Ben walked up to the building entrance where Richard waited to greet him.

"Anyone I know?" Richard asked.

"No," Ben lied. "Just an old friend."

Ben worried that Richard would have been rightfully suspicious of Jai. When the three had been in graduate school together, Jai had already developed a reputation for being slippery.

"Did you have them inside the lab?" Richard questioned.

"No," Ben said. He grew annoyed. "Would that have been a problem?"

"Perhaps," Richard said. "We both know that once the government sees our latest progress that we'll probably begin to be classified."

"But you have no problems letting your son wander around the lab nearly every day?"

"He's just a kid Ben."

"Even more reason that he shouldn't be nosing around."

"Look," Richard said, trying to diffuse the situation. "Things will be changing soon."

Ben heard the words from Richard's mouth differently than had been intended. In his mind, Richard had only confirmed his growing paranoia.

"What do you mean 'change?'" Ben asked, staring hard into Richard's eyes.

"Like Chris being around," Richard said. "I'm sorry Ben, but he does mean well. I've already told him that he can't be coming around like in the past. Morgan hates it and, you're right, it isn't appropriate at this stage."

"Tell him again then," Ben said, pointing out. "He was just here tonight."

Richard shook his head. He was surprised by the revelation and made a mental note to speak to his son again.

"I don't want to argue," Richard said. "I'll take care of it. Our focus needs to be on correcting whatever malfunction we still have in the system."

"We can only figure out this lag problem if we keep testing," Ben said. "I've been telling you that."

"Well," Richard concluded. "Let's get back at it then."

A short time later, Richard and Ben were inside the lab, preparing to run a test on the machine. Richard was already operating the machine via the helmet, while Ben stood back at the machine's control panel.

"Bring the power up to the problem level," Richard requested to Ben.

Ben complied. After Richard was able to wrestle mental control of the machine, a clear image appeared in the machine's viewing chamber. It was obviously Morgan and Richard's house where no one appeared to be at home.

"Morgan!" Richard yelled above the machine's powerful hum. "Are you there?"

Morgan responded through a conference speaker inside the lab. She had been monitoring over a telephone while they tested.

"Yes Richard," she said. "I'm right here in the living room"

Richard looked around inside the living room but saw nothing except the empty sofa and a littered collection of belongings.

As Richard turned around, Ben thought that he caught a glimpse of himself pass though the home's entryway and head upstairs. Ben assumed that it must have been Chris returning home, but he couldn't quite extinguish the thought that he'd seen himself in the image. Richard didn't seem to notice it, so Ben decided to keep quiet for now.

"Honey," Richard said to Morgan. "We're still not seeing anything, so we're going to shut down."

"I'll see you later then," Morgan responded as she signed off of the speakerphone. "Don't stay too late."

Richard concluded the test by motioning to Ben to cut the machine's power. He took off the helmet and sat it down nearby. Obviously frustrated, he picked up a towel to wipe sweat away from his brow.

Ben spoke up first. "We haven't had time to test enough at these power levels. We shouldn't be doing the presentation yet."

Richard didn't seem nearly as concerned.

"So we'll do it at the lower levels." Richard suggested. "That's where we'd been testing at for months now.

"As I have told you before," Ben scoffed. "We both know that the quality in the image won't be enough to impress them."

"The concept works," Richard said. "That alone should carry us."

"They'll be expecting something more significant than what they saw last time."

"And they'll get just that."

We're in a corner here Richard. We might not be better off than any of our competition."

Richard finished cleaning himself off. He was frustrated.

"We'll need to analyze the latest run logs then," Richard said, relenting. "Maybe something will show up."

"I'll look into it tonight," Ben said. "I have some things that I'd like to check first."

Day 3 {6:00pm}

☺ ↔ ☻

Under normal circumstances, entering Jessica's house would have been surreal for the real Chris. Given everything that had occurred over the past day though, the machine was instead at the center of Chris's thoughts. Thus, the experience hardly registered for him.

Jessica's parents were in their living room when she entered with Chris. Her father was a burly man, but his gruff exterior was betrayed by a teddy bear personality. In contrast, her mother had a dominant personality and was often critical of Jessica. While Jessica displayed traits from both of her parents, it was easy to see how she might have inherited some of the judgmental tendencies set forth by her mother.

After initial greetings, Jessica's father got down to business.

"I'm hoping you're able to have a big game Chris," Jessica's father said. "I always loved to shut down Westby. You know, back in the day."

Jessica's father liked to relive his glory years whenever he had the opportunity.

"Jessica tells me that you're not feeling well?" her mother butted in.

"Things have been a little off," Chris answered. "But I'm getting it figured out."

"Good," Jessica's mother said with icy determination. "You wouldn't want to embarrass Jessica."

Jessica flushed, obviously made uncomfortable by her mother's comment.

"Geez Mom," she said. "Try to be more subtle."

As Chris followed Jessica into her room, he couldn't help but be sympathetic toward who she was. After interacting with

Jessica and her family, Chris had come to realize that she lived a life different than he'd expected.

Jessica's Mother seemed to dominate the household and treated her poorly. They weren't a wealthy family, so it was easy to see why Jessica might be attracted to success. Chris thought that if he really were suddenly some sort of superstar, it made sense that they'd be dating. By the same token, it also made sense why the real Jessica might see Tyler and his family's wealth as a sort of escape from her reality.

While Jessica unpacked inside her room, Chris made a bit of smalltalk. Admittedly, Chris had no real idea how to make smalltalk with a girl whom he liked. Until now, he'd never actually had the opportunity.

"I didn't realize that you were such a hard studier," Chris said, unpacking his books. "Are you thinking about college?"

Jessica stopped what she was doing and walked over to Chris. She planted a kiss on him. Chris let it linger before she finally broke it off.

"We're really studying?" Chris asked.

"No," Jessica said, leaning in to kiss Chris again. "I just wanted you all for myself."

Chris and Jessica settled onto a small, tattered sofa that sat against one wall in her crowded room. They continued kissing and, at first it was exciting for Chris, but after a few minutes, his mind began to wander.

Chris simply couldn't keep from thinking about how he would get the machine going again. Despite the fact that he finally had what he wanted with Jessica, the sense that things in this world were entirely wrong kept distracting him.

Finally, Chris broke off the kiss with Jessica.

"I'm sorry," Chris said. "But I need to get going."

Jessica appeared to be floored by the announcement.

"What?" she said, annoyed and confused. "Where would you need to go?"

"There's something at the lab that I can't get out of my head and I wanted to help out," Chris said. "Trust me, it's for the best."

Jessica remained angry.

"What are you talking about?" she questioned. "You're acting so weird."

"I'm fine," Chris said. "Trust me."

Chris stood up and started to leave Jessica's room. He stopped when he realized that he had a problem.

"Can you take me back to the lab?" Chris asked.

When Jessica's car pulled into the lab's empty parking lot, Chris was pleased to see that all of the vehicles were gone for the evening.

"Why, again, are we here?" Jessica asked.

"I wanted to run a few tests on some old equipment." Chris responded.

Jessica was skeptical.

"Since when did you start having an interest in this stuff?" she challenged.

Chris smiled and offered. "It's been a while."

Jessica continued to press, saying. "I don't want to get into trouble if you end up breaking something."

"It'll be fine." Chris said, adding. "Trust me."

Jessica parked her car.

"Why didn't you bring this up…" Jessica s, her voice trailing off. Chris had already gotten out of her parked vehicle.

Jessica reluctantly got out too. She wasn't used to being treated this way, so she was annoyed when she caught up with Chris at the door to the lab building.

"How do you plan on getting inside?" Jessica asked, looking around. "There's no one here."

Chris punched in an access code and the doorway to the lab popped open.

"I left myself a way in." Chris said proudly, recalling his actions during their prior visit.

Once inside, Chris led Jessica over to the corner of the room where the old viewing chamber, control helmet, and other equipment were sitting in storage.

"We'll need something to move this closer to the control panel," Chris said, pointing to an empty space in the center of the room.

"You don't think that anyone might notice tomorrow?" Jessica questioned, skeptically.

"We'll just put it back before we leave," Chris replied, still not paying full attention to Jessica.

Rather, Chris was focused on the task at hand and excited to figure out a way to restore things to how they'd been before. After sizing up the situation, Chris realized that, without any wheels under it, the viewing chamber was too heavy to slide. Chris dug around in a back room until he found a hand loader that did the trick.

While Chris worked, Jessica looked on. She was alternatively bored, annoyed, and skeptical as Chris spent the next few hours connecting various wires. As the evening progressed, he also had to dismantle elements of the holographic movie projector in order to restore those parts missing from the machine. With the passage of time, the disarray inside the lab only grew.

Finally, Jessica couldn't hold back her tongue any longer.

"This really seems like a mess," she said. "I don't see how you're going to have time to put all this back together. I'll need to get home soon or my Mom will have the police out looking for me."

Chris finished tearing the movie projector apart, cherry-picking the last of the parts that he needed. While doing so, he paid Jessica only passing attention.

"We'll have to remember to put these back too," he said.

When it came time to perform a test, Chris realized that Jessica might actually be helpful to have around. He wasn't sure how smoothly he could operate this version of the machine alone.

"Can you help me with something?

Chris led Jessica over to the control panel and pointed to a red button.

"The machine should have some safeguards in place," Chris said. "But I'm not sure how sophisticated they are."

"That sounds encouraging," Jessica grumbled.

"I doubt that they spent much time refining that yet," Chris admitted. "All you need to remember though is to hit this button if I signal you or something goes really wrong."

"What do you mean 'really wrong?' And what is this button going to do?"

"It'll cut the power. Don't worry, I've used this before. It'll be fine."

Jessica appeared to grow more uncomfortable as she had more time to think through what Chris had been saying.

"This doesn't look safe," she observed. "Did Ben or your Mom show you how to do all this?"

"No," Chris said. "My Dad."

Jessica shook her head and pointed out. "Your Dad's been dead for five years."

Chris acted as thought this fact was no big deal. "Uh-huh."

Chris set the target power level on the control panel and the machine began to hum as it warmed up.

It was time to begin. Chris slowed down enough to notice how haphazard the machine looked. The worry on Jessica's face made sense. He was struck with a certain sense of loss. Assuming that Chris was able to 'reset' things, Jessica would assumedly no longer be his girlfriend.

Chris leaned in and kissed Jessica one more time. It wasn't a passionate kiss, but he assumed that he might not get another opportunity.

"I wish that I'd gotten to spend more time with you," Chris said.

"What's that supposed to mean?" Jessica shot back.

Jessica didn't get an answer though, as Chris took a position near the viewing chamber and put on the control helmet. He appeared fine at first but soon flinched in pain from the stress of the crude machine's power. The holographic projection in the viewing chamber started to appear, but Chris struggled to make it stabilize. This primitive version of the machine was much harder to control than the modern version. It was dangerous.

Jessica grew increasingly worried as she saw Chris in pain. She finally couldn't take it any longer and pressed the red button. Immediately, power levels dropped. The machine winded itself down.

Chris was taken by surprise when the machine stopped. He took off the helmet and yelled to Jessica. "What happened?"

Jessica looked frightened.

"I thought you were getting hurt," she said.

Chris looked exhausted. Despite his frustration after the aborted run, he still managed to flash a cocky smile.

"It was a little rougher than I was expecting," he admitted.

"I really think that we should go home," Jessica pleaded. "It's getting late."

Chris looked at the time and realized that they were already pushing their luck. If the test didn't work, Chris would be stuck having to put everything back as it had been and trying again at another time. He wanted another chance before giving up.

"One more try," Chris insisted. "And then we'll put everything back."

At this point, Jessica was thoroughly baffled by everything that had occurred that evening. She sighed, near tears, clearly at the end of her rope.

"I'm getting out of here," she said. "You're not making any sense and I'm not going to stand here and watch you hurt yourself."

Jessica stormed out of the lab, assuming that Chris would follow and that they could end the strange night. Of course, he didn't follow her. Instead, he decided to risk a run of the machine on his own.

Chris reset the power levels on the control panel and the machine again powered up. When Chris put on the helmet this time, he was ready for the jolt of the cruder machine's power. Again, he strained at first but regained control.

The viewing chamber soon sprang to life. Chris was overjoyed when he caught a brief glimpse of the lab as he knew it, in the real world. The image was incomplete though. Chris thought that it would take additional power to clear it up.

As Chris was thinking about his next move, a power surge caught him by surprise. The last thing that he saw before blacking out was an electrical breaker box shooting off sparks.

Day 3 {8:00pm}

♣

Earlier that same evening in the real world, Chris's parents were still not aware of what had happened to their son or that there was another Chris in his place. As soon as Richard walked through his home's front door, Morgan could tell that he was upset.

"What's wrong?" Morgan asked

Richard answered while removing his jacket.

"Just Ben," he said.

"Still nothing in the logs?"

"No," Richard said. "Ben's going to look over things from the last test, but we've been burning out and we're well past finding anything obvious."

Morgan was skeptical.

"Ben's actually helping though?" she questioned. "Not just saying it?"

"Yeah," Richard admitted. "If anything, he's more focused than I've seen him in a long time."

Morgan suggested. "Maybe the stress from this crunch will do some good to him."

"Maybe," Richard said. "But something still seems off about him. I mean, more off than usual."

Richard didn't take time to speculate further as he glanced around the house.

"Where's Chris?" Richard asked. "I have some things to speak with him about."

"He's upstairs," Morgan said. "I'm glad that you brought it up. Rachel has been telling me that he's acting strange at school."

Richard seemed surprised.

"What kinds of things?" he asked.

"I don't know if it might be this girl he's been interested in," Morgan said. "Or some test or just growing up."

Richard remembered that they'd been expecting test results from Chris's earlier visit to the hospital. "What'd the doctor say?"

"They called tonight and the tests were fine."

As she said the words, Morgan realized how worried she'd become. She'd never seen her son act as he had before and, given Rachel's concerns, she knew that it wasn't all in her head.

"I guess that you two aren't the only ones who've noticed something odd about him," Richard said, referring to Ben. "I just hope that this isn't something more serious than seeking attention."

"He looks to you for approval," Morgan said. "You realize that, right?"

"Yes Morgan," Richard said. "I do. But he also needs to realize that the world doesn't always revolve around him."

Richard went upstairs and, when he arrived at Chris's room, he knocked. After a moment, he heard the other Chris say. "Come in."

Richard opened the door and was surprised to find Chris taking down some of his posters. The room looked like it had been rummaged through and was in total disarray.

"What're you up to Chris?" Richard asked, clearly puzzled.

Chris was again stunned to see Richard alive. He didn't pass out this time and managed to sit himself down before that impulse struck. Chris was about to confront Richard and shout at him that he wasn't real, but he stopped himself when he noticed Morgan looking on from the hallway.

"What's going on Mom?" Chris stammered.

"We just wanted to talk with you about some things," Morgan said.

So far as Chris was concerned, he'd hallucinated a vision of his father coming into his room to counsel him. In a strange sort of way that only made sense inside his mind, Chris thought that maybe he could wrestle control of the situation in his head, on his own.

He knew that doing so would mean a careful game of not letting his mother know that he had issues. So far as he was concerned, he assumed that could get things to turn back to normal if he tried hard enough. First though, he decided that he just needed to ride out whatever was going to unfold.

"You know," Richard said. "You can talk to us if you have something on your mind."

Chris smiled and thought to himself how ironic the statement was.

Richard continued. "I need you to not come to the lab anymore."

Morgan piped in. "Please don't go down there anymore without our permission Chris."

Chris didn't hesitate.

"That's fine," he said. "I'll never go back there again."

Richard seemed surprised by Chris's reaction.

"It doesn't have to be like that," he said. "I'm just saying that I need you to not come down there for a little while."

"Okay," Chris said.

Chris wasn't sure what to do next. He hoped that, with the request agreed to, Richard might simply disappear.

Richard continued. "Your mother and I have been really worried about you."

"We're not the only ones who are worried about you," Morgan added.

Chris acted surprised and asked. "Worried about what?"

"You've been behaving strangely over the past few days," Morgan said. "Is there something that you're not telling us?"

Chris grew worried. He wondered if they were onto him or if he might just be imagining that too.

"No," Chris said. "I'm doing okay."

Neither Richard nor Morgan believed Chris. Based on the conversation thus far, they could both see that Chris clearly was acting strangely.

"You're not getting any pressure from kids at school to try things?" Richard tried to be gentle while asking.

"No," Chris said, going through his own explanations in his head. "I'm sure that it's just some stress or something, like the doctor said."

Richard and Morgan both looked unconvinced.

Richard said. "I need to get back to the lab, but I want you to rest. We'll talk tomorrow about getting you some help."

"Look," Chris said. "I'm not on drugs. I don't need to be on any either. Maybe I'm just tired or something, I don't know."

"We're not accusing you of anything," Morgan said. "We just think that you should take it easy for now. We'll talk about some options to help you out."

With that, Richard and Morgan both walked out of the room, leaving Chris to let his mind race with thoughts. That didn't last long though. Chris was overwhelmed, partially out of delayed shock and partially out of sheer exhaustion. He put his head down and fell into a deep sleep.

Day 3 {10:30pm}

☺ ↔ 😃

Jessica had waited by the lab door in the other world, furious that the real Chris hadn't come outside yet. She became alarmed when she noticed a surge of bright lights from inside the lab.

She ran back into the lab, arriving inside just after Chris had collapsed. At first, Jessica was terrified that he was dead, but she quickly noticed that he was still breathing. Realizing that he could still be hurt, she pulled out her phone and called for help.

Chris regained consciousness hoping that everything had been restored back to normal. The first thing that caught his attention was the sight of several paramedics kneeled beside him, asking if he was "Okay."

When Chris then caught a glimpse of Jessica, he knew that things still weren't fixed. And when he noticed both Morgan and Ben rush over to him, he figured that the situation might have actually grown significantly worse.

Morgan noticed Chris regaining consciousness and kneeled down alongside the paramedics.

"Are you okay?" she asked.

"Yeah," Chris said, sitting up. "Sorry about everything."

Tears streamed down Morgan's face. She tried to speak clearly, but the words barely choked out of her mouth. "What were you doing here?"

"I just wanted to help," Chris said. "I was going to fix it."

Morgan continued to cry. "You could have died."

Jessica cut in.

"I tried to get him to stop," she said. "I didn't think he knew about this stuff."

"Jessica," Morgan said in an icy tone. "Please just go home."

Jessica felt the obvious cold shoulder from Morgan. She thought about protesting – her boyfriend had nearly been seriously injured – but Morgan's frosty demeanor made her decide to obey. As it was, she was simply relieved that Chris was conscious and talking again.

"I'll see you tomorrow then," Jessica said to Chris. "I guess we have some things to talk about."

"Yeah," Chris said, adding. "Sorry."

Chris gave Jessica a weak smile and pecked him with a brief kiss. They both knew that he'd have a lot of explaining to do, so he was already dreading it.

Ben startled Chris by saying. "If you wanted to help with something, you should have asked. You're mother's right, the equipment here can be extremely dangerous."

Chris stood up with the help of a paramedic and dusted himself off. Morgan was still worried that something might be wrong and hovered nearby. Another paramedic handed Chris a cold pack and a towel.

"We're going to take you in," the paramedic said. "Just to check things out."

"I'm okay though," Chris said, turning to Morgan. "Really Mom."

Morgan had none of it.

"What has gotten into you?" she asked. "We're going with them, just in case."

While Chris was being led outside, Ben stepped over to the control panel and noticed where Chris had the settings.

"Honey," Ben called to Morgan. "Can you come here?"

Morgan joined Ben at the control panel.

"What's wrong?" she asked.

"Look," Ben said, pointing at the machine's power setting. "It was over the safeguard."

Morgan gasped, shocked at the implication. Ben then turned and noticed the damaged electrical box.

"We're lucky that we hadn't replaced those breaker boxes just yet," he concluded. "Or otherwise…"

Ben's voice faded. Morgan had a sad look in her eyes. She didn't want to think more about it and went to rejoin Chris with the paramedics outside.

Ben continued to linger inside the lab for a moment. He looked again back at the control panel and then glanced at the old equipment that Chris had set up. The gears inside Ben's head had started to turn as he began to understand what had been going on in the lab.

5:
Learning The Truth

Day 4 {7:00am}

☺ ↔ ☻

The real Chris continued to feel helpless after being released from the hospital in the other world. The nurse joked about remembering him, referring to him as a "repeat customer."

Since then, he'd been resting at home. Most troubling, Chris was essentially under the guard of Morgan. She was both concerned and angry that Chris would suddenly sneak into the lab and try to work on the old Machine.

The only upside of being under virtual house arrest was that it left Chris plenty of time to think about his situation. If a malfunction of the machine had been at the center of the changes to his world, then Chris knew that he'd likely need allies. He couldn't repair it on his own. Unfortunately, it didn't appear that he had many options.

Chris reasoned that confessing any of the strangeness that had been going on in his life to Morgan would only further concern her that something was wrong with him. And confiding to Ben seemed an even worse idea. Although Ben seemed like an entirely different person, Chris was still skeptical.

Morgan had insisted that Chris not go to school that day, but the decision created a couple of problems of its own. At one point in the morning, Chris overheard Morgan taking a call from the school.

"I wouldn't care if this were the biggest game in school history Coach Barns," Morgan said, pausing to hear an angry response. "Chris is resting. He's had some further complications, so I don't know if he'll be in school tomorrow either."

Over her lunch break, Jessica had tried to visit, but Morgan simply turned her away.

"I don't think that we need to be bothering Chris while he rests," Morgan said to Jessica. "Now do we?"

Jessica wasn't deterred quite that easily and said. "He hasn't been responding to any of my calls or messages."

"Ben and I decided to take away some privileges after everything at the lab," Morgan said. "Besides, he should be resting and not talking to his friends. I hope that you'll understand."

Day 4 {12:00pm}

♣

The situation was not much different in the real world, where Morgan had insisted that the other Chris stay home from school and, this time, he'd not resisted. With the big game against Westby occurring later in the day, the idea would have normally seemed ludicrous. However, in light of everything that he'd been experiencing, the game was hardly a concern on the other Chris's mind.

Morgan's insistence that they seek further professional help did remain a potential problem. Fortunately for Chris, he was able to convince Morgan that he was 'doing better' that morning and the doctor had suggested to Morgan that they delay any visit for one more day while he ordered further tests. This all seemed to appease Morgan, at least for the time being.

Of course, nothing had changed for Chris. Richard's visit with him the night before had felt real. Too real. Chris had hoped that the situation would have changed by morning, but Morgan continued to make references to Richard that assumed that he was still alive.

As the day wore on, Chris made up his mind that he wasn't going to stick around to find out what would happen next. With a bit of digging around Chris's bedroom, the other Chris was able to find a few stashes of money. He still couldn't log into his computer account, but he was able to log in via a guest account that allowed him to at least gain internet access.

From there, Chris's focus shifted to planning. He wasn't sure where he'd go, but he was going to travel somewhere to escape. Given his lack of funds, he knew that it would only be for a little while and not particularly far. But he was optimistic that even a little escape might be enough to clear his mind. When he did eventually return, he was sure that everything would be better.

Day 4 {1:00pm}

☺ ↔ ☻

In contrast, the real Chris had an entirely different plan in mind in the other world. By early-afternoon, he had been on what might have been considered to be his best behavior and Morgan relented enough to allow him to go back to school. Morgan insisted on driving him there, but that plan changed at the last minute. Ben had come home from the lab for a late lunch and found himself enlisted to help.

"Ben," Morgan said. "I have an appointment that I just remembered. Can you drop Chris off at School?"

"Sure," Ben said, grabbing his keys.

"I'll be at the lab later this afternoon," Morgan said to Ben. Then she turned to Chris and added. "I'll pick you up after school. Don't get any ideas either – I might be letting you attend class, but you're not taking part in any games tonight. I don't care what that coach says."

On the drive to school, Chris could tell that Ben wanted to talk about something, but he couldn't guess what. Instead, Ben kept making nervous conversation.

"Your Mom was getting an earful from that coach last night," Ben said.

"This morning too," Chris replied. "At this point, that's probably not a surprise."

There was an awkward silence for a second.

"So," Ben said. "Your Mom is worried that you're having a hard time dealing with you Dad's death."

"Why's that?" Chris asked, certainly curious. He'd hoped to fill in some of the blanks regarding what Jessica had told him about his father's apparent death.

"You know," Ben said. "The machine and the accident. I know that things haven't been the same since."

"I'd say," Chris said, grimacing at Ben.

Ben tried to let the remark roll away. He was unsure if Chris had been making a veiled sarcastic remark about his relationship with Morgan.

"Anyway," Ben said. "Your Mom and I wanted you to know that you can talk to us about anything."

"I just wanted to see if I could get the machine going." Chris responded.

Ben took a deep breath. It was hard for him to talk about what had become the foremost failure of his life.

"We're not going down that path again Chris," Ben said. "We can't."

"Why not?" Chris asked.

"Your mother and I tried. We spent nearly three years trying to make it work. I'm grateful for that time bringing us closer together, but it had to stop. Your mother couldn't handle it anymore and we had bills to pay."

"It was close though."

"Maybe," Ben said, hesitant to admit it even to himself. "I still think about it all the time you know. The accident."

Chris probed a little. "I still don't understand exactly what happened."

Ben was clearly not interested in reviewing all of the details, but he offered up a short explanation.

"When we were testing it for the first time," he said. "I mean thoroughly testing it, it just seemed as though the machine was too much. Your Dad was an incredible man. I don't know that anyone could have or should have tried to do what he did. It was just too dangerous and we were impatient."

"He didn't yell anything to you about changing the power levels?" Chris wondered.

Ben was taken aback by the question, confused as to how that might have made any difference.

"No," Ben said. "He never gave us any signs. He just fell down and, by the time the paramedics arrived…"

Ben's voice trailed off.

"He must not have been able to find his way through it," Chris said. "Or maybe it was too much here."

"Find his way through what?" Ben asked.

"The energy waves that the helmet puts off. It gets a little crazy inside a person's head."

Ben continued to be confused by how Chris could speak so authoritatively on the subject. He wondered if it were Chris's way of dealing with the loss and changes.

"Like I said," Ben stated. "Your Mom and I tried, but we couldn't pull it off without him. Neither of us wanted to push the machine hard after what had happened and, eventually, it just got too difficult to keep working on it without any progress."

Chris nodded. He was growing concerned that refining the machine to fix whatever had happened might be more difficult than he'd anticipated.

"Your Mom and I had to make some decisions to ensure that all of us were okay," Ben said. "I'm not going to lie. I could care less about some of the work that we take on now, but it pays the bills."

Chris pressed on.

"Don't you worry that you gave up on the machine too soon?" he asked.

"No," Ben said. "I was more concerned that we'd lose the house."

Ben laughed at his own remark and continued. "Maybe we'll get back to the machine someday. Your Mom has needed some time to pass and some distance. Maybe I have too."

For the first time, Chris actually felt pity for Ben. This was not the man whom he'd butted heads with over the past several years. The other Ben had an altogether different focus in his life. The outcome of the accident as it happened for Ben had left him a broken man professionally, even if he'd found a purpose with Morgan that might have otherwise eluded him.

Chris was surprised by feelings of wanting to do something to genuinely help. It would be one thing to fix things for himself, but, if he could, he wanted to help fix things for Ben and Morgan too.

"I will give you credit though," Ben said. "That was some pretty crazy setup that you had going in the lab."

"What do you mean?" Chris asked.

"The way you had everything hooked up. You might have had the machine working again with a bit of adjustment."

Chris wasn't sure how to respond. He had a decision to make and, going on his gut feel of how radically things in the other world differed from the norm, he made a choice that he hoped he wouldn't regret.

"It did work," Chris said.

When Chris arrived at the lab with Ben, he still wasn't sure how he'd get Ben to start up the machine.

"Just because we're coming here doesn't mean that you're not still going to school," Ben said.

"Uh-huh," Chris said, letting his voice trail off.

As Ben opened the lab door, he admitted. "Your Mom would be furious if she found us here working on it."

Once inside, Chris saw that the machine hadn't actually been moved from where he'd left it the prior day.

"So how'd you figure out how to put this back together?" Ben asked.

"I've studied it," Chris replied.

"Oh?

"Yeah, but this is like an antique."

Ben was surprised by the remark.

"I don't know about that," he said.

"It just doesn't have some things that you could add to make it easier to use," Chris paused before he added. "And safer."

Ben perked up and asked "Add what kinds of things?"

"Phase buffers, first and foremost," Chris said. "The power coming through to the helmet is probably a lot higher than you were expecting and it's dangerous for anyone wearing it."

After the last bit had come out of his mouth, Chris realized that he'd probably hit a bit too close to home with his point.

"Anything else?" Ben inquired, taking mental notes.

Chris pointed to the control panel and said. "We have to make sure that the power levels can quickly scale up and down."

"What do you mean?" Ben asked.

"If you were wearing it as it is," Chris said. "The initial power levels hits the controller all at once. It's like hitting a brick wall."

"Richard said something like that to," Ben said. "We'd intended to modify the delivery system, but we had deadlines and no time left. It would have been easy to add, maybe in a few hours, but we always had one or another thing needing our attention instead."

Ben stopped and took a long look at Chris before he continued. "You never wanted to talk about this stuff before whenever I've thought to bring it up."

"I guess that I'm a little different right now." Chris said. "All of that stuff, it wasn't critical though. If my Dad had just said to turn up the power more, he could have made it."

The suggestion seemed counter-intuitive to Ben and he didn't appear to buy it.

"I still don't understand what you think he was dealing with?" Ben said.

"It's like riding against a wave. Each energy wave needs to be overcome until you're at the next level. Then you're okay."

"Okay," Ben said, still not entirely understanding what Chris was saying. "I hadn't thought of it like that, but I can see how it might seem that way."

"Your rational inclination is to avoid the waves and stay where you're at. But when you're in there, you can't play it safe."

Ben cut in.

"We did some tests after the accident," he said, "when things were getting a little desperate. But we never turned the power levels up to the same point that he had."

"It's a bumpy ride when you do," Chris said. "But that's the only way you can get the image projection to work."

"That's what we thought, but we were afraid to push it, so we tried other approaches. Nothing worked."

"My Dad must not have made it because he stayed too long where he thought he was safe." Chris said. "The key is taking the power levels up so that you can get to the next level, where things operate much calmer."

"No!" Morgan said from behind.

Chris and Ben were startled. Both spun around to find Morgan standing behind them. Not surprisingly, she was mad.

"I thought that you were taking Chris to school?" Morgan asked Ben.

Ben knew that he was busted and replied. "We just got talking about things."

"So I hear," Morgan said sarcastically.

"I was going to take him to school in a few minutes," Ben said. "We weren't going to do anything."

Morgan shook her head while tears streamed down her cheeks.

"I thought that we said that we were done with all this?" Morgan pleaded. "I knew that we should have gotten rid of it."

Ben went over to hug Morgan.

"I'm sorry," Ben said.

Chris stood by, worried that he'd suffered another setback. Morgan might make it a priority to get rid of the machine and his only chance of figuring out what was happening might be lost.

"Chris," Morgan said. "We're going home."

And Chris knew that it was the end of the discussion.

Chris spent the remainder of the afternoon in his room. Morgan and Ben turned to deliberating Chris's fate downstairs.

"We might need the parts," Ben insisted. "We don't have the money right now to be throwing good equipment away."

Morgan was quiet.

Chris crept out of his room to see what was occurring below. He watched as Ben hugged Morgan.

Ben continued. "Tomorrow we'll look into what we can re-use and sell the rest."

Alarms of panic went through Chris's mind. He considered drastic moves that he might need to make to prevent the machine from being broken up and sold.

A moment of silence in the house was broken by a knock to the door.

Ben went to answer the door, while Morgan stepped into the kitchen to wipe tears from her face. She was embarrassed that she might be seen by someone in her current state.

When Ben opened the door, Chris was surprised to see Tyler waiting outside. Standing behind Tyler was an older, beefier man who was clearly Tyler's father. He had a beet-red face and short-cropped hair. It was clear that he used his large build to intimidate people.

"Is Chris home?" Tyler asked Ben

Ben didn't appear at all intimidated, at least not at first.

"He's still not feeling well," Ben said.

"We're hoping to talk," Tyler's Father said.

"He's resting upstairs," Ben said, annoyed at their pushiness.

"Maybe we could go up?" Tyler asked.

A standoff ensued for a long moment. Chris realized that they wanted something and that they were only going to escalate tension until they got to him. He decided to speak up.

"What did you guys want?" Chris asked as he walked down the staircase.

"Wow," Tyler said. "You look just fine to me. The way we've been hearing it at school, I'd thought you were nearly dead."

What's been going on the past few days Chris?" Tyler's Father said. "You've been letting the guys on the team down. Us boosters too."

"I've been to the hospital twice in the last three days," Chris said. "That should count for something."

"We're heading to the game," Tyler said. "That should count for something too."

Tyler's Father cleared his throat and cut him off. It was obvious that he lorded over his son.

"What my son is trying to say is that we're going to need one of our best players against Westby tonight," Tyler's Father said, getting rolling. "The whole team, heck, the whole school, is counting on you to be a man and a leader. We need you to play at the kind of level that we all expect."

Morgan, who had stood at bay, stepped forward to her son's defense. She let all of her anger from earlier in the day flow through her, as she directed it at Tyler's Father.

"You do not have the right to come into my house and make these sorts of statements to my son," Morgan said sternly.

While the stinging words rapidly came out of her mouth, Morgan stepped forward through to the doorway. Instinctively, Tyler and Tyler's Father stepped backward onto the porch.

"Chris will be returning to school and returning to your baseball team," Morgan added sarcastically. "When his doctors and I say so."

With that, Morgan shut the front door. It slammed hard. Chris looked impressed by Morgan's handling of the situation.

"Wow," Chris said. "That was the coolest thing I've ever seen you do."

Morgan wasn't amused by Chris's gushing appreciation.

"Chris," Morgan commanded. "Go to your room."

Chris didn't immediately walk away though. He figured that it was as good of a time as any to make his drastic move.

"I will," Chris said. "But we need to talk about something first."

Morgan and Ben both gave Chris confused looks.

Ben finally asked. "What?"

"I know that this is going to sound crazy," Chris admitted, holding his breath. "But I think that I've somehow altered my reality."

Both Ben and Morgan glanced at each other, sharing concerned looks. This wasn't what they were expecting to come out of Chris's mouth.

"I think that it had something to do with the machine," Chris said. "I was using it at extremely high power levels. The next thing that I knew, I was here and everything about my life was totally different."

Morgan teared up again. She couldn't handle hearing such claims from Chris. His words only further made Morgan certain that something was seriously wrong with him.

"Chris, are you feeling okay?" Morgan asked. "I know that things have been crazy the past couple of days."

To offer some comfort, Ben put his hand on Morgan's shoulder. He had a curious look on his face though and didn't' outright dismiss Chris's assertions.

"Honey," Ben said. "The Chris who we know wouldn't know how to do what he's done at the lab with the machine. I think we should hear him out."

"I haven't met the guy," Chris said. "But after living his life for a couple of days, I'd agree."

Between sniffles, Morgan said. "But the machine didn't work. It never did."

"It did where I'm from," Chris pointed out. "At least, most of the time."

Morgan was confused and wondered how any of this could be possible.

"But how?" she asked, quietly.

Ben added a question of his own. "That's what you were talking about earlier Chris?"

"Yes," Chris said, trying to regain control of the conversation. "During the machine's first successful test, my Dad got into trouble with it, but he saved himself by requesting that the power levels be turned up at the right time. He had to think fast and that saved his life."

"But that's not what happened," Morgan pointed out, confused. "Richard died."

"I know," Chris said. "I'm not sure why he didn't do the same thing here. I just know that the machine does work."

"If what you're claiming is true," Morgan said. "Why didn't you tell us sooner?"

"I didn't realize anything was wrong," Chris said. "At least not at first. I woke up in my room and noticed that it was different, but I thought that it was a joke or something being played on me. At school, people were all treating me differently and I liked it. It wasn't until I got home that first night and Ben was here that I knew something was incredibly wrong."

"Why?" Morgan questioned, regaining her composure.

"Because my Dad never died and the Ben who I know isn't exactly a nice guy."

"I'm not?" Ben asked, surprised.

"I just don't know what's going on anymore," Morgan said. "Chris, I knew that something was wrong, but this is just…"

Morgan couldn't get the rest out. Ben held her closer.

"I know that this sounds crazy," Chris said. "But I need you try to trust me. Let me prove to you that I'm not crazy. Don't get rid of the machine just yet. If I could get some help in the lab with a few things, I think that we could have the machine running and then you could see for yourself."

"No Chris," Morgan said. "We need to take more time to sort this out."

However, Ben was more enthusiastic about Chris's suggestion.

"Chris mentioned some modifications to me earlier that might work," Ben said. "They made sense."

Morgan wasn't sure what to do next. Ben seemed to be ready to help Chris, but she also knew that Ben had never quite let his hopes for the machine go.

Chris could tell that Morgan still didn't entirely believe him.

"Look," Chris said. "Let's just try this out and, if I'm crazy, we can go see the doctor or whoever. You can get me drugged up or treated."

Morgan didn't think that Chris's play for humor was funny. She looked hard at Ben and then Chris, taking a moment to sort out the situation.

"Okay," Morgan said. "We'll listen to what you're saying for now."

Looking at Ben again, Morgan then concluded. "Let's go to the lab."

Ben grabbed his jacket and added. "Chris, I'll try to find the parts that we talked about."

Chris nodded. Things were in motion and he was ecstatic.

Ben said to Morgan. "I'll meet you guys at the lab."

During their car ride to the lab that evening, Morgan didn't say much to Chris. She was still processing his claims in her mind. Once they were inside the lab though, working on repairing the circuit box that had blown earlier, she began to open up.

"When did you say this started?" Morgan asked.

"A couple of days ago," Chris said. "The day that I fell down the stairs, after seeing Ben."

Morgan reminded him that she was still skeptical. "You understand why this is hard for us to believe, right?"

"Oh," Chris said. "I'd probably think that I was crazy too."

"I didn't say that," Morgan insisted, despite some hesitation. "Like Ben said, I know that my son wouldn't normally be able to put the machine back together like you did."

In many ways, Morgan had spent the time since Chris's revelation denying to herself that his words could at all be true.

Because of the possibilities that he was suggesting, part of her wanted desperately to believe him though. That desire crept out.

"How is he then?" Morgan asked. There was still doubt in her voice.

"Who?" Chris responded.

"Richard. Your father. You said he's alive"

Chris smiled. Her question was more difficult to answer than he had expected. Like most sons, he had a complicated relationship with his father.

Chris began. "His work is brilliant. Right now, he's been under a lot of stress. The project is counting on more funding. He works late, but he still finds time for us."

"He's taught you things? About the machine and our work?"

"Oh yeah. He lets me hang out at the lab and sometimes even lets me help out. Ben hates it when I'm around though and you get upset when you find out that I'm at the lab."

The remark surprised Morgan.

"Why's that?" she asked.

"After the big breakthrough during the first test of the machine, you got worried about something happening in the future to either you or Dad. You mostly stopped working at the lab after that."

"Hm" Morgan said, losing herself in thought for a moment. "I could maybe see that."

"Anyway," Chris continued. "You have your own projects at home, working on genetically-enhanced gardens. The stuff doesn't always turn out right."

Morgan smiled for the first time that evening.

Chris shrugged. "You seem happy though."

Morgan nodded. It was so odd for her to consider that any of these revelations might be real. It wasn't every day that someone learned what might have been.

Chris wasn't sure what to tell Morgan. He was focused on getting things in his life back to normal. Yet, he also wondered if it might be of benefit to know more about how things were different.

"So," Chris said. "You're happy too?"

Morgan reflected and then she answered. "It's been hard without your father. The project struggled without him. I struggled without him."

Morgan motioned to the machine. "Ben and I just didn't have enough of what it took to keep this going."

Chris pointed out the movie projection system, or at least what was left of it after he'd taken back of the borrowed parts.

"Ben said that you're doing other projects now."

"Yes," Morgan acknowledged. "We needed to do something and it worked out pretty well."

Morgan noticed Chris give her an odd look.

"Then this must seem pretty weird, I suppose," Morgan said.

"What?" Chris asked, not sure what she meant.

"Seeing me with Ben."

"Oh that? Yeah, it's really messed up."

"Ben's been good to me," Morgan said. "I wouldn't have been able to keep it all together without him.

"I'm fine with it though?" Chris wondered, referring to the other Chris.

"You didn't like it at first. Not you but Chris. I mean. You know what I mean."

Chris nodded and said. "I'm still trying to keep it all straight too."

"It just happened though," Morgan said. "I wouldn't have guessed it in a million years."

Morgan smiled and said. "Ben's a different guy than he was a few years ago. I think that Chris is fine with it, most of the time. He's been so busy with sports since Richard died that it probably isn't on his mind much anyway."

"Yeah, I hear that I'm pretty awesome."

"We can't keep up with the college recruiters. I wish we could have made it to more of his games. Things have been hard though and we've been too busy."

"He probably understands."

"I hope so."

Morgan paused and continued. "This has been the oddest conversation of my life."

Ben returned to the lab and found Morgan working hard with Chris to set up the machine.

"We were lucky," Ben said. "I got the parts, right as they were closing."

Chris nearly cheered when he realized that the night was looking up for him.

Morgan walked over to Ben and said, softly. "You're right. I'm not sure what's gotten into him, but he's been doing all of the work on the circuit box."

"Well?" Ben shrugged.

"Maybe it's true," Morgan admitted.

Chris dug through the parts that Ben had returned with. He called over to Ben and motioned to the machine. "Could you help me set these up?"

"Sure" Ben said.

Day 4 {10:30pm}

♣

From her bedroom window in the real world, Rachel noticed the other Chris sneaking down from his room, backpack in hand. She'd been studying and had actually intended to head next door soon to check on Chris. The more she'd replayed the events of the past few days in her head, the more she realized how odd Chris had been acting.

Now Rachel was curious as to what he might be up to next. Rachel felt that she'd done virtually everything that she could do to raise concerns about Chris to his parents regarding his strange behavior. Of course, she hadn't confronted him. At least not outright.

In large part, her hesitation had revolved around not being able to imagine life without Chris. They were best friends, so she barely admitted to herself that she wished that their relationship was more than that. Chris's remarks about Jessica had been annoying, if innocent enough in the past, but his recent behavior towards Jessica had only made Rachel feel more crushed than ever.

While it certainly wasn't odd for Chris to be sneaking out, it was unusual for him to be carrying a stuffed backpack. He was obviously up to something and Rachel determined that she'd find out what it was.

Rachel went to the garage and started up her car. She thought about where he might have been going while she backed her vehicle onto the street. It didn't take her long to spot Chris walking quickly to the end of their block. He had not tried exceptionally hard to conceal himself nor did he appear to be going anywhere in a particular hurry.

Rachel pulled her car up beside him and yelled through the open passenger window. "Need a ride somewhere?"

Chris seemed startled and replied with a simple. "No."

"Where are you going?"

"I'm just out for a walk."

"Uh-huh."

Rachel pulled her car over to the curb and parked. She got out and caught up with Chris midway down the next block.

"You can go home. I'm fine and just want to be alone," Chris said to Rachel.

Chris was annoyed to have Rachel following him. She was persistent.

After composing the words in her head, Rachel blurted out. "You haven't been acting like yourself for days now. I'm worried. Is it something that I did?"

Chris had no idea what Rachel was talking about. "Look," he said. "I'm sorry if you think that we're supposed to be good friends."

"This is exactly the kind of stuff that I'm talking about," Rachel said, exasperated. "We are good friends, regardless of if you want to redefine that or not, so stop being a moron. You're not acting like yourself."

"Well," Chris shot back. "You and everyone else aren't acting like yourselves either."

"What does that mean?"

"Ben's a jerk, Jessica's cheating on me with Tyler, and coach is acting like he's never seen me play before. None of the guys on the team even acknowledge me and now you're suddenly my best friend."

Chris paused before figuring out how to word the next part. "I keep imagining that my Dad's still alive and I don't know why. I think I'm hallucinating"

Rachel's heart sank. She was convinced that Chris had serious mental issues and she feared that he needed help immediately. She debated if she should try to take him home or to the hospital. She knew that, either way, he'd put up a struggle and there was a risk that he'd simply run away. Rachel decided to take a softer approach.

"I know that sometimes things can be confusing," Rachel said, hoping that it didn't sound as hollow as she feared.

Chris replied. "That's just it, this shouldn't be confusing. These are basic things that no one understands."

"I want to understand Chris."

"No one is listening. It's almost like I'm in another dimension or something."

That statement made something click inside Rachel's head. She remembered what Chris had said a few days before about the machine and seeing himself with Jessica. She wanted to kick herself for not connecting it the morning when she'd picked Chris up at the lab. She recalled how he'd acted disoriented then.

"You think I'm crazy don't you"?" Chris asked.

"No," Rachel replied, knowing that she had to play things cool. "But I need you to try to remember what you were doing before everything started to seem wrong."

"Okay."

"Were you using the machine at all?"

Chris was confused. "What machine?"

"You know," Rachel said. "The machine that they have at the lab."

"No, I don't really know what goes on at the lab."

His statement surprised Rachel.

"Really?" she asked.

"I've been swamped with baseball practice lately. There's a big game coming up."

"Against Westby?"

"Yeah."

Rachel realized that her theory regarding what was going on might be more complicated than she'd originally suspected.

"So you were at practice," Rachel said. "We had a test the morning that I picked you up at the lab. Do you remember studying for it the night before?"

"No," Chris said. "I figured that I wouldn't have to worry about it."

Rachel thought that it shouldn't be a surprise that some things were consistent about Chris.

"What were you doing instead?" Rachel asked.

Chris said. "I was with Jessica."

"For how long?"

"I don't know," Chris admitted. "It wasn't too late. Her parents are kind of, you know, strict about things."

Rachel raised an eyebrow.

Chris continued. "I walked home and went right to bed. We'd had an intense practice and I was exhausted."

"Here's the deal," Rachel said. "What you just described sounds nothing like how the Chris who I know spent his time a couple of nights ago. The machine must have done something to you, er, him. Both of you."

"I don't know anything about that stuff."

"That's the crazy part. You're not imagining any of this. Me. Your father. Ben. This is real. I'm not saying that what you're describing isn't real, but there is obviously some wire that got crossed."

Chris looked on, still confused. Rachel was empowered, as her conclusion became clearer.

"You know that this happened on an old episode of 'Star Trek,' right? Captain Kirk and Spock both got sent to another dimension. Their versions from the other universe, the alternative one, were evil and they caused all kinds of trouble in the real world."

"I'm not evil," Chris said.

Rachel chuckled and responded. "I'm not saying that you're evil. I'm just saying that something happened. The reason that you think that you're not you is that you're actually not you."

Chris became nervous. Rachel's explanation was not remotely something that he'd have considered. Of course, he knew that his parents had been involved in some extremely unusual experiments that had failed. It didn't make sense to him, but it seemed a better plan to explore at this point than simply running away from home.

"Then what're we supposed to do now?" Chris asked.

"We need to bring this up to your parents," Rachel said. "There's no way that they'd have thought about it this way. I've been too busy covering for you."

Chris gave Rachel a quizzical look.

"I meant Chris," Rachel said. "The other Chris. He'd been sneaking around and messing with the machine while no one knew about it."

Chris was uncomfortable with Rachel's suggestion. He hadn't expected confessing his problems to Morgan and Richard to be her brilliant suggestion.

"Hang on," Chris said. "We don't need to be telling them about all this.

"If I'm right," Rachel said. "They're the only people who can help you."

"I just don't want to go to the doctor again." Chris said.

Rachel smiled and said. "Some doctor isn't going to be able to help you out with this. At least not the kind that they have at the hospital."

Day 4 {10:30pm}

☺ ↔ ☻

It took longer than the real Chris had expected to get the machine set up again in the other world. Of course, he reasoned, they were dealing with older technology and its many quirks. It was late in the evening by the time everything was ready to test.

"Do you really think this will work?" Morgan asked Ben.

Ben wondered if so many of their earlier failures with the machine were about to pay off.

"It's worth a try," Ben said.

Chris overheard their discussion and chimed in.

"It'll work," he said. "It worked before."

"You passed out," Morgan pointed out.

"These new modifications should help prevent that." Chris replied.

Despite everything that Chris was saying and doing, Morgan was still worried. There was an unusual excitement in the air, but it was tempered by a certain element of concern over the inherent dangers involved.

Chris reached for the control helmet first, but Morgan stopped him.

"Don't you think that one of us should be doing this instead?" Morgan asked Ben.

"I'll be fine," Chris interjected. "I've done this a few times now and I know how to operate it. Besides, you two need to make sure that the machine runs fine."

Morgan couldn't stop thinking about how insane it all was. Chris noticed the fear on her face.

"I want to fix things and I think I know how." Chris continued, adding a wink to Morgan. "Trust me."

Morgan finally relented. Deep down, she wanted things to be right too. She wanted Chris back.

"If there's any sign of trouble," Morgan said. "And I mean any sign. Then we're shutting this all down."

Chris agreed and took his place near the viewing chamber.

"Chris," Ben said. "Your Mom is right about being cautious. The power levels that you're talking about are well beyond anything that we would consider safe."

"It'll hold together," Chris said. "It did before."

Chris signaled Ben to turn up the machine's power levels. The machine hummed to life.

With the modifications that had been made, Chris noticed that the machine was easier to operate.

"The ride is much smoother!" Chris yelled over to Ben.

As its power level was increasing, the machine became more mentally strenuous to operate. Chris had to try hard not to show the strain. He knew that Morgan was tentative about him operating the machine. Her natural cautiousness would look for any reason to shut everything down.

Chris managed to hold on though, as the machine went up to the designated power level. The viewing chamber had already filled with static and then a rudimentary image appeared. Everything occurred so quickly that Ben could scarcely appreciate it. Morgan knew how hard they'd tried in the past and she wished that her Richard could have been there to see the dream finally accomplished.

The viewing chamber's image grew clearer until the power in the system leveled off. The screen showed what looked like the lab. Ben noticed the real Ben pass into view.

"Hey that's me," Ben said.

In the viewing chamber, Ben could be seen at work in the real world's lab. Morgan shook her head, as it was clear that Chris was right about their world being different.

"That's not you," Morgan said to Ben. "And that's not our lab."

"Turn up the sound!" Chris yelled.

Ben complied and everyone listened in on the conversation.

The arch's view showed the real world, where Jai was conversing with Ben.

Jai said "Don't be so upset. I know it isn't pleasant, but I can assure you that it's necessary"

"I just didn't realize that this had to be part of the deal," Ben said.

"Don't be a fool," Jai said. "He'll expose us and destroy everything. We need him distracted or, better yet, eliminated."

"When does this need to be done?" Ben asked, reluctantly.

"You have a presentation with your sponsors coming up," Jai pointed out. "That would seem like a perfect opportunity to do something that might redirect the spotlight off of us and take Richard out of the picture."

"Richard's no fool," Ben insisted.

"But he still trusts you and that will be his weakness." Jai said.

Before the pair could continue talking, the viewing chamber filled with static and the machine's power levels fell. The humming sound decreased until it disappeared.

Ben noticed a plume of smoke coming out of the back of the control panel and moved quickly to grab a special fire extinguisher. He flipped open a hatch behind the control panel and put out the fire on a smoldering circuit board.

Chris took off the helmet and rushed to Ben's side.

"What happened?" Chris asked.

"It just overheated," Ben said. "These are old circuits and we should have had better ventilation."

Morgan appeared to still be distracted by what she'd witnessed in the viewing chamber.

"What was happening there?" she asked.

"It didn't sound good," Ben added. "Was that me?"

"Yeah," Chris replied.

Ben was taken aback.

"Who was I talking to?" he wondered. "Was that Jai?"

"Yeah," Chris said. "He's the kind of guy you hang out with I guess."

"Really?" Ben responded, clearly disturbed by the revelation.

"Did he say that they were going to hurt Richard?" Morgan asked.

"That's what it sounded like," Chris said. "I thought that he might be up to something, but I didn't imagine that it was this bad."

"I still don't understand what we just saw," Morgan said. "Was that really happening?"

Ben had been quiet during the exchange. He tried to piece together what he'd just witnessed.

"I've got some ideas," Ben said. "I don't think that the machine changed our reality. I think that the machine somehow tapped into a parallel universe."

"How is that possible?" Morgan said.

"We weren't ever pushing the research this far, but there's always been some speculation in physics circles about it. We'd never seriously considered that it might be a side-effect though."

Morgan only grew more concerned. Knowing that Richard was alive, at least somewhere, made her desperate to prevent him from being harmed.

"Then we have to warn Richard!" Morgan exclaimed.

Chris said, assertively. "We need to get this all switched back to normal. We still weren't quite at the power levels that I'd set the machine to when things happened."

"We're going to need a lot of new parts to replace the damaged ones," Ben said, while he looked over the scorched circuits. "If we're going to take it up another level, we'll need to add more capacity."

"Chris," Morgan said. "What were they talking about? A presentation?"

"There's a big presentation coming up," Chris said, pausing to work out the timing in his head. "The government sponsors are going to be there. It's in a couple of days."

For the first time in years, Morgan suddenly had a renewed drive to get the machine working. She wasn't going to let it be a failure this time, not with the stakes so high.

"Then we don't have time to waste," she said.

"You guys finally believe me?" Chris asked.

Ben and Morgan nodded.

"I'm still not clear how the machine was responsible for switching you with Chris," Morgan said.

"Well, the machine zapped me here somehow," Chris said. "Maybe it opened a portal or something and I fell through it."

Ben wasn't satisfied with that theory. "Did you bring anything with you?" Your clothes? Something in your pocket?"

"No," Chris replied. "I woke up in bed here. I didn't recognize anything."

"That's it then," Ben said, proudly. "Your consciousness was switched!"

Ben, Morgan, and Chris stood thinking about the statement for a moment and then all said in unison. "Wow."

Chris looked at the damaged control panel. "Where are we going to get parts at this time of night?"

"I'll make some calls and see what we can round up," Ben said. "We can stop at home too. There are at least a few things that we can use in the garage."

Day 4 {11:30pm}

♣

Ben was alone at the real world's lab, working late. He had spent the evening continuing to analyze the data, trying to figure out what had been going wrong with the machine. They'd long tested the machine at moderate power levels and it had performed well enough. But, with rumors of competitors nipping at their heels, well enough wouldn't be good enough.

Given Jai's earlier offer, Ben had felt a renewed pressure to get things right. His heart hadn't been in the project for some time, but the interest of Jai's employers had changed this enthusiasm overnight. If Ben was going to sell out, he'd need to have a functioning machine.

Jai seemed to know enough about the project to be interested, but Ben suspected that he didn't know the whole truth. They might be satisfied with a rudimentary machine, at least for a while. Once they demanded more sophisticated viewing capabilities, they would insist on increasing the machine's power levels and they'd learn that it didn't work. And then, Ben wondered, what would happen to him?

Thus, as Ben's anxieties grew, and what appeared to be a lack of focus by Richard had only further annoyed him. In fact, he'd fought with Richard all afternoon, reminding him that they should be focused on the project and not ancillary distractions.

Richard had a mid-afternoon meeting with their government contacts, preparing for the particulars of the upcoming presentation. Ben was frustrated that he'd not been involved. Richard's job during the meeting had been to lower expectations, just in case they didn't sort out the machine's bugs in time. While Richard was with them, he aimed to project a sense of calm confidence.

Ben resented that Richard had left him to work alone in the lab that evening. He continued to sense a lack of urgency from Richard. He knew that Richard would be returning soon, but he was impatient.

As he waited, Ben decided to duplicate their last test. It wouldn't be as efficient without Richard around, giving them a second set of eyes to catch clues, but Ben was running out of time and willing to take chances. And somewhere in his paranoia, Ben thought that perhaps Richard was part of the problem. It wouldn't surprise him if Richard had been doing something wrong while operating the machine.

Soon after Ben had put on the helmet and was about to start up the machine, he received a surprise incoming call from Jai. Ben switched on a viewing screen and transferred the call from his mobile phone, onto the control panel.

A screen on the panel came to life and he saw Jai appear, ready to talk. This was the same conversation that the real Chris and the other Ben, along with the other Morgan, had just spied pieces of.

"Hey buddy," Jai began. "What're you doing up so late?"

Ben took off the helmet and responded. "I was going to ask you the same thing."

"Listen," Jai said, wasting no time with further pleasantries. "My employers are getting a little impatient."

Ben's guard went up. "What does that mean?"

"It means that they're impatient people. They want to feel comfortable knowing that you're fully committed to them with, you know, your talents."

"You mean my assets?"

"Yeah," Jai said, becoming serious. "That too. Look, I'll admit that I've had a hard time explaining what the holdup is. I thought that we had a deal, but you've been distant in our communications."

"I'm not ready to hand things over," Ben admitted. "I thought that we'd agreed that doing so would cause an unfortunate stir."

Jai became testy and applied more pressure by asking. "Is there some problem with the machine?"

"No," Ben lied. "It's working fine. Just fine."

"What is it then?" Jai pressed. "Are you still thinking over our conversation about Richard?"

Ben continued to hesitate. He wasn't a skilled poker player.

"Yes," he said.

Jai said "Don't be so upset. I know it isn't pleasant, but I can assure you that it's necessary"

"I just didn't realize that this had to be part of the deal," Ben said.

"Don't be a fool," Jai said. "He'll expose us and destroy everything. We need him distracted or, better yet, eliminated."

"When does this need to be done?" Ben asked, reluctantly.

"You have a presentation with your sponsors coming up," Jai pointed out. "That would seem like a perfect opportunity to do something that might redirect the spotlight off of us and take Richard out of the picture."

"Richard's no fool," Ben insisted.

"But he still trusts you and that will be his weakness." Jai said. "Do I need to remind you of what your life has been like because of him and his family?"

"No," Ben said.

"I should tell you that some of my employers' people," Jai said and then stopped to correct himself. "Our employers' people are monitoring and they're in a position to make this transition occur seamlessly."

Ben's brow furrowed. If he hadn't already felt like his agreement with Jai had spiraled out of control, now he certainly did.

"This is all going to work out," Jai said. "I'll contact you again in the morning."

"Okay," Ben responded, his voice emotionless.

"Just be ready," Jai concluded.

With that, Jai signed off.

In the minutes that passed after his conversation with Jai, Ben began to realize that he was trapped, having told lies in several directions. It was with a greater sense of urgency that he resumed his earlier test. The machine hummed to life, warming up while Ben put on the control helmet. He'd set the power levels to those that he'd been testing at with Richard during their last failed run.

At first, Ben had a hard time controlling the machine. He wasn't used to 'piloting' it by himself. He and Richard had long ago established their routine, so it had been quite some time since he'd last felt the energy from the machine bombard his mind.

Just the same, he was experienced enough to know how to mentally navigate through the pitfalls that the machine presented. Eventually the viewing chamber's image came together, showing Richard and Morgan's home. Ben thought that it made sense to spy on Richard. If anything, he might get a clue as to Richard's motives.

Ben was surprised to find no one at home. He thought that perhaps it was another example of the suspected 'lag' problem. He noticed the real Chris walk by and didn't think much of it until he saw the other Ben follow behind him. Ben was flabbergasted.

Through the machine's speakers, he heard the other Ben say. *"The parts should be in the garage."*

Ben changed the image to follow Chris and the other Ben through the house and into the garage. There was a work room in the rear of the garage that contained stacks of electronic equipment. Ben clearly knew that it wasn't himself working with Chris, but he had no explanation for what he was witnessing.

What he observed next was even more revealing. Ben listened intently while the other Ben and Chris dug through a pile of electronic parts.

"I always wondered what it'd be like if I got sent to another dimension," the other Ben said. *"I've been familiar with the theories, but I never thought we'd just happen onto it."*

"It's not everything that it's cracked up to be," Chris responded.

The other Ben perked up at the remark.

"When this is all over," he said. *"Things are going to change, aren't they? I mean, Morgan and I won't have to worry about money or any of that anymore."*

"Probably not," Chris said, thoughtfully. *"I have a feeling that life is about to get a whole lot more complicated."*

"I suppose we need to get you back home first," the other Ben said, shifting gears. "Right?"

The real Ben looked on in bewilderment. His doppelganger was referring to Chris getting sent to another dimension. His mind raced as he wondered how the machine could have transported Chris into the other dimension. It didn't take long before he overheard the answer.

"We're going to have trouble getting your machine up to the power levels that we need to get me back," Chris said. "That had to have been the key to it. I really wish that we had the machine that I used to get here."

"We've been making improvements though," the other Ben asked. "What else makes their version of the machine so much better?"

"Back home, it is just much more refined. I was able to take the power levels to points that hadn't really been tested yet. Dad and Ben were just working out the kinks on their latest version and hadn't tested the upper limits like I did when I was messing around."

The other Morgan interrupted the conversation and the other Ben casually said to her. "Hey honey, I'm just getting Chris set up back here."

"We should get over to Ian's before it gets too late," the other Morgan said.

The other Ben replied. "Just a few more minutes."

Ben reached over and squeezed Morgan's hand softly. She smiled.

"What?" the other Morgan asked softly.

"Ask me later," the other Ben said.

In the real world, Ben's heart leapt. He was stunned to see that his doppelganger was obviously carrying on a romantic relationship with the other Morgan. Clearly Richard was not an obstacle inside this other world. It was a place where he wouldn't be meddling with the project.

The other Ben continued speaking to Chris.

*"You really think that it was just the power?" he asked.
"Cranking it up?"*

*"Maybe," Chris said. "When I saw my life here, I wanted it
to be real. I mean, really, really wanted it to be possible."*

"I wonder what Chris is doing right now."

*"If my consciousness is in his body, then he's probably
inside my body and wondering why his world is upside down."*

*"He's not like you, you know, hanging out at the lab or
anything like that."*

"Then he's probably thinking he's lost his mind."

When the strain of keeping the viewing chamber active
became too much to bear, Ben took off the helmet. The machine
began to shut down. After collecting himself, Ben realized that the
other Ben and Chris had been discussing the other Chris whom
he'd been interacting with. Everything suddenly made perfect
sense to Ben. The other Chris had treated Ben differently than
Chris had ever done. And why not? They'd clearly gotten along
just fine in this other world.

Ben flashed back to the morning when he'd discovered the
other Chris passed out in the lab. He'd been too angry and too
determined to rid the other Chris from the lab to realize what had
occurred. Ben thought it was no wonder that Chris had been so
confused that morning. The other Chris undoubtedly had no idea
how he'd ended up in the lab.

Earlier remarks that the other Chris had made to Ben
concerning Richard also fell into place. The other Ben was
married to the other Morgan because Richard was clearly dead or
entirely out of the picture. If that were the case, then Ben realized
he suddenly had an opportunity.

The life that Ben had witnessed play out in front of him
looked much more ideal than his own. In fact, it would have been
hard for him to imagine a better situation to take advantage of.
Jai's offer had initially looked like a perfect opportunity too, but it
had started to come with strings attached. Ben dreaded the idea of
having to kill or incapacitate Richard. Deep down, Ben wasn't an
evil guy. He simply wanted an escape.

And there would be no better escape than if he could
somehow travel to this alternate-world. Knowing what he did

about building the machine, he could finish their version of it and claim it as his own. He'd be the lone hero in their world.

Everything suddenly made sense to Ben regarding why his machine had been appearing to malfunction. Given the physics that they'd been dealing with while building and testing the machine, Ben felt like a fool. He'd never considered the possibility that the machine was tapping into another reality. The apparent lags that they were seeing in the remote images weren't defects. They were the greatest breakthrough in science of their era.

Ben imagined that if he could get into this world itself, he could polish their version of the machine a bit further and sell to it the highest bidder. No harm, no foul. And, along the way, he could be hailed as the most brilliant scientist of his era.

The one problem in this quickly-developing plan would be Chris. Ben worried that he might need to get rid of him at some point. And bringing the other Chris back to the parallel universe wouldn't necessarily be the best plan. Since Chris appeared to be in the middle of trying to get himself back to the real world using that dimension's machine, Ben reasoned that perhaps an 'accident' could be arranged to get rid of him.

Ben was so intent on working through his plan that he almost didn't notice Richard return to the lab. He'd turned on the building's sensor to alert him if someone entered, so it had been triggered when Richard arrived. Ben took off the helmet and pretended to be reviewing data at the control panel.

Richard walked into the lab a few seconds later and said to Ben. "Sorry about that, I got caught up with some stuff at home."

Ben looked exhausted, having spent the past few minutes operating the machine at high power levels. Richard noticed immediately.

"Were you running some tests on your own?" Richard asked.

Ben didn't answer right away, as his mind was still spinning in many directions. He was paranoid that it might appear that he was trying to look as though he'd been hiding something.

"That's right," Ben said. "I wasn't sure when you'd return and wanted to collect more data."

Richard didn't entirely buy Ben's explanation, but he also didn't want to pick a fight in the middle of the night. He recognized that Ben had been under the same stresses that he was, but he planned to keep an eye on him, just the same.

"Did I miss anything?"

"No," Ben said, taking another moment to collect himself. "We don't have much time, so I think that we should focus more on clearing up the image at the lower power levels."

Ben had no intention now of letting Richard test the machine at the higher power levels, given that he might piece together what had been going on. Or, worse yet, chance a sighting of a similar interaction between Chris and the doppelganger that he'd just witnessed.

Richard simply said. "Okay."

As Richard settled into his lab station, his phone rang. He answered it and discovered that Morgan was on the other end of the line.

"What's going on?" Richard asked. "I just got back to the lab."

"I'm sorry," Morgan replied. "But can you come home?"

Richard was confused. "Why?"

"Something's come up with Chris again," Morgan said. "Just come home as soon as you can, okay?"

"Okay," Richard said, concerned. "I'll leave right now."

After he hung up the phone, Richard turned to Ben.

"Sorry," he said. "I've got to get home. Again"

"Something wrong?" Ben asked.

"I'm not sure," Richard said. "Morgan seemed to think that it was important. Chris I guess. I'll try to be back later. Get some rest if you need it though."

Richard rose to leave. Ben couldn't help but worry that something had happened at Richard's home involving the other Chris. Something that might jeopardize the secret that he'd just learned. Events were happening too quickly for comfort and Ben suspected that he might have to make his decisions sooner than later.

6:

Temptation

Day 5 {12:00am}

☺ ↔ ☻

The real Chris and the other Ben and Morgan grew tired as the evening carried on. As the real Ben had witnessed in his viewing chamber, they'd returned home to their garage workshop. The trio salvaged what parts they could find. After cataloguing them, they compiled lists of parts left to acquire.

At one point, Chris noticed that Morgan lingered against a pile of electronic parts.

"You okay?" Chris asked.

"I'm fine," Morgan said, not truthfully. For the first time, Chris seemed like a stranger to her. If everything that they'd witnessed earlier was true, then everything had suddenly changed inside her own world. It looked like that was the case.

Morgan continued. "This is just all surreal."

"Tell me about it," Chris said, wearily.

"This is possibly the biggest discovery made in centuries. Maybe ever. Chris, there's a parallel universe and we can travel to it."

"Yeah," Chris agreed. "Everyone's going to be famous. Unless the government covers it all up."

"I feel as though we should tell someone," Morgan said.

"I'm sure that we will."

"No," Morgan insisted. "I meant right now. There's no reason to keep this a secret."

That thought hadn't actually entered Chris's mind, at least not practically.

"Who would we call?" Chris asked.

"Maybe our old project sponsors," Morgan said. "They have people and money. I'm sure they'd be interested in helping."

Ben had been listening to the conversation and interjected.

"Don't you think that they'll just think we're crazy?" he asked.

"Why?" Morgan contended. "We'll show them that the machine works. In fact, it works better than they'd ever expected"

Something about the plan seemed wrong to Chris. Everything was happening so fast that there were too many variables to consider.

"What about my Dad?" Chris pointed out.

"They'll help us save him," Morgan said.

Ben wasn't as optimistic.

"There isn't time," Ben said. "We know that the machine works and that Richard is in trouble. There'll be time for all that other stuff later, but let's take a shot ourselves."

Morgan nodded and said. "I just don't want to lose him again. I feel like we only have one shot."

Chris said, confidently. "We can do this."

Morgan nodded in agreement.

Ben looked at scribbles on a notepad in his hand and said "I've got the full list of parts."

"We'll be able to get everything?" Chris asked.

"I called my friend Ian and we should be able to get the important ones from his workshop," Ben said. "I might have some explaining to do about why it's so urgent at this time of the night, but I'll deal with that."

Ben handed Chris some additional notes.

"We'll have to split up to make this happen fast," Ben said. "Chris, do you know what these things are?"

Chris looked over the list and smiled. These were basic parts and rough instructions.

"Oh yeah," Chris said.

"Good," Ben said, pointing to the pile of electronics in front of Morgan "Stay here. You should be able to find the stuff on that list here in the workshop. Call us when you're ready."

"Where are you going?" Chris asked.

"We have some friends to drop in on," Ben said.

Morgan said to Ben. "Maybe I should stay with Chris?"

Naturally, she didn't want to leave him alone.

"I'll need help tearing into Ian's stuff for parts," Ben insisted, realizing that he wasn't fully convincing her. "Don't worry, we won't be gone long."

"I'll be fine," Chris assured Morgan.

Ben headed outside to get their car while Morgan lingered with Chris.

"I'm sorry that we put you through all that," Morgan said.

"What do you mean?" Chris said.

"About thinking that something was wrong with you," Morgan said.

Chris chuckled.

"You're not the only one," he said. "I don't know that anyone expected something like this to happen. It was sort of a random accident."

Morgan philosophically waxed for a moment. "Accidents in science lead to significant discoveries all the time. Electricity, penicillin, microwaves."

"I just hope that it wasn't some fluke and that things are stuck this way," Chris said.

Day 5 {12:30am}

♣

Richard arrived home to find Morgan, Rachel, and the other Chris waiting for him in the living room. Chris looked up at Richard as though he were a ghost.

"What's wrong?" Richard said. "We were in the middle of some important things at the lab."

Morgan motioned for him to join her on the sofa.

"Take a seat honey," she said. "We're in the middle of something important here too."

Morgan turned back to Rachel and continued. "Maybe you could tell Richard what you told me."

Richard thought that it was all highly unusual. He reluctantly settled in next to Morgan and waited for Rachel to explain what was wrong.

Rachel began. "You know how Chris has seemed a little bit 'off' lately?"

Chris gave Richard a weak smile.

Richard responded. "Maybe."

"Well," Rachel said. "There are some things that I'd forgotten to share with you and Mrs. Jennings."

"I don't know about forgotten," Morgan prompted.

Rachel continued. "Chris hadn't wanted me to say anything, but he snuck out to the lab to use the machine to eavesdrop on Jessica Aalgaard."

Richard quickly grew angry. "You what?"

"I didn't do any of this," Chris said.

"Oh, just wait Richard," Morgan added. "It's only going to get worse."

Richard continued to glare angrily at Chris.

"Ben mentioned that he'd found Chris in the lab, but he didn't mention any of this." Richard said

"I don't think that he knew about it," Rachel explained. "The reason Chris was so interested in using the machine was because of something he'd seen when using it the night before."

Richard gritted his teeth, furious that Chris had been using the machine on his own. He knew that Chris was curious, but such behavior was outrageous. Richard was also annoyed with himself for being so sloppy as to allow such a security lapse to occur.

"What did you see?" Richard asked.

Chris kept pleading innocence. "I didn't see anything."

"He thought that he'd seen himself dating Jessica in the viewer," Rachel answered on his behalf.

Richard turned to Morgan. "I thought that you said that Chris is dating Jessica?"

"I said that he thought that he was." Morgan replied.

"I am dating Jessica," Chris said. "Or at least I was."

Rachel could feel the conversation tumbling out of control. She decided to spring her conclusion on them.

"He isn't Chris," Rachel said. "At least not our Chris. I think that our Chris is in another dimension."

The words trickled out of Rachel's mouth too quickly for Chris's parent to react at first. Richard sat stunned for an instant, trying to make sense of it all. Morgan was surprised as well, having not yet heard that part of the explanation.

"What?" Richard said, dumbfounded.

Rachel continued. "Chris had some sort of accident with the machine. When I picked him up in the morning, he was all disoriented and then he started acting all weird. He actually did think that Jessica was his girlfriend and that Ben was married to you Mrs. Jennings."

"What?" Morgan said. She put her hands up and shook her head. The conversation became increasingly odd.

Rachel looked at Richard and said. "He thought that you were dead."

Richard turned to Chris for confirmation, but he merely shrugged.

"Don't you think that we should be taking him in to see the doctor?" Richard asked Morgan, before turning back to Chris. "Rachel, I don't know how these ideas got into your head. I'm sorry Chris, but there is obviously something seriously wrong with you and Rachel is only making this worse."

"We have an appointment for tomorrow morning to go over more tests," Morgan said. "There's only so much that they can do right away."

"Rachel," Richard said. "It's late, so I'm going to have to ask you to go home."

Rachel continued to try to convince them. "Isn't there any chance that something happened with the machine?"

"Yes," Richard responded. "Chris could have given himself brain damage. This nonsense about another dimension though? Not likely."

Chris sensed that Rachel's theory was still his best hope of finding a quick explanation for the present circumstances. He wasn't going to let it be ignored.

"I know that this sounds crazy," he said. "I don't even really understand it all myself, but I know that a lot of stuff is very wrong. I'm starting to wonder if you guys are messing around with bigger things than you realize."

Rachel added for emphasis. "Chris said something about watching your tests. Apparently they hadn't been quite right."

Morgan looked at Richard. She knew that Chris had been at the lab, but not the full extent of his visits there.

"That's right." Richard admitted. "We've had some glitches."

"So you've been seeing things that seem unusual or different?" Rachel questioned.

"Not really," Richard said, but then he admitted. "Some things have seemed off. We haven't been able to explain the lag that we're seeing."

Morgan said. "The images don't match up."

"Maybe we could at least check it out?" Chris pleaded.

Richard took a long look at Chris and agreed.

"Fine," he said. "Let's go down to the lab and see if you remember anything."

Day 5 {1:00am}

☺ ↔ ☻

The real Chris was in the other world's garage, still gathering parts when he heard a knock at the window. It startled him, but then he realized that the person behind the noise was Jessica.

Chris went around to a side door to let Jessica inside and immediately asked "What are you doing here?"

Jessica was taken aback and delivered the same question right back at Chris.

"What are you doing here?" she exclaimed. "I can't believe that you skipped the game!"

At this point, Chris wasn't going to try too hard to justify his actions.

"I was working with my Mom and Ben on something at the lab," he said. "I guess we got caught up on it."

"There were scouts and recruiters at the game," Jessica pointed out. "You suddenly don't care about college?"

That news did make Chris feel guilty for an instant. He didn't want to screw up the other Chris's life, but he also realized that he needed to consider a much bigger picture. The priority had to be getting things back to normal.

"You look awful you know." Jessica added, looking up and then down at Chris's appearance. He was quite haggard from working non-stop at the lab.

All that Chris could muster was to say. "Thanks."

Chris continued working, somewhat ignoring the conversation with Jessica. He was still a man on a mission, but Jessica wasn't one to be ignored that easily.

"Are you cheating on me?" Jessica asked, abruptly. "You disappeared and don't return my calls. You skipped the biggest game of your life. All of this secret stuff is downright weird."

Chris took a breath while gathering the last of the parts that he needed. He didn't have time for this sort of drama.

"I'm sorry that I haven't been around," he said. "But we've got some really important stuff going on."

"What could be so important?"

"I really don't have time to get into it all, but maybe it'll make sense at some point."

"I don't even know why I came over here." Jessica admitted, clearly near the end of her rope. "Tyler said that he figured you might be with Rachel again or something."

Despite everything, the mention of Tyler still managed to annoy Chris. And Jessica knew that dangling the reference would get Chris's attention and he played right into it.

"Don't get upset," Jessica said. "He was just being a friend."

"Yeah," Chris said. "The kind of friend who's trying to hit on you."

Jessica's phone rang loudly and interrupted their conversation. While Jessica spoke on her phone, Chris sorted through the parts one more time to double-check that he had everything.

"Some guys called looking for Tyler." Jessica said. "I guess he'd heard that you were at the lab with your Mom and Ben."

Chris was dumbfounded and wondered how Tyler knew that information. This was a new low for Tyler in any reality.

"What?" Chris said, thinking aloud. "Is he stalking me now?"

"I guess that the guys were drinking and someone said he was going to teach you a lesson. They thought that he might be coming here or the lab, but they weren't sure."

Chris was concerned that the distraction might further complicate the evening. He didn't need additional problems.

"Don't you think that we should call the police?" Jessica asked.

Chris thought for a moment and said. "And tell them what? That we heard a rumor about a guy from school who might be about to commit a crime?"

"Yeah."

"Look," Chris said, trying to keep his calm. "Let's head over to the lab and check it out. You can give me a ride, right?"

Jessica said reluctantly. "I guess."

Chris gathered up the parts that he'd placed into a large bag. Morgan and Ben would be returning to the lab soon and Chris didn't want to leave either of them wondering where he'd gone. He dug a cell phone out of his pocket.

Jessica remarked, annoyed. "Oh, so you do have your cell phone?"

Chris gave her a sheepish smile and dialed Morgan's phone.

While it was dialing, Chris said to Jessica. "My battery's about to run out, so I've had it off. Sorry."

Morgan answered her phone.

Through the phone, Chris heard Morgan ask. "Chris?"

"Hey Mom," Chris said.

"Is everything okay?" Morgan asked.

"Yeah, I've got what we needed," Chris said and then he looked over at Jessica. "Jessica stopped by and she's going to take me back to the lab, okay?"

Morgan grumbled and inquired. "You haven't told her anything, have you?"

Jessica couldn't hear Morgan's side of the conversation, but she still gave Chris a curious look.

"No," Chris said. "Of course not. Look, we should get going here."

"Ok," Morgan said. "We should be done gathering up everything soon. We'll see you shortly."

Chris hung up the phone a moment later.

"I still don't think it's a good idea to try to confront him if Tyler's up to something," Jessica said.

Chris seemed undeterred.

"Tyler's stupid," Chris concluded. "But he's not a criminal."

While Jessica didn't agree with Chris's assessment of the situation, she also didn't want to stand around arguing. Chris and Jessica headed out to the street, where her car sat waiting.

Day 5 {1:00am}

♣

Ben had begun preparing another test of the machine in the real world. He'd grown more convinced than ever that there was an opportunity for him in the other world. The challenge that remained was to duplicate Chris's method of getting there.

As Ben struggled to solve that problem, an alarm sounded on the machine's control panel. Ben realized that a proximity sensor had noticed that someone was coming into the building. He switched a monitor to show an exterior view and immediately saw Chris, Morgan, Rachel, and Richard all approaching the lab.

"Oh no," Ben muttered to himself.

The thought instantly occurred to Ben that something significant was obviously happening if Richard had brought his entire family to the lab in the middle of the night.

Ben feared that Richard must have figured out what had been wrong with Chris over the past few days. If that were the case, then he also would be aware of their connection to the alternative universe. With Jai's pressures and now Richard, literally, about to walk through the door, Ben knew that circumstances had reached the end of the line for him.

Thinking fast, Ben engaged the lab's door locks by keying in a series of commands that denied Richard access. After that task was complete, Ben redoubled his efforts on the machine. The immediate crisis would be handled, but now he would truly be committed to his latest plan.

Out in the hallway, Richard was surprised to learn that his lab entry pass code suddenly wasn't working. The lab door's display simply said that the password that he'd entered was not valid. Richard tried entering it again but received the same message.

"That's odd," Richard said.

"What?" Morgan asked.

"My pass code isn't working."

Richard turned on the intercom, assuming that Ben might still be inside.

"Ben," Richard said into the intercom. "The door isn't opening. If you're in there, can you please let me in?"

There wasn't an answer and that surprised Richard. He had noticed Ben's car out in the parking lot, so it was a safe bet that he was inside the lab and could help. If anything, Richard thought, Ben might be just as intrigued as he was to determine if what Chris and Rachel were claiming was true. The machine, with an ability to transport people to a parallel dimension, changed everything.

"He's in there?" Morgan asked. "Right?"

"I think so," Richard replied. "His car was parked outside."

Rachel piped up. "The only reason he'd ignore us is if he was up to something and didn't want us in there."

Morgan considered the conclusion, her natural inclination already leaning in that direction.

"He has to be up to something then," she said.

Richard scolded them both. "Don't just rush to any conclusions. Maybe he's working and can't hear the intercom."

Morgan grumbled, not buying the excuse.

Chris kept quiet during the exchange, still unsure of everything. He simply wanted this nightmare of sorts to end, but he also wasn't one to sit idly watching and he wanted to help.

"Aren't there any other ways inside?" Chris asked.

"No," Richard shrugged and said. "We tried to keep it simple."

As the machine powered up, its humming grew loud enough inside the lab that everyone could hear it in the hallway.

"Isn't that the machine?" Morgan wondered.

Richard recognized the sound and was concerned.

Morgan continued. "What if he destroys it?"

"Why would he do that?" Richard asked.

Day 5 {2:15am}

The other Tyler had wondered what was wrong with Chris. He'd never been incredibly close to the other Chris, but they'd still been teammates for years and clearly knew one another extremely well. Chris had always been the team's star player and Tyler had always been second best. It gnawed at him to be number two, but the truth was that Tyler had never been talented enough to carry the team entirely on his shoulders.

Without Chris, the team had fallen on its face against Westby earlier that evening. Coach Barns had looked to Tyler to carry the team to victory, but he'd failed.

Tyler had never seen his father as angry with him as he'd been after the game. His father had been the Chris of his era, but now he was the head of the local police department. His father was successful by most standards, but he still lived his life in glory days gone by. That was what was important to him and, by extension, that was what was important to Tyler.

Only Tyler was never fully able to live up to his father's expectations, because Chris had always been in the way. And Tyler resented Chris for it. Tyler resented that his father had made him go to Chris's house before the game against Westby and virtually beg him to play. It was embarrassing.

Even more embarrassing was that, despite the talk, Chris had still had the nerve to skip the game. It was unheard of. Yet, Chris's absence should have provided Tyler with his moment to shine, but the spotlight made Tyler melt. The disappointment in Tyler's father's eyes after the game was something that Tyler would likely remember for the rest of his life.

The game had started close for a few innings, and Tyler had an opportunity to be a hero early, with the bases loaded. But, he'd struck out and the team was never able to get into the same position again.

After the game, Tyler and some of the guys on the team decided to forget the disappointment by tossing back a few beers. For Tyler though, drinking didn't help. It actually made the situation worse, as his anger toward Chris only grew stronger. Finally, Tyler decided that he needed an outlet for all of that frustration and that outlet became Chris himself.

Tyler, against the wishes of some teammates sober enough to realize the stupidity of his plan, decided to pay Chris a visit.

Chris and Jessica were back at the lab, waiting for Ben and Morgan to arrive and they'd not noticed Tyler anywhere. Chris assumed that the rumors that he had come to the lab were unfounded and had already started working on putting the newest parts in place. Jessica looked on over his shoulder and noticed the melted circuits inside the control panel.

"What have you guys been doing here?" Jessica wondered.

"Working on the projector," Chris said.

"Your Mom was fine with that? Jessica said, seeming surprised.

"She understands."

Another minute went by until there was a knock at the lab's door. Jessica was startled by it.

"Tyler?" Jessica asked.

"It's likely my Mom and Ben," Chris responded.

Jessica followed Chris to the lab's main entrance and they found Tyler waiting outside. Chris was angered by the distraction.

"Hey Buddy," Tyler said. "Open up!"

Chris yelled. "We're busy!"

Chris looked at Jessica, who seemed more annoyed than frightened.

Tyler laughed and said. "I know. You missed the game man."

"He's not going to leave," Jessica said to Chris.

"So we'll call the police," Chris said.

"His Dad is the police," Jessica reminded him.

Chris tried to keep Tyler at bay.

"I don't have time to talk right now," he said.

Tyler glared at Chris and replied. "I'm going to be out here until you do."

Chris knew that Morgan and Ben would return to the lab any moment. When they did, he assumed that they could all deal with Tyler together.

"He looks like he's drunk," Jessica said. "He's probably harmless. If he's inside, we can keep an eye on him."

Chris noticed that Tyler still had a baseball bat in hand. That didn't seem so harmless.

"Why don't you leave that outside if you want to come in?" Chris offered, indicating the baseball bat.

Tyler set the bat aside outside and came inside. As he looked around the lab, he feigned being impressed. In the back of Chris's mind, he couldn't help but wonder if he'd just let a fox into the henhouse.

"Quite a place you have here," Tyler said.

Tyler wondered farther inside the lab.

"So," Chris asked, impatiently. "What did you want to talk about?"

"Oh," Tyler replied. "I just wanted to understand what was so important that you'd let us all down?"

From the tone in Tyler's voice, Chris quickly grew concerned that he might get violent.

"Some things came up, so I'm trying to help my family out," Chris said. "You can understand that, right?

Jessica cut in. "Just go home Tyler. You're drunk. I can drop you off."

Tyler's voice boomed at Jessica. "Shut up!"

Chris wasn't intimidated and yelled back. "I think it's time you left or we're calling the police."

Tyler chuckled and said. "Police? They won't care now that my Dad's not happy with you. Do you think that any of them are behind you after you let this whole town down?"

Chris didn't entirely believe the threat, but anything he did to get rid of Tyler wasn't going to be easy.

"I thought that maybe you were a nice guy inside somewhere, but you're not," Chris said. "You're a jerk."

"I'm the jerk?" Tyler replied. "You're the guy who hasn't been at practice all week and then you skipped the biggest game of the year. But I'm the jerk?"

Chris didn't say anything in reply.

"Good luck having a future after this week buddy," Tyler continued. "Scouts. Everyone at the game. Now they all know what kind of guy Chris Jennings actually is."

Tyler had gotten himself wound up to a point where it seemed as though he might explode. He wondered over near the viewing chamber and mock-admired it. Then he picked up the machine's control helmet and looked it over.

Tyler grinned and asked. "What's this? Some sort of crash helmet?"

"Put it down and stop fooling around!" Chris ordered.

Tyler simply smiled and said. "Okay."

With that, Tyler slammed the helmet down onto the lab's floor. It made a crunching noise as it struck the hard surface.

Chris responded without thinking, rushing at Tyler. With his momentum, Chris managed to knock Tyler down. A scuffle followed on the floor.

Tyler was a better fighter than Chris, but he was also still a bit drunk and his swings were slower than they would have otherwise been.

The sloppy fight that ensued worried Jessica. She stood by at first and watched as Tyler struggled to crawl atop Chris. Tyler wanted to gain the advantage, although Chris was able to prevent his first few attempts.

Eventually though, Tyler struck Chris with a couple of punches that sent him reeling. After he had Chris off balance, Tyler pulled off the reversal and soon Chris was pinned down under him. Tyler pulled his arm back to punch, but, by that time, Chris had gotten his wits about himself and was able to block the blow.

The pair continued to wrestle. Jessica wanted the conflict to end and decided to take action. She thought that she might be able to get between them, but that didn't prove to be a wise idea.

"Get off of him!" Jessica yelled while tugging at Tyler's arm.

Tyler shifted his weight and his fist accidentally jerked into Jessica's head. The blow made her body go limp and she fell down behind Tyler and Chris.

"We have to help her you idiot!" Chris yelled.

Tyler looked back at Jessica for a moment, but then didn't pay her additional attention. Like an animal, he was focused on Chris.

Chris used the distraction to shift his weight enough to toss Tyler off of his body. Chris was on his feet an instant later and made sure that he had created some distance from Tyler, who was getting up off of the floor.

Thinking fast, Chris went to the machine's control panel and had a few seconds to punch in a series of commands before Tyler lunged close enough to try at tackling him again. Chris got away from Tyler and next ran over to the broken control helmet. He pulled out the main power cord from the helmet's top and then held the cord out in front of himself.

"Keep back," Chris said. "Or else you'll get hurt."

Tyler snorted. "You're trying to scare me with a wire?"

Tyler lunged forward, but Chris held out the cable as though it were a weapon and Tyler flinched back. Chris started to back up and lured Tyler into stepping through the viewing chamber. The machine could be heard humming as it powered up, but the viewing chamber was still empty when Tyler stepped inside it. Chris stood strategically opposite Tyler, holding the helmet's power cable out as though he might strike with it. This threat kept Tyler in position near the viewing chamber.

Tyler quickly grew frustrated and said. "Fight me like a man Jennings."

Chris stood by waiting. He hoped that his plan might work, but timing would be the key to its success.

"What're you doing?" Tyler asked. "Standing there all..."

Tyler was cut off when the viewing chamber sprang to life and energy flowed from it into his body. He was instantly shocked. His body jerked and twisted from the force of the energy until he fell unconscious to the floor.

Chris ran over to the control panel and shut down the machine. He then went over to Jessica's side and helped her as she regained consciousness.

"What happened?" Jessica questioned Chris as she rubbed on her head. "My head hurts."

"Tyler is taking a nap for a while," Chris replied. "Are you okay?"

Jessica looked at Chris with a groggy expression and said. "I feel like my face is about to fall off."

Chris noticed swelling on her cheek and said. "We might want to get you looked at."

Chris stepped over to Tyler's motionless body and used some nearby wire to bind his hands and feet. Jessica walked over to help.

"Pretty impressive," Jessica said after looking down at Tyler.

"I'm going to call the police," Chris said to Jessica. "I don't care what Tyler said."

Chris heard commotion come from the building's front door and looked up to see Ben and Morgan step into the lab. They were both carrying armloads of parts for the machine and stood dumbfounded at the scene.

Morgan asked Chris. "What's going on now?"

Day 5 {3:00am}

♣

Inside the real world's lab, Ben had the machine powered up to nearly the level that he guessed was needed to make the switch into the other dimension. He'd recalled the level that Chris had left the machine at when he'd caught him in the lab. The viewing chamber was already projecting an image while Ben tried to find his counterpart, assuming that that was part of the triggering process.

It was a long shot, as Ben had no specific idea regarding how to trigger his travel to the other dimension. He'd overheard the mention of reaching certain power levels, but had little more to go on. Unfortunately for Ben, nothing had happened yet. He was straining under the power at such a high level, so he wasn't sure how much longer he could hang on.

Ben tried to check at the lab in the other world, but the image that appeared inside the viewing chamber was of an unrecognizable location. Ben realized that the lab must have been in a different location in the other world. Of course, he had no idea where that might be.

Before starting the machine, Ben had programmed it to not power down when it reached certain temperature alerts. With the machine operating at high power levels, it would soon overheat. He expected that it would fail just after he'd left for the alternate dimension, but his plan also left him a second way out of his predicament. It was undoubtedly the other world or bust. He might have only one shot, but felt that it was worth the risk.

If he could transport over to the other world, then destroying the machine in the real world would help Ben never be bothered again. He'd switch bodies with the other Ben, leaving him stranded in the real world. With the machine destroyed, the project would be halted. No sponsor would fund a project that had appeared to have destroyed itself. Richard, along with Ben by association, would be disgraced. Neither would have a chance at stopping Ben's plans in the other world.

That plan wasn't working though and, standing under the strain from the machine, Ben wondered if he might simply die. He'd been pushed into executing his plan without fully understanding the mechanics involved. As the strain increased, Ben was resigned to his fate. Touched by a final feeling of regret, he acknowledged the intercom line that Richard had opened.

Out in the hallway, the group heard Ben's voice over the intercom. His voice was barely audible due to the machine's loud hum.

"I'm sorry," Ben said, weakly.

Richard shouted into the intercom. "Let us in!"

There was no reply. Morgan looked concerned.

"He's finally lost it," she said. "Hasn't he?"

Richard didn't have a reply for her. He was dumbfounded as to what might be going on inside the lab. Regardless, it seemed clear that Ben had somehow betrayed them. Richard felt powerless.

From behind everyone, Rachel spoke up.

"Now what're we going to do?" she asked.

Back inside the lab, Ben was nearly overwhelmed by the machine's power. He couldn't help but continue to feel that he'd failed. More than anything else in his sad life, he'd wanted to find himself transported to the other world. He'd wanted so badly to escape.

And then he did.

Ben's body collapsed near the viewing chamber. The viewing chamber went from displaying a clear image to mere flickers as Ben's consciousness lost contact with it.

Out in the hallway, no one had yet realized what had happened with Ben inside the lab. Richard focused on alternate means of getting into the lab. He tapped feverishly at the control panel.

The others noticed that Richard seemed to be up to something.

"What're you doing?" the other Chris asked Richard.

Chris was used to being a leader amongst his peers, but the events of the past couple of days had thrown him off. He'd been scared that he'd lost his mind, but now it was increasingly looking like Rachel was right. Something about the experiments that were being conducted had resulted in his current situation. That realization gave him the confidence to not lurk in the shadows any longer.

Richard glanced back at Chris.

"One needs to leave a back door," Richard said. "At least whenever possible."

"You have a way inside? Chris asked.

"I thought of something that I'm going to give a try." Richard said, turning his full attention back to the console. After Richard had completed a series of keystrokes into the console, he stood back, expecting the door to open.

But nothing happened. The door didn't open.

"What happened?" Chris asked.

"It didn't work," Richard replied, simply.

Richard put his head down. Ben had known to block his best hope of access. The sound of the machine inside began to worry Richard. He knew that it could actually destroy itself, but he didn't realize that that was actually Ben's plan.

Morgan had known Richard long enough to realize when he was stumped.

"There has to be another way inside," Morgan suggested.

Rachel piped up. "I know that Chris had an account."

Richard's head jerked up in realization.

"Yes he did," Richard said, looking at Chris. "Try to think of what it might have been."

Chris was tired of standing around in the background. He wanted to help, but it didn't seem possible.

"I have no idea," Chris admitted.

Chris thought for a moment and then punched in a series of letters and numbers into the keypad. Unfortunately, the combination didn't open the door. Richard continued to grow weary of the sound of the machine's hum.

"Don't try to guess what our Chris might have used," Richard suggested. "Just punch in what you would have used."

Chris thought of something else and punched it in. This time, it worked and the lab door rose open. Richard and Morgan ran inside. Chris and Rachel followed close behind.

"Nice thinking loser," Rachel yelled over to Chris. "Something about Jessica?"

Chris shrugged in affirmative.

Richard noticed Ben's fallen body first and pointed Morgan over to him.

"See if he's still breathing!" Richard yelled. "I need to stop the machine!"

Morgan ran over to where Ben was unconscious. While she tended to his situation, Richard noticed that the machine's control panel was lit up like a Christmas tree.

Chris and Rachel stood behind Richard and immediately noticed the array of blinking lights.

"This looks really bad," Chris said.

The situation was obvious enough that Rachel knew that they were in trouble.

"Maybe we should just get out of here," she said.

Richard worked intently at the panel, hoping to shut the machine down.

He said to Chris. "Ben turned off the automatic shutdown."

Richard typed feverishly into the control panel, but he couldn't get anything to happen.

"You can't stop it?" Rachel asked.

An error message popped up repeatedly on the screen. Richard tried a few other tactics without success.

"He's locked it down with a series of passwords," Richard revealed.

"What's wrong?" Morgan yelled across the lab to Richard.

Richard decided that it was too late and that things were too dangerous. They needed to get out of the room as quickly as possible.

"Get back!" he yelled. "The machine is going to blow! It'll fill the room with debris!"

Chris and Rachel ran back into the hallway. Richard waited for Morgan to reach him before running out of the lab together.

Once everyone was safely in the hallway, Richard typed a sequence into the hallway control panel. He'd assumed that the lab door would shut, but it didn't. Richard watched as the control panel's screen flickered.

"The machine is draining too much power," Richard said. "It's overloading the electrical system."

Morgan ran down the hallway and tried to open the building's main entrance, but it didn't budge.

"This panel must be overloaded too!" Morgan yelled to the others. "We need something heavy to break it!"

Richard heard the cry and ran back into the lab to grab an array of tools. He found a large, steel wrench that he'd hoped might be enough to shatter the exterior entrance's glass.

"Step back!" Richard said, winding up and then swinging the wrench.

The wrench slammed hard into the door's glass, but it ricocheted off the surface, leaving no more than a scratch to the glass.

"It's secure glass," Richard said. "It isn't supposed to break."

Morgan looked back down the hallway, into the lab, and could see that the control panel was entirely red in color. She felt the machine's hum ring loudly into her ears.

Chris stepped up to Richard and held his hand out for the wrench.

"Can I give it a shot?" Chris asked.

Richard handed Chris the wrench, assuming that it was worth a shot. Chris stepped into a perfect batter's stance and took a particular swing at the glass. It shattered upon the wrench's impact into a spider web pattern that Chris was then able to kick open.

Chris, Rachel, Morgan and Richard used the opening to run outside, getting away from the building. As they fled, they heard the machine's screeching hum reach its apex.

7:

What Could Have Be(e)n

Day 5 {3:00am}

☺ ↔ ☻

Police in the other world led Tyler out of the lab in handcuffs. Inside, the real Chris was still being interviewed by an officer.

"We've gotten statements from both you and Jessica," the officer said. "One thing that doesn't quite make sense to me is why Tyler would have wanted to cause you any trouble."

"He was still upset that I'd missed the game," Chris pointed out.

"Which game was that?" the officer inquired, before suddenly recognizing Chris. "Oh hey, you're that Chris Jennings kid."

Chris hesitated to answer, not wanting to bring the wrath of the police department onto himself. He still assumed that Tyler's earlier bluff about having the police in his back pocket might be true.

"Yeah," Chris said, sheepishly. "That's me."

The officer chuckled. "Well, I grew up in Westby, so you feel free to take a night off whenever you want."

The officer finished up his notes and then added, sarcastically. "Captain Wentworth isn't going to be happy about his boy getting brought in again."

"You guys don't like the captain?" he asked.

"Just between you and me?" the officer confided.

Chris nodded.

"We can't stand him. We can't stand his kid Tyler either. This'll be the third time this year we've brought him in and it is a pleasure."

Chris smiled. He was satisfied that justice would be served.

"Good to hear," he said.

"Don't worry." The officer added. "We'll take care of it."

Day 5 {3:15am}

♣

Richard, Morgan, the other Chris, and Rachel waited outside the real world's lab building for an explosion, but it never occurred.

Rachel listened closely for the hum of the machine and noticed when it began to wind down.

"What's happening in there?" she asked.

Richard listened closely for a moment and then replied. "One of the circuits must have blown out before it could overheat and explode."

Chris wondered. "Is it safe to go back in?"

"Let's give it another minute," Richard said. "Then we can assess the damage."

While they continued to wait outside, Rachel looked at Chris with starry eyes.

"You saved us," Rachel said.

Chris blushed.

"If you hit anything just right," he pointed out. "It'll shatter."

Chris looked around at the lack of any obvious damage and added. "Besides, it doesn't seem like there was much of an explosion to be saved from."

After waiting a few more minutes, Richard gave the all-clear for the group to go back inside. The group rushed into the room, with Richard and Morgan both returning to see what condition Ben was in. They were both surprised to find Ben moving. Morgan knelt down by his side.

"Ben, can you hear me?" Morgan asked, loudly.

Richard held him down.

Ben stirred and said. "My head. What just happened?"

Ben was disoriented because he was actually no longer Ben. Rather, he was the other Ben, having switched consciousness with the real Ben.

Richard left the other Ben in Morgan's care and surveyed the control panel

"There's plenty of damage though," Richard observed. "He turned off the safety override and it overheated."

Morgan said. "We're lucky he screwed up one more thing."

"Hey babe," the other Ben said to Morgan. He then smiled at Morgan, not realizing that she wasn't his wife. In fact, it was reassuring to him to have her at his side.

Richard noticed that Ben was cognizant and angrily said. "You tried to destroy the machine."

"What?" Ben said, not immediately recognizing Richard's voice.

"You idiot," Morgan said. "You'll go to jail for this."

Ben sat up and looked around. He realized that he had no idea where he was at.

"Hey," he said. "Where am I?"

At first glance, Ben thought that his surroundings looked like a lab of some sort, but not one that he recognized.

"Am I dreaming?" Ben continued, soon noticing Richard. "Richard, how're you here?"

Richard ignored the question and said to Morgan. "We need to call an ambulance."

"Why?" Ben said, continuing to look around. "This is the lab that I saw with Chris, isn't it?"

"What are you talking about?" Richard asked.

Ben realized what had occurred and exclaimed. "Oh no, he's with Chris now, isn't he?"

Morgan looked over at Chris, who was keeping a distance with Rachel.

"Who?" Morgan said in a concerned tone. "Who's with Chris right now?"

Putting more pieces together, Ben grew concerned and blurted out. "Don't you see what's happened? Ben from my reality just switched places with me."

Ben laid back down in frustration.

"This is ridiculous," Richard said, still not convinced of Ben's claim.

Ben sat up again and spotted the other Chris.

"Are you okay?" he asked. "Your mother and I have been worried about you. I'm here now and we'll figure out a way to get back."

Richard remained confused by Ben's behavior and initially assumed it to be a ruse of sorts.

"Ben," Richard said. "This charade needs to end."

"Charade?" Ben balked. "What're you talking about? Your son has been trapped in a parallel universe with me for the past few days. He's in danger now."

Richard and Morgan exchanged uncertain looks.

Ben continued. "Look, I didn't believe this either until Chris used our machine to show me what was happening here. Your Ben was about to double-cross you with Jai and some people he's been working with. We were working to save you, but your Ben must have figured things out too and escaped to my dimension."

Richard looked confused at first, but then it all started to make sense.

"We tried to send him back to warn you," Ben said. "But our machine still needs some work. I wasn't entirely sure if it'd be possible to send him back with it anyway. Now I'm here."

Morgan gasped and looked over at Richard. They were both coming around to believing that what Rachel had been saying was true.

Ben said. "We need to get things going again if we're to have any chance of getting Chris back safely and stopping my counterpart."

"Let's say that we believed you," Morgan said to Ben. "Where is our Chris right now?"

"He's still in my universe," Ben said. "Probably at our lab, working with your Ben and maybe not even realizing it."

Day 5 {3:30am}

☺ ↔ ☻

After the police had left the other world's lab, Jessica readied to head home. By this point, it was nearly the middle of the night, so her parents had potentially noticed that she'd snuck out. As it was, there were going to be questions aplenty regarding the black eye that she was sporting from Tyler's errant blow.

"I'm sorry about everything," Jessica said. "Freaking out and all that.

"That's okay," Chris said. "In the future, just do me a favor?"

"What?"

"Don't forget what a jerk Tyler is."

Jessica scoffed.

"That shouldn't be too hard," she said. "I'll see you tomorrow then?"

Chris looked over at Ben and Morgan and wondered what they might do next.

"Maybe," Chris replied. "I'm not sure if I'll be back in school just yet."

Jessica kissed Chris goodbye and said. "Just don't forget about me again, okay?"

"Don't worry," Chris smiled and said. "You're not easy to forget."

"Good."

After Jessica had left the lab, Chris checked in on Ben and Morgan. Ben was examining the control helmet.

"Is it bad?" Chris asked.

The helmet was clearly badly battered.

"It could have been worse," Ben said. "We'll need to repair a few things inside, but nothing major."

"That's good, right?"

"Yeah," Ben confirmed. "I was more worried about the viewer. That wasn't meant to be used for zapping people, but it should be fine."

Morgan looked over at Chris again and asked him. "You're sure that you're okay? We could take you over to get looked at."

"No," Chris said. "I think I've been looked over enough lately."

Without any warning, Ben passed out. His unconscious body jerked for a moment and then stopped. This was caused by the real Ben 'arriving' and taking the other Ben's place in the alternate dimension. Morgan rushed to his side and helped him as he woke back up. Ben – now with the real Ben inside his body instead – was disoriented.

"What's wrong?" Morgan asked, naturally concerned.

The real Ben shook off his dizziness. He hadn't anticipated how jarring the transfer experience would be.

"I'm fine now," Ben assured Morgan, hedging an excuse. "Don't worry, I must have just not had enough to eat tonight and got up too quickly. My batteries have been running down."

Ben last remembered desperately wanting to be in the alternate dimension. Then there was a white flash of light and he suddenly found himself in this other reality.

Through his new eyes, Ben marveled at his unfamiliar surroundings. It was exactly as it had looked through the viewing chamber. He smiled at Morgan, but then noticed that the real Chris was also nearby. He knew that he'd have to be careful around Chris, at least until he'd dealt with him.

Morgan helped Ben to his feet and suggested. "I think that we all need to go home and rest."

Chris protested. "I thought that we were in a hurry, right? You know, because of my Dad maybe getting killed?"

Chris's efforts were futile though. Ben was exhausted from the transfer and wanted time to reorient himself, so he simply agreed with Morgan.

"We need to get some rest Chris," Ben said. "Or we'll make mistakes and fight against ourselves."

"Can't we at least take the helmet with us?" Chris asked. "We can work on it later at home."

Morgan thought about the request for a moment before relenting.

"Bring it along," she said. "But you're still getting some sleep."

As they were all leaving the lab, Ben reached over and kissed Morgan.

Morgan made sure that the kiss was short and asked Ben. "What was that for?"

"Oh," Ben said. "I'm just happy to see you."

Morgan wasn't in the mood for such affection though and simply said. "I'm glad that you're feeling better."

Chris noticed the oddly-timed kiss and immediately thought that it was unusual. It certainly didn't yet cross his mind that the real Ben might be in the alternate dimension with him, but he did wonder about the unusual show of affection. Ben turned to Chris and watched him as they exited the lab together.

"Don't worry Chris," Ben said. "Our focus right now is on getting you home."

Day 5 {6:00am}

♣

It was morning at the real world's lab, but that wasn't apparent from inside the windowless room. The other Chris and Rachel were asleep in a corner, while the other Ben worked with Richard and Morgan to make what repairs they could to the machine.

Ben had admired the sophistication of this universe's machine, musing. "It really is everything that we'd hoped it would be, isn't it?"

Richard replied. "The general approach never actually changed, since our theories were always close. But we've used the extra funding that we've received over the past several years to enhance it."

While Ben continued to work at his tasks, Morgan took Richard aside.

"You believe him then?" Morgan asked.

"Yes," Richard said. "I would have been more skeptical if Chris hadn't been acting strangely too. Something is going on here Morgan."

Part of Morgan still wasn't entirely convinced. She needed a sounding board to sort it out.

"Let's say he's for real," Morgan said. "Do you really think it's as easy as turning up the power levels? Our Ben was the one who made the switch happen, not him."

"I know honey," Richard said. "But we need to give it a try. We'll figure this out."

"And he can help?"

Richard looked back at Ben, who was consumed by the work, and said. "He seems to be fine."

"Fine," Morgan said. "I'll be back in a bit with the rest of the replacement parts."

Morgan kissed Richard and turned to leave the lab. Ben spun around in time to witness her leaving and got a curious look on his face. It was strange for him to see Morgan back with Richard.

In the corner, Chris and Rachel woke up from their naps. Rachel noticed Richard walk over to help Ben continue repairs on the machine.

She motioned to Ben and asked him. "You trust that creep?"

"Yeah," Chris said. "I'm glad he's here, so everyone doesn't think that I'm crazy anymore."

"Well," Rachel said. "Maybe he's just another figment of your imagination."

Chris gave Rachel a half-concerned look.

"Just kidding loser," Rachel continued with a laugh. "You should have seen the look on your face."

Rachel and Chris both got up and went over to observe Richard and Ben working. Ben noticed Chris approach and stopped for a moment.

"You must have had a crazy last couple of days?" Ben asked Chris.

"Yeah," Chris said. "I thought I'd lost my mind for a while there."

Rachel asked Richard. "How are things going?"

"Morgan's getting the parts that we need," Richard said. "Once those are in place, we should be able to give it a try."

"What are we trying out?" Chris wondered. "Sending me back?"

"No," Ben answered. "I'll go back. We need to stop their Ben first. Then we'll switch you back with their Chris."

After Morgan had returned to the lab with the necessary parts, she pitched in where she could with the repair tasks. Despite not having everything at their disposal, she was surprised by the progress that Richard and the other Ben had made in a relatively short period of time.

Ben noticed the progress too. He remarked to Richard. "I'd forgotten just how strong of a team we made. I wish that we could have stayed longer."

Richard hadn't had time over the past few hours to reflect on the work. When he did, he agreed that something had indeed been missing in his most-recent work with the real Ben. The swift progress with the other Ben was undeniable.

He responded. "Maybe there'll be a next time?"

Ben smiled. "Maybe."

"You're certainly easier to work with," Morgan added, having overheard the exchange.

Ben seemed surprised by the remark. "What do you mean? Am I usually a slacker evil-genius here or something?"

"No," Richard replied. "But let's just say that you have a very different attitude."

By later in the morning, the machine was finally ready and little time was wasted getting it ready to perform. Morgan continued to be concerned that their plan to swap the other Ben back with the real Ben could even work.

The other Ben put the control helmet on and got into position. He was nervous about how it would work. He understood what he needed to do while wearing it, but there would undoubtedly be small differences when operating this version of the machine.

"You haven't operated the Machine at these power levels, have you?" Morgan asked Ben.

Ben conceded. "No."

Richard remained confident though. "Don't fight it when the energy waves start coming in. You'll know what I mean. We'll level it out at a point where it'll feel like you've hit a calm in the storm."

Ben nodded as Richard started up the machine. It was the first time in a long time that he'd used the machine. Ben tried to push memories of the other Richard's fatal accident out of his head.

When the first energy wave hit Ben, he was surprised by how smooth it felt. He was used to testing with his primitive machine years before and, in comparison, this machine was a breeze to operate.

It wasn't long before an image of his lab in the other world appeared in the viewing chamber. Since Ben knew where the lab was located, it made sense to check there first.

"That's our lab," Ben yelled over to Richard.

Ben looked around inside, but nothing stuck out. It was deserted. Ben thought about where everyone might be. Their home seemed the most logical explanation and he checked there next.

An image of the other Morgan making breakfast at home in the kitchen appeared in the viewing chamber. The real Chris was seated nearby at the dining room table, where he was examining the control helmet.

"It should mostly be fixed," Morgan said, indicating the control helmet.

Chris smiled while inspecting Morgan's repair work. She'd had trouble sleeping and stayed up to fix it that morning.

"I'm impressed," he said.

"You should be," Morgan replied with a wink. "I spoke with Ben and, since you guys got some rest last night, you're going to head together to the lab. I'll catch up with you later today after I've had a chance to sleep."

"Ben!" Morgan called upstairs. "Breakfast is ready!"

Still observing in the real world, the real Morgan got goose bumps upon hearing her doppelganger's words. Understandably, it made her uncomfortable to witness her alternate self call out for Ben. Although the other Ben had seemed pleasant enough, she still couldn't imagine being married to him.

Both Morgan and Richard were dazzled to see the machine displaying images of the other world. The first time they saw Chris in the dining room made both of their hearts ache. As soon as they heard Morgan's mention that Ben and Chris would be heading to the lab together, they knew that such action would mean trouble.

Over the hum of the machine, Morgan yelled to Richard. "We need to help Chris!"

Richard replied. "We'll stop this."

The other Ben's perspective soon left the dining area and headed upstairs.

The real Ben's voice was heard calling out. "I'll be down in a minute!"

The viewing chamber's image moved into the master bedroom and they discovered the real Ben getting dressed.

The real Ben looked like he was already comfortable in his new life and the other Ben was furious to see this stranger inhabiting his world.

"Are you ready?" Richard called over to the other Ben. "We're taking up the power."

"Do it!" the other Ben yelled back.

As smooth as the machine had been, the jolt from the extra energy boost hit the other Ben hard. At first, he feared that he might black out, but he was soon able to wrestle control. The strain showed on his face.

"Nothing's happened," Morgan observed to Richard. "He doesn't look like he can handle it much longer."

"Give him another minute." Richard replied.

In the viewing chamber, the real Ben continued to groom himself. The other Ben wasn't sure what he should do. As he watched the real Ben on the viewing chamber, he grew upset. The other Ben regarded the real Ben as a thief who had stolen his life. That anger caused the other Ben to fixate on the real Ben, wishing that he could switch back.

As if on cue, the real Ben fell to his knees. He put his hands on his head, clearly in terrible pain.

"Get out of my head!" Ben yelled.

Richard immediately realized what was happening and said to Morgan. "It's working!"

The real Ben's pained voice echoed through the viewing chamber's speaker, but he seemed to resist the reversal. Richard's excitement waned.

"He must have been ready for it somehow." Richard said. "He's fighting it."

"How is that possible?" Morgan asked.

"I don't know," Richard said. "Maybe he knows something we don't."

With the real Ben resisting the switch, the other Ben couldn't take the strain much longer and soon pulled off the control helmet. The connection to the viewing chamber ended with the image of the real Ben on his knees ceasing. The other Ben sweated profusely, clearly overcome by his battle of wills.

"What just happened?" the other Ben asked. "I thought that we were about to switch back."

"He knew what you were doing and was able to block you," Richard replied.

"But how?" Ben asked.

"Try to remember what happened when he switched with you," Richard said. "Could you feel anything?"

"I don't know," Ben said. "Maybe for an instant. I knew that something odd was happening, but I just didn't know what."

"Hmm," Richard said, lost in thought.

The other Chris spoke up. "Can't we send me back instead? I could warn my Mom."

Richard considered the proposal.

"Do you remember the switch?" Richard asked.

"I was sleeping," Chris said. "So, no."

"I just wonder if Chris might resist it too," Richard said. "Not realizing that we were trying to help."

"Besides Chris," Ben interjected. "You're not trained to use the machine. It could be dangerous."

Chris said. "But I want to do something to help."

"We need to figure out a plan," Morgan said to Richard.

Day 5 {10:15am}

☺ ↔ ☻

The real Chris was on his way to the other Chris's room when he heard Ben cry out. He went into the master bedroom and found Ben on his knees. By the time Chris arrived in the room, Ben was regaining his composure, having successfully foiled the other Ben's attempted switch.

Chris yelled down to Morgan. "Ben's hurt again!"

Morgan ran up to the bedroom, but by the time she arrived, Ben was on his feet.

"What's wrong?" Morgan asked.

"It's nothing," Ben lied. "Just a migraine. I'll take a couple of pills and be fine."

Chris didn't believe Ben, knowing that what he'd witnessed was clearly more than a simple headache.

"But I heard you yelling," Chris said. "You were on the floor."

Not surprisingly, Morgan was concerned. She'd already had Chris's health to worry about and now Ben.

"Ben," Morgan said. "We should get you checked out. Maybe it's something to do with the machine."

Ben hesitated. He didn't want to arouse suspicion, so he decided to play along.

"I'll stop in at the clinic," Ben offered. "Okay?"

"I can take you there," Morgan suggested.

"No honey," Ben said. "You need to get some rest. I'll take Chris along, just in case, and then we'll head over to the lab."

This plan seemed to appease Morgan.

Ben had assumed that the real world's machine had been destroyed after he'd switched over to the other world. In light of that, he wasn't sure how someone could have possibly tried to reverse the switch. If the machine hadn't been destroyed, he knew that it would be a significant problem for him.

Alternatively, he wondered if what he'd felt had instead been a side-effect of the switch that he'd not previously considered. He decided that it was something that he'd need to investigate

Ben looked to Chris and asked. "You're okay, right Chris?"

"Yeah," Chris said. "Why?"

"Just wondering," Ben said calmly. "We've all been around the machine quite a bit lately and the technology is still experimental."

Morgan said. "I'll feel better after you get checked out."

Ben stepped away from the others.

"I'll go get the car Chris," he offered.

Chris went to the other Chris's room to grab a couple of clothing items and Morgan followed him.

"Is it just me or does something seem odd with Ben?" Chris asked Morgan.

"He's under a lot of stress," Morgan said. "He gets this way sometimes. We're not used to this sort of thing. I do remember Ben getting headaches in the past when times were tough."

"Maybe I'm overreacting, but he seems different somehow."

"Make sure he gets checked out," Morgan insisted. "He can be stubborn. I'll see you guys later this afternoon."

Of course, Ben had no intention of going to the clinic. He planned to take Chris straight to the lab, where he could eliminate Chris from the parallel universe in a 'lab accident.'

As Ben backed the family car out of the garage, he realized that his plan had hit an immediate snag. He'd been hasty in suggesting that they drive to the lab. He hadn't immediately remembered that he wasn't sure where the lab was located in this dimension.

Ben hurriedly searched around inside the car. There was stray mail and little else. Shipping boxes referenced an office suite, but that wasn't much to go on. Fortunately though, the car's dashboard had a navigation device. Ben turned it on and searched the address history until he found one that matched two of the packages' address. It appeared to be the correct location

Their lab was in a lower-rent area, but Ben made a note to himself that such modest surroundings would change soon enough. He memorized the route to the lab on the map and switched off the GPS as Chris got into the vehicle.

Day 5 {11:00am}

♣

"I've got an idea," Richard said.

"What?" The other Ben asked.

The situation in the real world had continued to seem lost until Richard decided to take a chance.

"It's something I'd been toying around with now for years," Richard said. "We'd always wanted to extend our theories to make the viewing chamber into a teleporter, but it was, you know, the long term. Ben helped with it, but we'd never seriously pursued it yet."

"I wish that I could have been able to come up with that," Ben said, as he gave Richard a crooked smile.

"We never talked about the portal?" Richard asked Ben, referring to the other Richard.

"A little," Ben said. "But it seemed as though it'd be a long way away in development. We were focused on getting the viewing chamber to work at the time, so it seemed years out. After the accident, we couldn't even get the viewing chamber to work and that didn't matter anymore."

"We are petitioning to start the portal phase here," Richard said. "After we received our next round of funding. It was planned as a promise for the future in our presentation."

Ben gave Richard a curious look.

"Even with funding, it would take months to retrofit the machine, right?" Ben asked. "I never doubted the theory Richard, but it just wouldn't seem viable right now."

"What if I said that we'd already incorporated most of the work into the machine already? We managed to get ahead with the funding that we already had. We've always worried about rivals catching up with us."

Ben's jaw dropped.

"Did it really work?" he questioned.

"We haven't had much time to test it," Richard admitted. "But we thought so. A ball goes in, then it pops out someplace else of our choosing. That sort of thing. We only tried it a couple of times because it ended up causing a black-out of most of the west coast."

Rachel had been sitting nearby, listening to the conversation. She hadn't followed much of it, but that revelation caught her attention.

Rachel interrupted. "That was you guys?"

"Yes," Richard confirmed. "It was a short. We worked it out, so it shouldn't happen again. Anyway, since then we've been distracted by the viewer itself not appearing to function."

"How is being able to teleport across the country going to help us?" Rachel asked.

Ben tried to remember back to their preliminary discussions of the theories around it all.

"Richard," Ben conceited with a big grin on his face. "So you want to try to use it to send one of us over to the other side?"

Morgan asked Richard. "What are you thinking?"

"We're going to open a portal to the other world and use it to rescue Chris," Richard said.

Day 5 {11:15am}

☺ ↔ ☻

The real Chris had expected that the real Ben would first drive to the clinic, so he was surprised when Ben immediately drove to other world's lab.

"I thought we were getting you checked out?" Chris asked Ben.

"Oh," Ben said, curtly. "You know how your mother gets sometimes."

"But…"

Ben cut Chris off. "It's nothing, really."

Chris decided not to argue, but he took further note of Ben's strange behavior. Chris's mind had been otherwise distracted with thoughts of getting home. He felt as though they'd wasted too much time resting the prior evening. The repaired control helmet sat on Chris's lap and, even though he'd been impressed with the work Morgan had done on it overnight, he couldn't help but feel as though they were only running further behind.

Once at the lab, Ben and Chris got to work swapping out the remaining control panel parts that still needed replacement. Chris seemed to take charge and Ben let him work. Ben thought that it was almost too easy. Chris was enthusiastically fixing the machine that would soon lead to his demise.

As the afternoon went on though, Ben began to realize that killing or severely injuring Chris wasn't going to be as easy as he'd assumed. In his heart, Ben was a coward, not a criminal. His cowardice and desire had given him quick rewards after years of frustration, but those same decisions had continued to put him deeper into a corner.

Yet, Ben knew that he'd have a choice to make and it would prove to be a hard one. All of the ingredients for his long-term happiness were in place in the other world. Chris was the only element that needed to be purged and that purge would be necessary to avoid everything else falling apart. He would have to convince Morgan that Chris was dead, both in this dimension and the other.

Had Ben decided to sacrifice Richard for the sake of Jai's deal, there would have been great rewards in the end for that too, but it was an imperfect plan. Potentially being branded a traitor and a wanted man were chief amongst those imperfections. On the other hand, simply removing Chris from the equation would eliminate any potential risks. It wouldn't be pleasant, but Ben hoped that any guilt that he felt after the incident would swiftly fade away.

Day 5 {1:00pm}

♣

Morgan looked on as the other Ben and Richard worked through calculations that would enable them to open the portal. Their working together gave a glimpse of what the two colleagues might have accomplished if the real Ben hadn't gone astray. Together they were the best that they could have been, in an ideal world.

"We don't know what'll happen with sending a person through the portal, let alone sending someone to another dimension," Ben said. "Are you really sure that you want to risk this Richard?"

Richard didn't hesitate in his answer.

"I'm not going to sit here and watch," he said. "Not when we can do something to help Chris."

Ben took a deep breath.

"I should go Richard," he offered. "You know more about operating this machine anyway and I belong back there."

Richard stopped what he was doing and said. "It's my responsibility, not yours. You have a family to think about as well."

Off to the side, Chris came up behind Ben.

"You guys need any help?" he asked.

"No" Richard said, looking at the viewing chamber, "Maybe in a bit though."

While the others continued working, Rachel whispered to Morgan. "Do you know anything about this?"

Morgan said, with a half-hearted smile. "Enough to be worried."

"So you're as nervous as I am about it?"

"Yes," Morgan said, putting an arm around Rachel.

It was several hours before it was finally time to begin. Chris helped Richard and Ben move the viewing chamber into a more centralized location in the room. Richard wanted to give it some space, as he knew that it would need it when opening the portal.

While Ben started to warm up the machine, Richard went over to Morgan. He motioned at Ben when he spoke to her.

"He might need your help," Richard said. "I'd feel safer if you were assisting."

Morgan hadn't gotten over her discomfort around the machine, but now wasn't a time to fret about such things.

"I will Richard," Morgan said.

"Thanks," Richard replied, pausing to reflect. "We're doing the right thing?"

"It's our only option." Morgan said, simply. "Bring him home, okay?"

Morgan teared up and hugged Richard. They held one another close.

As Chris watched, he didn't fully understand what was about to happen, but he could tell that it might be the last time that he saw Richard. He'd never gotten the chance to say goodbye to his father, so he wasn't going to let another opportunity pass him by. Even if this Richard wasn't quite the one who had raised him, Chris still felt a connection to him.

Richard and Morgan let go of one another so that he could get into position. Richard began walking towards the portal, but Chris stopped him.

"I just wanted to thank you for everything." Chris said. "I'm glad that I was able to see you again and I wanted to say that I'm sorry."

"Sorry for what?" Richard asked.

"You wanted me to be like you, but I'm not."

Richard realized what Chris had awkwardly tried to say.

"No," Richard said. "I would have wanted you to be whatever you wanted to be."

Chris took the words to heart and started to choke up. He hugged Richard.

"Thanks," Chris said.

"And don't worry," Richard assured him. "This won't be the last that you see of me."

Chris let go of Richard. Rachel, who had been standing nearby, fought away tears of her own and stepped up to hug Richard.

After briefly embracing her, Richard let her go and finally moved into position. He was nervous, for sure, but he was able to use his self-confidence to push away thoughts of failure. In his mind, he had every reason to trust what he'd help build.

Morgan took her place at the control panel while Richard handed Ben the control helmet. Ben put it on and gave Morgan a thumbs up sign.

"You're sure you can bring up the location?" Richard asked Ben.

"Yes," Ben said. "I'll take care of it."

"Remember, it's going to be rough at first at these power levels, but stick through it and you'll be fine."

Ben nodded. A few moments later, he felt the energy hit hard against his mind, but he concentrated and was soon past it.

The viewing chamber image became clear, with the other dimension's lab appearing. Chris and Ben were working together in the lab, making the last of the repairs to their machine. It surprised Morgan to see Chris interacting with Ben, unaware of the threat that he posed.

"Now!" Richard yelled to Morgan. "Do it!"

Morgan entered a series of commands into the control panel and the machine hummed louder than it had been heard to sound before. The viewing chamber stopped displaying a full image of the lab. Ben and Chris could still be seen in a corner of it, but the majority of the image became pure energy.

The energy's pattern solidified inside the viewing chamber to what appeared like a sheet of water. In this state, it was still and reflective like a mirror.

Richard looked at Morgan and mouthed to her under the violent noise of the machine. "I love you." He then walked tentatively up to the waiting portal.

The strain of holding the position was already getting to Ben.

"I'm not sure how much longer I can hold on!" he yelled.

Richard reached out his arm and pressed his fingers up to the portal's wall of energy. Instead of being shocked when he touched it, the energy seemed to absorb his fingers. Richard stepped forward, putting his entire arm into the plane of energy. Then he took one more step, putting his body through the wall of energy. With that, he'd disappeared.

As soon as Richard was gone, Morgan powered down the machine. She was happy that the portal had appeared to work, but she dreaded what was to happen next. She hoped that Richard could confront Ben in such a way that no one was harmed.

Ben took off the helmet, his head drenched in sweat. He was exhausted from the entire session. Chris joined Morgan to ensure that Ben was okay.

"That was pretty intense Ben," Chris said.

"Glad I could impress you for once," Ben said with a smile. "But I think Richard did most of the work."

Morgan handed Ben a bottle of water. Ben drank from it while wandering over to rest in a nearby chair.

Rachel was still standing in the same spot behind everyone, struggling to take it all in.

Finally, Rachel yelled. "That was amazing!"

Everyone chuckled in agreement.

"So where is he now?" Chris asked Ben and Morgan.

"Hopefully," Ben said. "Inside our lab, helping Chris and stopping their Ben."

Morgan's anxiety continued to fester. She couldn't keep her mind off of wanting to know what was going on with her husband and son. She knew that Ben wouldn't or shouldn't be ready to use the viewing chamber again for a while. Yet, she needed his help in pinpointing their lab's location and she was hoping that he'd be rested enough soon.

"When you're ready," Morgan said. "I want to find out if Richard made it."

Ben looked up at her. He knew Morgan well enough to understand Morgan at a basic level. So far as he guessed, she was likely near-frantic about protecting her husband and son.

"Give me a few minutes," he said. "And I'll be ready again."

Day 5 {5:00pm}

☺ ↔ ☻

The real Chris couldn't help but notice that Ben hadn't said much throughout the entire afternoon.

"You've been awfully quiet," Chris observed, still not aware that the Bens had switched realities.

Not surprisingly, the statement made Ben paranoid. He wondered if Chris suspected something, but then decided that he was perhaps simply not playing correctly to the part.

"I was just concentrating," Ben said. "You know, we wouldn't want anything to happen to you when we test the machine."

"Don't worry," Chris chuckled and said. "I'll plan on double-checking everything."

Ben nodded and said back. "I'm glad that you're here."

In his rush to flee to the other world, Ben knew that he'd had virtually no time to study the other Ben's behavior. He knew little about how the other Ben normally behaved, yet it had been clear that the other Ben was happy-go-lucky in nature. Ben knew that he could try his best to imitate such a demeanor, but he'd soon be found out due to one misstep or another. He was thankful that the ruse wouldn't need to last much longer with Chris.

After the repairs had been completed and Chris had checked everything over with Ben, the machine was finally ready for another test. Ben picked up the repaired control helmet and plugged it into the machine. He offered it to Chris.

"Ready to go?" Ben asked.

Chris admitted. "I'm a little nervous testing it right away like this."

"It'll be fine," Ben said. "We need to get you going, right?"

Chris paused for a moment and said. "You can run it alone?"

Previously, the other Morgan had been necessary for Ben to operate the machine. If anything, Ben had been a bit rusty. Chris gave Ben a curious look, but let it go.

Chris had hoped for an opportunity to say goodbye to Morgan, but they'd already lost enough time that it didn't make sense to wait for the sake of pleasantries. Chris knew that she'd understand and, so far as he still knew, time remained of the essence if he hoped to save Richard.

Chris put on the helmet and got into position near the viewing chamber. Ben started warming up the machine at a lower power level.

Morgan walked into the lab and was surprised to see the machine already running.

"Ben," Morgan said over the hum of the machine. "What's going on?"

Ben was startled that Morgan had arrived at the lab. He'd expected that she would have slept longer. Unfortunately for Ben, her presence for what would follow was both unfortunate and complicating.

Day 5 {5:30pm}

♣

The other Ben soon felt rested enough to attempt using the real world's viewing chamber again. Morgan took her place behind the control panel and started up the machine. Ben put the control helmet on and worked through the different levels of energy that initially bombarded him. Eventually, the viewing chamber showed the lab.

On the screen, they could see both the real Chris and the real Ben preparing to run their machine. The other Morgan had yet to enter the room and, even more importantly, Richard was nowhere to be found.

"Where's Richard?" Morgan yelled over to Ben.

"I don't see him," Ben confirmed. "He might not have landed where we'd hoped."

Morgan fought the urge to panic. She knew that that might be reassuringly true, but it also served to raise many more questions.

An idea quickly popped into the other Ben's head. If he tried to reverse his consciousness again, he wondered if he couldn't catch the real Ben off guard. At the very least, perhaps he'd warn Chris.

"I want to try the switch again!" Ben yelled.

Morgan wasn't sure what he had in mind, but if he felt up to it, she supported him.

"Okay!" Morgan yelled in reply. "I'm turning it up."

Morgan changed the machine's power output to the appropriate level. After a few seconds, Ben felt the increased energy hit him hard. He had braced for it better this time though and navigated through its waves without much issue.

Ben concentrated, trying hard to trigger the switch. He fought harder this time, thinking that he was close to realizing the switch, but ultimately it didn't work. Ben had to back off when the strain became too much.

Morgan realized that Ben had been pushed to his limit and powered down the machine.

"It didn't work" Ben said exhaustedly as he took off the helmet. "But let's hope that it still helped."

Day 5 {5:30pm}

☺ ↔ ☻

With the other Morgan looking on, the real Ben and real Chris were ready to begin their test. As Ben started the machine's power-up sequence, the other Ben's actions - taking place simultaneously in the real world - caused him to fall to the ground.

"Get out of my head!" Ben screamed.

That exclamation from Ben allowed Chris to put everything together. It finally became clear to him that the Ben now with him was not his new friend.

Chris tore off the control helmet, knowing that he didn't want to be standing with it strapped to his head while Ben was at the control panel.

Morgan noticed a change in Chris's demeanor right away.

"What's wrong?" she asked.

Chris looked right at Ben.

"You're him, aren't you?" he questioned.

"What are you talking about?" Ben said with a nervous chuckle.

"You weren't going to send me home," Chris said. "Were you?"

"What's wrong Chris?" Morgan repeated. She looked confused at Ben and added. "What does he mean Ben?"

"I don't know honey," Ben said. "He must be losing touch with reality. I just hope that a side effect of the machine isn't mental instability."

Morgan went over to Chris to calm him.

"Everything is going to be okay Chris," Morgan said. "Just take it easy."

Chris ignored Morgan's attempts at comfort and kept his attention focused squarely on Ben.

"How were you planning on getting away with this?" Chris wondered.

Ben said nothing. He knew that he needed to diffuse the situation, before Morgan began doubting him.

Chris continued. "What happened? I thought that you were going to kill my Dad. Did you chicken out and come here thinking that it would be easier to get rid of me?"

Ben's face turned red with anger. Chris knew that he had him, but Morgan wasn't yet convinced.

"Stop it," Morgan said, "Both of you, you're scaring me."

"It's okay," Ben said to Morgan. "He's just having an episode."

Chris was upset with himself for not noticing it all sooner.

"You blacked out when the switch happened," Chris said. "Didn't you?"

Morgan spoke calmly to Chris, hoping that she could diffuse their confrontation. She wasn't yet sure why he was suddenly acting so abrasive toward Ben.

"Put down the helmet Chris," Morgan said. "Let's talk about this."

Chris kept the helmet in hand while walking over to the control panel. He also kept eye contact with Ben.

"Is that why you didn't want to go to the doctor on the way over?" Chris said, motioning to Morgan. "Or were you just in a hurry to get rid of me and figured she'd never know?"

Morgan turned her attention back to Ben. She was angry and he knew he'd have to explain his actions.

"Is that true Ben?" Morgan asked.

Ben decided not to try to cover up the truth.

"Yes," he admitted. "But I did it for Chris. I'm fine, really. I knew that we were behind and needed to get caught up."

While Ben was distracted by the conversation, he stepped away from the control panel. The machine had continued to run at its warm-up power level throughout the conversation. Chris took the distraction's opportunity to reach over and subtly turn up the power levels on the machine.

Chris had a feeling that Ben might try something, so he went on the offensive. He unplugged the open end of the power cable from the helmet. Morgan was the first to notice that the cable had sparks flying out of it.

"Chris," Morgan said. "What are you doing?"

Chris ignored the question and motioned the cable at Ben.

"Get away from her," Chris said.

Ben stayed calm and replied. "Now Chris, don't be doing anything that you might regret. You could hurt someone."

Chris remained locked on Ben, refusing to back down.

"How did you think you'd get away with this?" Chris asked. "I'm sure that the other Ben has already told my Dad what happened. They'll just switch you right back any minute."

Chris addressed Morgan. "I'm trying to make it so that he can't hurt anyone, don't you see? It's Ben from my world. He came here and now he wants to get rid of me."

"I have no idea what you're talking about," Ben said, continuing to lie. "I'm concerned that the process that got you here might have made you mentally unstable. If you'd wanted to see your father, I'm sure that we could pull him up on the viewing chamber. It seems unlikely that anything might have happened to him recently."

Ben hoped that the bluff might actually work, but Chris seemed unfazed. Just the same, Ben realized that he might be able to convince Morgan that Chris was insane. The realization gave Ben confidence that he would succeed after all.

Ben stepped closer to Morgan, pretending that he might somehow protect her from Chris. Chris responded by lurching at Ben with the sparking cable. The motion forced Ben to back up, stepping away from Morgan.

"Chris!" Morgan yelled. "Put that down now!"

Despite Morgan's protests, Chris kept after Ben. Ben continued to backpedal. Chris led him over near the viewing chamber.

The machine's power levels had just risen high enough that energy was surging inside it. Ben didn't notice though, since his back was facing the viewing chamber. It was the same gambit that had worked on Tyler.

"Even if you sent me home," Chris yelled. "We'd just come back and get you. We know what you wanted to do to my Dad, so you probably had the same thing in mind for me."

Chris almost had Ben trapped inside the viewing chamber. Ben took a few more backward steps toward the waiting energy field. Then he stopped short.

"What do you plan to do Chris?" Ben asked. "Kill me? Everyone knows that you're having a tough time right now. You'll either go to jail or to an asylum."

Chris looked down to see the sparking from the cable go dead. Ben smiled and looked over to Morgan at the control panel. She'd shut down the machine.

"Thanks honey," Ben said.

"Chris," Morgan said. "This is over."

Ben stepped close enough to Chris that he was able to grab Chris's arm.

"I'll take care of him," Ben said, turning back to the energy-filled viewing chamber. "You really thought that I was that stupid?"

Ben didn't realize that Chris had a stronger body in the other world. Chris easily shook Ben's hand away, surprising Ben. It didn't matter much though, as Chris's heart sank. His gambit had failed. He was stuck without any allies.

"Stop with the fighting Chris," Ben said. "Everything will be okay."

An aluminum bat made a quick 'thunk' when it came down like a club on top of Ben's head. Ben's body dropped to the floor and, as he was sinking, Richard was revealed standing behind him. Richard held Tyler's baseball bat in hand.

Chris was overjoyed to see Richard.

Chris hugged Richard and asked, sarcastically. "What took you so long?"

"I got dropped across town," Richard said. "Another bug to work out."

"Richard!" Morgan yelled. "Is that really you?"

Richard smiled, but hesitated when remembering that the other Richard had been dead in this reality for a number of years. Before Richard could answer, Morgan passed out from the shock of seeing him.

"Oh no," Richard said.

Richard rushed over to the floor next to Morgan and quickly had her in his arms. Chris followed close behind him.

"Is she okay?" Chris asked Richard, who was checking Morgan's pulse.

"She's breathing normally," Richard said. "Her heart's pumping."

"This kind of thing has been happening a lot lately," Chris said.

"Seeing dead people?" Richard asked, still holding Morgan's head.

"No, people passing out."

"Yeah," Richard said, thinking back to the first time that he'd met the other Chris. "Seems to be common for us too."

Morgan regained consciousness a moment later. She was still groggy, so Richard thought it best not to shock her again.

"Can you take over here?" Richard said to Chris. "I'll get Ben restrained."

"Ok," Chris replied, taking Richard's place at Morgan's side.

Richard went back over to where Ben was still unconscious. He rummaged around for wires until he found several long enough to tie Ben up.

"How'd you get here?" Chris asked Richard, suddenly realizing how odd it was that his father was somehow in the other world. After all, he knew that the other Richard was supposed to be dead in the other world.

Richard replied while still securing Ben. "I worked with their Ben to open up a portal."

"A what?" Chris said, sounding as if it were the first he'd heard of such a thing.

"A portal," Richard said. "Something extra that Ben and I had been working on. It hadn't been thoroughly tested yet."

"Wow," Chris said. "Wasn't that dangerous?"

Richard looked long at Chris before answering. "Yeah, it was. But I needed to make sure that you were safe."

Richard's words struck deep inside Chris. Doubts that Chris had had about his father were washed away by the selfless courage that Richard had displayed for him.

"Thanks," Chris said, struggling to hold back his emotions. "You'll have to tell me how that works when we get back."

Richard smiled. "Sure thing. I just hope that they can get the portal reopened so that we can go back home."

"How do they know when to open it?"

"Hopefully," Richard said. "They're monitoring what's happening here right now."

Chris looked concerned and asked. "Shouldn't they have opened it by now?"

By this time, Ben had regained consciousness and realized that he was captured and bound.

"They're probably dead," Ben said.

"What?" Richard asked, reflexively.

Richard looked down at Ben and anger filled his eyes.

"They're probably dead," Ben repeated, quietly. "And Jai's people have the machine now. I'm sorry Richard, I truly am."

Richard looked as though he was about to shake Ben violently.

"What did you do Ben?" he asked.

"It's not what I did," Ben said. "I fear it's what Jai might do."

Richard thought back to Jai's presence a few days before and sighed.

Ben continued. "I thought I'd destroyed the machine and nothing would happen. I got in too deep Richard."

Richard shook with anger as he said. "You betrayed us."

Chris had never seen his father so upset before.

"That's why I came here," Ben admitted. "They wanted to hurt you and I couldn't let them. It seemed so much better here. And if I left, it fixed everyone else's problems."

"No Ben," Richard said. "It solved your problems, at least for a little while. In the end, it made all of your problems that much worse."

Ben looked stunned and repentant, but Richard was not sympathetic.

Richard yelled over to Chris. "Did he hurt you?"

"No," Chris said. "But he tried."

"I'm sorry Richard," Ben repeated.

Chris yelled at Ben. "You tried to kill me!"

Ben perhaps believed it when he said. "I wasn't going to kill you."

"Why Ben?" Richard asked. "What did I ever do to you to deserve this?"

"I wanted to be the one who people admired," Ben said. "I was going to sell out the project to Jai, but then I needed a way out after things got too complicated with his people. I just wanted a way out of it all."

"You could have said something to me," Richard offered. "It never should have come to this Ben. We can't make this all go away now."

Ben was speechless. He knew that he was in trouble, so he felt like an even bigger failure than ever before.

"There has to be a way back, right?" Ben quietly offered. "There's time."

Chris suggested. "Maybe something went wrong and they're having a problem."

Richard had worried that Chris might be right. He'd known that, in leaving to save Chris, he'd have to trust in the reliability of the machine. Even with Morgan around to assist, he knew that it would be difficult for Ben if something went wrong.

Chris looked hard at the alternate reality's machine.

He said to Richard. "What about this machine?"

Richard finally started to think again.

"Does their machine work?" Richard asked.

"Yeah," Chris replied, looking at Ben. "That's how we learned what he was up to. That you were in trouble."

Chris picked up the helmet and plugged the cable back into it.

"It doesn't have the portal circuits."

"No," Richard confirmed. "But at least we could get a look at what's happening at home."

By this point, Morgan had sat up, away from Chris.

"Richard?" she asked, still groggy. "Am I dreaming?"

Day 5 {6:00pm}

♣

The other Chris and Rachel had been sitting together, watching as Morgan and the other Ben decided what to do next. Given all of the activity of the past hours, they hadn't spoken a great deal since their conversation the night before.

"Did you know anything about this?" Chris asked Rachel. "All these experiments and other dimensions and stuff?"

"This is sort of over my head," Rachel admitted. "If I weren't worried that Chris and his Dad might die, I'd probably think that it was pretty cool."

"How does no one know about this kind of stuff going on?"

"I knew that Richard and Morgan were involved in some crazy projects and Chris talked about his Dad working on this viewing chamber thing. I'm not sure that they quite knew what they had on their hands though."

"My parents were working on something similar. That's how my Dad died. Their stuff never ended up working, so I figured it was just some crackpot idea that ended up getting my Dad killed. I couldn't take it all that seriously, you know?"

Rachel nodded.

"I understand," she said. "I didn't realize that it had gotten to be anything like this. I just thought it was sort of creepy anyway."

Chris seemed satisfied with her answer.

"Okay," Chris said. "Are we in trouble then? I mean, is the government going to arrest us or lock us up somewhere so that we don't tell everyone about this?"

"No," Rachel said. "They'll probably just wipe out our memories."

Chris got wide-eyed in response.

"Are you serious?"

"No," Rachel said. "You're a lot more gullible than Chris is."

Chris was half-annoyed. It hardly seemed to be a time for joking around.

"Uh-huh," Chris said, changing the subject. "So are we dating here or something? I mean, you and Chris are always hanging out, right?"

Rachel thought about the question

"Yeah," Rachel lied. "Of course we're dating. I thought you knew that."

"I figured that something must be going on if you're always with Chris. You seem like a nice girl, don't get me wrong."

"What's that supposed to mean?" Rachel shot at Chris.

Rachel had the realization that this was the first opportunity of her life to understand Chris. Sure, he wasn't actually Chris, but she would take what she could get. Luckily for her, the other Chris wasn't the type of person to hold back.

"You're Rachel from next door," Chris said. "It'd just be weird if we were dating."

"Why?"

"Where I'm from, you're great. We had a lot of fun growing up together, but you just weren't right for me. After I started playing ball, you sort of got jealous and stopped talking to me."

"So I wasn't enough fun for you, was that it?"

"No, no. We never dated or anything. I never thought about you that way."

"Did you ever really give me a chance?"

Chris thought hard about the question.

"Maybe not," he admitted. "I wasn't thinking about girls back when we were friends. And when I started to, you weren't around. I guess I got distracted by other girls, like Jessica. They just stood out."

"Great," Rachel said, thinking how she couldn't ever seem to step out of Jessica's long shadow. "It sounds like your life is perfect then. A big star with the dream girl."

Chris smiled for the first time in many hours.

"It's okay," he said. "I sort of lost myself in all that stuff, you know? After my Dad died."

"I'm sure that Jessica had no problem finding you. She tends to do that with the cool guys."

"Do you know her?"

"I don't need to, I know the type."

"She's cool, but she's always trying to get me to study and think about the future and stuff."

"Ah," Rachel sneered. "Sounds like a doomed high school romance."

Chris's face crinkled at Rachel.

"That's not very funny," he said.

"I'm sorry," Rachel said. "It's just that I know what kind of girl she is, that's all. If you're into that, fine. But I'd respect you more if you weren't."

"She's a smart girl, studying all the time. If anything, she's got things a lot more figured out than me. I probably wouldn't be able to play ball if she didn't make me study for tests or get papers done."

This answer seemed to surprise Rachel.

"I thought that you didn't have to worry about that sort of thing?" she asked.

"Oh," Chris scoffed. "Maybe not from Coach Barns, but some of the other teachers seem to have it out for me. It balances out."

"So she makes sure you're all taken care of, is that it?"

"Sometimes," Chris said. "I just feel like when she gets the chance, she'll leave me behind, you know? She'll move on to bigger and better things that are more appealing to her."

Rachel had no idea what Chris was talking about. This was not at all the Jessica whom she had in mind.

"Oh," Rachel said. "I doubt that. She wants to be the trophy wife to someone famous."

Chris dismissed what she was suggesting. "Hey, I'm a good ballplayer, but I doubt I'm going to be some rich or famous guy. She knows that."

Rachel looked at Chris like he'd suddenly turned on a light switch in her mind. He could have been speaking for her and all of the fears she'd had over the years in wanting Chris to notice her affections.

Deep down, Rachel always knew that, if they were dating for a while, he might just get bored and move on. Chris's behavior seemed to confirm that fear. Yet, she couldn't help but feel as though he was facing the same concerns in his own life.

    While Rachel and Chris continued to talk, Morgan approached the still-resting Ben.

    "You okay to go again?" Morgan asked Ben.

    Ben looked exhausted, but he wanted to keep working. He'd been resting in anticipation of another check on Chris.

    "I can," Ben said.

    "We'll look in on Chris and see if we can find Richard." Morgan continued. "Did you want to check the house this time? Maybe Richard turned up there?"

    "We can, but I'm not sure why he would have gone there."

    Morgan felt defeated. She was ready to try anything at this point. After a few minutes, Morgan had the machine humming at the correct power level. Ben struggled to stabilize an image of the other dimension's lab. The image that eventually appeared in the viewing chamber happened to show the climactic standoff between Chris and Ben. Morgan looked horrified for Chris.

    "He's going to hurt him!" Morgan yelled out.

    A moment later, Richard appeared to knock out Ben.

    Morgan was overjoyed. "It's Richard!"

    A few moments later, they heard Richard talking to Chris about how Ben and Morgan would be monitoring them. When Richard spoke about the portal needing to reappear, Morgan got ready to open the portal again.

    "I'm initiating the portal!" She yelled to Ben.

    "Go for it!" Ben yelled back.

    After Morgan had entered a series of commands, the portal opened. Through the viewing chamber, a reduced image of Chris and Richard showed them still talking about their worries that the portal hadn't appeared.

    "They don't see it!" Morgan yelled.

    Ben was straining under the helmet, but still tried to understand what might be the problem.

    Ben yelled back to Morgan. "It must be opening the portal somewhere else!"

    Chris had been standing with Rachel directly behind Morgan and got an idea of his own in his head.

"I'll go through!" Chris yelled. "Ben, I'll bring them back!"

Morgan thought about his offer for an instant. While part of her thought that any help would be worthwhile, the risks of sending people back and forth through the portal weighed on her.

Ben didn't get a chance to respond before the lab's power turned off. In the blink of an eye, they were all standing in the dark. A moment later, emergency lighting came on.

"What's happening?" Ben yelled over to Morgan.

"We lost main power," Morgan said. "The machine cut over to the backup batteries, but they're only designed to power it down."

"Do you think the portal caused another blackout?" Rachel asked Morgan.

That question was the first thing that had come to Morgan's mind. She knew that they'd optimized the machine, so that it shouldn't have caused any future problems. If it did cause a blackout thought, the group would have a difficult time reopening the portal. At the very least, it could be hours before power was restored or until one of their government liaisons made a visit.

"I hope not," Morgan responded. "But we have to check."

Morgan turned to the other Chris and continued. "Chris, I want you to run outside and see if power is off in the neighborhood."

"Got it," Chris said.

Outside the lab, it was dusk. The neighborhood still had power and streetlights reflected off of Jai's sedan as he drove into the lab parking lot. He was trailed by several black cargo-sized trucks. After he and the trucks had parked, the rear door of one truck opened to reveal two dozen men wearing functional black outfits. The men waited for their signal to move out.

Jai examined the lab building from inside his car. A grumpy, overweight man sat next to him. His name was Mr. Chu. So far as the particulars of their relationship, he was Jai's employer and he was also an extraordinarily impatient man.

"They're all here then?" Mr. Chu asked.

Jai had noticed Richard's vehicle in the lot parked near Ben's car.

"That's how you wanted it," Jai replied. "Right?"

Chu noticed Chris up ahead, peeking out through the glass of the lab's main entrance. Chris looked confused by the additional vehicles in the parking lot.

"Who's that kid?" Chu questioned Jai. "We have to deal with some kid too? How are we going to make this look like an accident now?"

"He won't be a problem. He pokes around here enough that if something happens to him too, it won't be much of a surprise to anyone."

Chu held a radio up to his mouth and asked. "Power's cut?"

A voice on the radio hissed back, "Nothing going into the building."

Chu motioned to the lights in the hallway where Chris was standing and said. "What's still on?"

"Must be a generator." Jai replied. "That won't last long."

Chu again spoke into his radio. "Have you jammed the communications yet?"

"No," the voice in the radio said. "They have some form of encryption. We're having a hard time with it."

"Call me when you've cracked it," Chu said before he signed off.

Inside the building, the other Chris had made his way back down the hallway, returning to the lab itself. He wasn't sure why the parking lot had looked so crowded, but he could swear that he'd seen someone moving around in a sedan.

"The power's still on in the area," Chris said.

Morgan took his words as the first positive news that she'd heard in a while.

"That's a relief," she said.

"Hey," Chris added. "Do you know why there are some large trucks in the parking lot?

"No," Morgan said as she pulled up a security camera's video on one of the control panel's screens.

At first, they only saw the video of the trucks themselves, but Morgan switched cameras until she found a better view. They soon noticed the men waiting near one of the trucks.

Morgan immediately turned to the hallway door, expecting to see some of the men already entering the building, but none of them had tried to enter yet. Chris was still standing near the lab's inner door.

Morgan shouted to Chris. "Shut the door!"

Chris punched buttons on the door's control panel, trying to close it, but nothing happened.

"It won't shut!" Chris yelled back at Morgan.

Morgan typed a series of commands into the control panel, routing emergency power to the door.

"Try it now!" Morgan said. "I opened a new power channel to it."

On the security view screen, Morgan observed the men converging toward the building. Then the screen blinked out.

Morgan knew that it meant trouble and immediately called for outside help. She thought of one of the military contacts who Richard had on file and dialed their office number.

"How can I help you?" a young, junior staffer answered her call.

"Is McPherson in?"

"No ma'am," the junior staffer said. "Everyone is home for the day, but I can take a message.

"Listen," Morgan said, while she tried to remain calm. "We have foreign agents invading our lab."

"Hang on miss," the junior staffer said, sounding as though he was shuffling papers in order to start taking notes. "How do you know that?"

"I need you to listen carefully," Morgan said. "This is Richard Jennings's lab and we're under attack by someone. I don't know who, but we need help now."

The junior staffer's tone shifted to sounding as though he was only half-paying attention. It was likely that he thought that the call might be a prank.

"Can you wait on hold for a moment miss?" he asked.

Before Morgan could respond, the sound from the other end of the line switched to hold music.

Glancing down at the control panel, Morgan could see that the remaining power levels were about to be diminished. She looked around for the other Ben.

"Ben!" she yelled. "Go get some supplies out of the cabinet!"

Morgan pointed to a small supply closet across the room. Ben could tell from her voice that it was urgent, so he acted fast.

Across the room, Chris had tried the door controls again, but the door still didn't budge.

"It's jammed!" Chris said.

Chris had no idea what to do, but then he remembered the succession of screens on the door's access panel. Richard had gone through the screen earlier in order to enter an administrative password. Chris tried to remember what he'd seen entered. He navigated through the screens until he reached the point where he inputted Richard's administrator password. It worked and the door slid shut.

Once the security door had shut, things were quiet for a moment. Rachel looked on, amazed at Chris.

"When did you learn how to do that?" she asked.

Chris seemed impressed with himself and said. "I memorized my Dad's keystrokes earlier."

"Oh," Rachel seemed surprised. "So you're not a total idiot?"

Back at the control panel, Morgan heard the junior staffer come back on the line.

"Miss," he said. "How do you spell that name? Jennings, is that with a 'G' or a 'J?'"

Before Morgan could reply, the communications line died. A moment later, the power blinked out and the room was pitch black. Ben clicked on a flashlight and then tossed several other spare flashlights to others around the room.

"I take it," Ben said. "That was the last of the reserve power?"

8:
The Fix

Day 5 {5:45pm}

☺ ↔ ☻

After school ended in the other world, Jessica headed straight for the other world's lab. She hadn't been able to concentrate all day long. Most of her classmates were busy gossiping about Tyler's arrest and Chris's recent absences. Of course, Jessica had been advised by the police not to say anything at school.

Most concerning to Jessica was that Chris wasn't acting at all like the Chris whom she knew. She'd spent much of high school wishing that her life could be different and exciting, but this wasn't what she'd expected. One way or another, she'd made up her mind that things needed to get back to normal. Little did she realize that they were about to get much more complicated.

When Jessica walked into the lab, her jaw dropped at the scene. Everyone turned to see her bemused expression.

Automatically, Jessica asked Chris. "What's going on?"

"Hey," Chris said, smiling awkwardly. "Quite a bit, actually."

Richard stood nearby with Morgan. Chris wasn't sure what to say to Jessica about him.

Richard leaned over to Chris and whispered. "Jessica? You got her involved here too?"

"Too?" Chris asked Richard.

"The other Chris was busy chasing after her."

Chris groaned, knowing how that would be another problem to deal with. At least, if he ever got home.

"I'll talk to her," Chris said.

As Chris walked over to Jessica, he worried that he would be screwing something up by saying what he was about to tell her.

"My Mom was just having some people over to help out on some things," Chris said to Jessica.

Jessica examined Richard.

"That guy looks like your Dad," she said. "He's really alive?"

"You can keep a secret," Chris said to Jessica, still trying to come up with an alibi. "Right?"

Jessica gave Chris a quizzical look. She couldn't understand why he was so evasive lately.

Chris started to explain. "There are some things that I' haven't been completely honest about."

Jessica's heart sank. This was the rejection that she'd feared. She'd hoped that Chris's strange behavior had all just been in her head.

Chris continued. "I'm not the Chris who you know."

"You haven't been him lately," Jessica said. "That's for sure."

Jessica kept looking around the lab and finally noticed Ben tied up.

"Hey," she said. "What're you doing to your step-dad?"

Chris realized that he didn't have much of a choice. Things were already too complicated and the time was too short to keep lying to Jessica.

"Oh," Chris said. "He's not my stepdad."

Jessica grew scared. She worried that Chris and his mother had gone crazy and that she'd stumbled into the middle of something bad.

Chris felt her tension and tried to reassure her. "You know how my family builds things?"

Jessica nodded nervously.

"Well," Chris continued. "They built a machine that can somehow send people to a parallel universe."

Jessica quietly asked. "A what?"

"You know. Another world where everything is sort of the same, only it isn't?"

"Okay," Jessica said, clearly not understanding.

"I accidently came from my universe to this one and the Chris who you know is stuck back where I'm from."

Chris pointed at Ben.

"He's not a nice guy back home and he came here to escape from some bad things that he was involved in back there," he said, adding with a motion to Richard. "And that's my Dad. He's here too."

"Your Dad is dead Chris."

"Not where I'm from."

Richard waved at Jessica and then resumed working at the control panel.

"You expect me to believe all this?" Jessica said, wanting desperately to run away.

"I'm sorry," Chris said. "I know that you don't believe me, but after you see the machine in action, maybe you'll change your mind."

"I'm ready Chris," Richard called over.

Day 5 {6:15pm}

♣

Jai was still in his sedan outside the real lab, fully expectant that their raid on the lab had been a success. He was less than pleased when the team inside radioed Mr. Chu.

"We're in the hallway, but they've locked the doorway."

Chu grew angry and turned to Jai.

"You said that this would be a simple operation," he barked. "That your man would let us in without hesitation."

"He's likely not the problem. If Richard is in there, he might have suspected something."

"If we knew that this would turn into a siege, we'd have brought more men and equipment."

"We'll be fine."

Jai thought through the situation before saying more. Chu was someone whose influence, rightfully, frightened Jai. Chu had supported Jai in the operation, despite the protests of his peers. The payoff, if the project were for real, was too incalculably high to ignore

"We've jammed their communications, so they have no choice but to deal with us."

Chu objected. "We don't know their capabilities. Waiting them out may not be a swift process. And it could prove a disaster now that we no longer have the element of surprise."

"We still have a chance," Jai insisted.

"What do you propose?" Chu asked.

"I want to speak with them."

Jai knew that Chu's impatience had led to what had thus far been a foolhardy plan. Jai had been concerned about drawing attention too quickly, so the lack of discretion by Chu's men had only justified his worries.

Jai went into the building, deciding to call the shots himself. Chu's men were waiting for him next to the sealed lab door.

"You've restored power to the intercom?" Jai questioned one of the men.

"Yes," the man said. "It was on its own circuit."

The communications panel glowed with power.

Inside the lab, Morgan, the other Ben, the other Chris, and Rachel all sat in virtual darkness. Only Ben used his flashlight, the other's conserving their only sources of light.

"Who were they?" Chris asked. "The government?"

"They must be the men who Chris and I saw Jai talking about" Ben said, referring to his own portal test with Chris.

"Power and communications are both down," Morgan confirmed. "They wanted us sealed off."

"So they're going to kill us," Rachel said, panic rising in her voice.

"I think that we know what they want," Morgan said, indicating the machine. "We're just in their way."

Chris was frustrated.

"What're we supposed to do then?" he asked. "Wait in here until they leave?"

Morgan tried to calm everyone down.

"We have enough food and water around here to last a few days," she said.

Rachel's mind raced through their options.

"You called for help though," Rachel said. "What about help from outside?"

"Yes," Ben said. "You were calling someone in the military, right?"

"They didn't sound very convinced," Morgan admitted. "And then I got cut off."

Jai's voice came into the room through the intercom.

"Ben?" Jai asked.

Everyone looked at Ben, but he hesitated to reply.

"Pretend you're him," Morgan suggested.

Ben went over to the intercom. Before he could respond, Jai's voice again boomed into the room.

"I thought that we had an agreement?" he continued.

Ben only knew what he'd seen referenced earlier in his machine's old viewing chamber. It wasn't much to go on, but he at least understood Jai's willingness to sell the machine and the request to betray Richard.

Ben said. "The deal's off."

"And why," Jai said, clearly angry. "Is that?"

"I know that it would be a really bad decision," Ben said. "So just leave us alone."

"We can't really do that anymore Ben."

"Why not?" Ben pressed. "We don't want trouble any more than you do. Just leave and we can all forget this ever happened."

During a pause in the exchange, Chris said. "Really give it some punch Ben."

Jai responded. "Ben, we're just going to wait out here until you change your mind."

Ben said, forcefully. "We've informed the military! They're on their way! If you don't leave now, you won't have a chance to forget that this ever happened."

A longer pause ensued.

"Maybe they got scared and left," Rachel said.

Jai finally again spoke into the intercom.

"We were monitoring your communications before we jammed them," he said. "Based on your conversation, you can't expect us to take that threat seriously, can you?"

Ben looked at Morgan and could tell that she knew that Jai was probably right.

"Last chance Ben," Jai said, his voice echoing.

Ben let the words hang in the air without any reply. Jai didn't wait long before retracting his offer.

"Fine," he said. "Have it your way."

Before the intercom cut off, they could hear a loud whine. Chris said. "Did anyone hear something?"

"Yeah," Ben replied. "It's sounded like a high-powered cutting laser. How secure is that door?"

Morgan said. "It's like a bunker in here. We modified the lab so that, just in case any accidents happened, it would contain the explosion."

"Okay," Ben said. "We might have a little time then, but not long."

Rachel looked at Chris and grabbed him. She planted a long, hard kiss on his lips. Chris pulled back from her, shocked.

"What was that for?" Chris asked.

"I'm not going to die without that," Rachel said. "And if we do manage to get out of this, just remember me when you get back home? I'm sure I like you there too."

Day 5 {6:00pm}

☺ ↔ ☻

The other Morgan remained in shock while witnessing Richard appear in the flesh again in the other world, still unsure exactly what to believe. Even though Richard had explained what had just happened, it continued to all be surreal to her.

While Richard and Chris prepared to start up the machine again, Morgan noticed that the other Jessica had a similarly uncertain and confused look on her face. Morgan walked over to Jessica and was warmer to her, seemingly for the first time.

"It's a lot to take in," Morgan said. "Isn't it?"

"I just keep thinking that any moment I am going to wake up from this crazy dream," Jessica said.

Jessica looked at Morgan and said. "You don't think Chris is crazy?"

"No," Morgan said. "There was more going on than we realized. I don't know if I have it all straight yet, but they're not crazy."

"Is that Mr. Jennings?" Jessica asked. "I mean, Chris's Dad?"

"Yes."

"But I thought that..." Jessica's said, her voice trailing off.

"He did," Morgan said.

"I'm sorry."

Morgan tried to be strong and replied. "Don't be."

"It's true though," Jessica said. "About their being from some other dimension or wherever?"

"I think so," Morgan confirmed.

"Where are our Ben and Chris then?"

"Somewhere else," Morgan said. "They're going to try to get them back."

The pair continued to watch as Richard and Chris busily prepped the other dimension's machine. Given the work that Chris and Ben had already performed on it, they didn't have much further to go.

"I think it's mostly ready Dad," Chris said.

Richard looked longingly at the old machine. Working on it gave him a sense of déjà-vu.

"This old machine," Richard said. "I feel like I've been working on my first car."

"We got it working earlier," Chris said. "But it wasn't holding together."

"Their Ben said that you were instrumental in getting the machine going," Richard said, proudly. "They hadn't been able to get it going without you here."

"Well," Chris said. "They didn't have very far to go."

Richard knew that Chris was being modest.

"Just the same," Richard said. "After we get all of this sorted out, maybe you'll help me out a bit more?"

Chris was overjoyed at the offer, but part of him still hesitated.

"What about Mom?" he said. "She's going to kill me when we get home."

Richard winked at Chris and said. "We'll figure something out."

As work to ready the machine wrapped up an hour later, Morgan went over to help Richard. Chris noticed that Jessica was left alone.

Part of him couldn't help but wish that events had turned out differently. He wanted more time to spend with her, but he knew that it wouldn't be possible.

Chris had not initially realized how different of a person Jessica would turn out to be after actually getting to know her. He knew that she wasn't the same person at home, not after having dated Tyler for years. Given that realization, a part of Chris regretted putting so much effort into longing for Jessica, at least his world's Jessica.

Chris walked over to Jessica and said. "I'm sorry that I wasn't honest with you.

Jessica gave Chris a half-smile.

"If you wanted to break up with me," she said. "You know there are a lot easier ways to do it, right?"

Chris didn't realize that she was being sarcastic.

"I wasn't trying to do that," he said.

"I know," Jessica said. "I was just kidding. I've never seen you look like this before."

"Well," Chris said. "You'd never met me before, right?"

"I guess not," Jessica admitted.

There was an awkward pause before Chris continued.

"You know," he said. "You're a lot different than I thought you'd be."

Jessica was surprised by the remark and asked. "Aren't we together where you're from?"

Chris thought about lying for a moment, but resisted the urge. He'd gotten to pretend that he was Jessica's boyfriend for a few days and maybe learned a few things in the process. But life was confusing enough already and he didn't need to complicate it even more.

"No," he admitted. "You've been dating Tyler for quite a while."

Jessica went wide-eyed at the remark, looking disgusted.

"No wonder you acted so uncomfortable around me," she said. "That's disgusting."

"That wasn't it," Chris said. "I was just nervous spending time with you for once. I guess I did wonder about her judgment a little. I don't have a girlfriend."

Jessica seemed surprised.

"I find it hard to believe that you don't have anyone interested in you," Jessica said. "You are smart and you're a nice guy."

"I'd like to think so," Chris said, without much shame. "But sometimes it seems like Rachel's the only one who gets me."

The earlier occasions when Chris had tried to talk to Rachel made more sense to Jessica.

"So you take her for granted?" Jessica more so stated, rather than asked.

Chris thought about her words for a moment before replying. He realized that he probably had taken Rachel for granted at times, at least her loyalty.

"No," he said. "Well, maybe."

"About the only person in my life supporting me is Chris," Jessica said. "He's a good guy. Maybe you might want to be a bit more interested in those supporting you, instead of wasting time on someone who is just concerned with themselves."

Chris gave Jessica a quizzical look. The brief conversation had gone in several odd directions. He had a lot to take in.

Richard called Chris over. "We're nearly ready."

"Let's talk more later," Chris said as he leaned in to give Jessica a hug. "Okay?"

Jessica smiled at Chris.

"Deal," she said. "But only if I can bring my Chris back."

Chris walked back to Richard, who had the helmet in hand.

"I'm still not comfortable with you doing this Chris," Richard said.

"I used this machine before," Chris said. "It was a little rough, but I figured it out. I need you running the controls. You know it better than me, especially since it seems touchier."

Richard suspected that something additional was on Chris's mind.

"You want to try to switch back," Richard suggested. "Don't you?"

"Maybe," Chris admitted.

"We're not going to push this old beater very hard," Richard said. "I just want to find out what's happening."

"Fine," Chris relented.

"We were pushing our own machine to make this happen," Richard said. "I don't know if it'll hold together long enough to get you home anyway. We can't risk an accident."

Chris put the helmet on and stepped into position. After a few minutes, the machine was warmed up and ready to go. Richard stood with Morgan at the control panel, both closely monitoring different readouts.

"You're ready?" Richard asked Chris.

"Yes!" Chris shouted, bracing himself. "Do it!"

Richard increased the power levels. The change caused Chris to jerk as he struggled to deal with the incoming energy waves. Chris was able to navigate the waves in his mind and, ultimately, found calm in the energy storm.

The machine's viewing chamber showed the real world's lab sitting in darkness. The image wasn't exceptionally clear, due to the lack of light.

Chris yelled to Richard. "Turn up the power!"

Richard hesitated at first, but then complied. The viewing chamber's image improved, but it still only showed the lab and its occupants sitting around the soft light from Ben's flashlight.

"What're they doing?" Morgan asked Richard.

Richard replied. "It looks like the power is out."

Chris continued to watch those in the lab on the screen but could only hear vague remarks between them regarding the machine. A distortion of Jai's voice could be heard in the background.

"You guys haven't upgraded the sound processor?" Richard asked Morgan.

"No," Morgan said, disappointed. "We never got that far."

Chris continued to be fixated on the scene back home. He knew that they were in trouble, but wasn't sure how to help them. The higher energy level was getting to him. He was desperate to make things right.

Soon, Chris felt the surge of the transfer trigger as he saw white flash in his eyes. His body fell limp. The image in the viewing chamber vanished.

Morgan and Richard began the power-down sequence on the machine and rushed over to see if he was okay. They could tell that he was regaining consciousness and assumed that the strain had gotten to him.

"Are you okay Chris?" Richard asked.

Chris mumbled something unintelligible as he came to. But it wasn't the real Chris though. Rather, the other Chris had switched back into his old body.

"Where am I now?" he asked.

"You're here in the lab Chris." Richard said.

Chris sat up and looked around.

"I'm home?" Chris asked.

Morgan looked into Chris's eyes and wondered if her Chris were now back where he belonged.

"Is that you?" She asked.

"Yeah Mom," Chris replied.

Morgan began to cry. She was overjoyed to have her son back again.

Chris was still confused and curious.

"Did you stop them somehow?"

"Stop who?"

"We were locked in the lab. Some guy named Jai had cut off the power and was trying to get inside. We were trying to open the portal for you, but we got cut off."

From the corner of the room, Ben's voice rang out. "I can help you Richard."

Richard was annoyed by the interruption.

"We don't need your kind of help Ben," Richard said. "We've already had plenty of it."

"Let me switch back too," Ben persisted. "I can handle them. I might be able to do something to save them."

Richard was tempted by his offer but said nothing. He turned to Morgan."

"We need to get the viewer going again."

"But even if we do, we can't help him."

"I know, but we can't just sit here waiting."

Day 5 {7:15pm}

♣

At that exact moment in the real world, the real Chris's consciousness arrived back in his real body, triggering the other Chris's consciousness to switch back to his 'normal' body. Rachel caught Chris's body as it fell limp. The other Ben rushed over and helped her lower Chris to the ground. After a few seconds, Chris opened his eyes and took in his surroundings.

"I'm home?" Chris asked.

"What?" Rachel questioned back.

"It's me!" Chris said, growing happier. "I'm back!"

Rachel was confused at first, but soon understood.

"How did you get back here loser?" she asked.

"Dad was with me," Chris said. "We knew that you were in trouble and I wanted to come back to help."

Ben grew excited.

""It worked then!" he said. "Our machine worked!"

"It did," Chris said. "But we have to get the portal going again to get Dad back home."

"That might be a problem," Rachel said.

"Jai's people cut off all power to the building," Morgan explained.

"Then we'll reroute the power and tap into an auxiliary line," Chris offered.

"No," Ben said. "They cut it all off."

"Where are they at now?" Chris asked.

As if on cue, the first stream of light from the laser cutter entered the lab. Jai's men had reached them and were about to succeed in cutting through the door's locks.

"That's not good," Chris deadpanned.

With the door's main lock cut, Jai's men pushed the heavy door open with ease and flooded into the lab. Chris's first instinct was to do something to stop them, but such thoughts seemed foolhardy to consider. Within seconds, the men had everyone inside at gunpoint.

Jai strode into the room and surveyed the situation. Through the light from various flashlights, Jai identified Chris, Ben, Morgan, and Rachel standing together near the machine's control panel. The gunmen kept the group together.

Using a communications device, Jai called out to Mr. Chu.

"We're inside and everything is secure," he said. "Restore the power."

After a few moments, power had returned to the building. The lights in the lab came back on.

With everyone in the room clearly visible, Jai walked over to Ben and said. "I fear our 'friendship' has come to an end."

Understandably, Jai had mistaken this Ben for the Ben he made a deal with. Ben said nothing to correct him, at first standing silent.

"So," Jai continued. "You decided to wait until now to break our agreement?"

Ben continued to remain silent for another moment, unsure how to reply.

"I changed my mind," Ben finally said. "I'd like to forget about all this."

Jai smiled. It wasn't actually a discussion anymore.

"If this were just between us Ben, I might have let it go," Jai said. "But, unfortunately, that decision isn't in my hands anymore."

Morgan spoke up, asking. "What're you going to do with us?"

"I am not sure," Jai said. "That is up to my employer. He may not be as lenient as I would be."

Chris noticed that Rachel looked terrified. She was fairly certain that they'd all be killed soon. Besides Ben, the rest of them offered little real value to Jai and his men.

Any such actions won a slight reprieve when Mr. Chu entered the lab. He didn't appear overly impressed.

"Is this your idea of a joke Jai?" Chu barked.

Jai was taken aback by the implication. The old man had long annoyed Jai and now he'd called his competence into question.

Of course, the lab did look as though it was in shambles. All of the recent activity had left such an appearance that no one would have believed that a cutting edge project existed there. At least not one that was still functional.

Mr. Chu looked at the machine's control panel and said. "Does this pile of rubble even work?"

Jai turned to Ben, looking a slight bit insecure.

"Surely it wouldn't be a problem to give us a demonstration?" he suggested.

Ben looked around at the men with weapons and realized that he had little choice but to comply.

"Yes," he said, unsure how successful using the machine in its current state might be.

A couple of the gunmen motioned their weapons towards the control panel. Ben did as he was asked.

"I need help running it," Ben said.

Jai considered the request, wondering if it weren't a trick. "Who?" he asked.

Ben pointed to Morgan and Chris. Chu nodded to allow it.

"Fine," Jai said.

The group was slow to get the machine re-started. There didn't seem to be much reason to rush.

Within minutes though, Chu grew impatient.

"There will be consequences the longer you delay," he warned.

Jai motioned one of the gunmen to Rachel and the man pulled Rachel close, pressing his gun into her side. Rachel tried not to hyperventilate. Chris looked on, worried about what might happen to her.

"Move faster." Jai said.

A few more minutes passed, with the group working harder to prepare the machine. Finally, Ben stepped into position and put on the control helmet. At the same time, Morgan and Chris started up the machine. It hummed to life as the demonstration began.

Day 5 {7:30pm}

☺ ↔ ●

While Richard and the other Morgan prepped the other world's machine for another run, the other Chris rested in a chair near the control console. Jessica came over to speak with him. She tried to help him get up, but he was still too weak to stand.

The couple's reunion had been awkward for more reasons than either cared to admit at the moment. Both knew that something had changed between them as a result of the many recent events. Unfortunately, it wasn't the most appropriate time to sort all of that out.

"Is everything okay in there?" Jessica asked as she pointed to Chris's head.

"I think so," Chris said.

There was a long pause, as both struggled with what to say next. Chris still cared a great deal for Jessica, but he'd gotten a new perspective on his potential future path while living Chris's life. He wasn't sure how that might affect their futures together. Jessica had a different perspective as well and a new-found appreciation for Chris. Life wasn't going to be the same, so they'd need to sort out what that meant.

Finally, both said at the same time. "We should probably talk about things."

Both seemed surprised at one another's remarks.

"You're in a lot of trouble with all this," Jessica said. "Aren't you?"

"I don't know," Chris said. "I'd like to think that it'll be a good thing. Probably a great thing. I just think that things might be different from now on, you know?"

Jessica sat wondering what he had meant.

"Do you want me to leave then?" Jessica asked, sounding disappointed.

"I'm not sure what's going to happen next," Chris said. "But I want you to be a part of it, okay?"

Jessica knew that neither of them had much of a notion as to what she might be agreeing to. Yet she couldn't help but feel a bit of excitement underneath her fear.

"Deal," she said.

Chris felt strong enough to stand and, once he did, Jessica hugged him.

Across the lab, Richard checked over the work that Morgan had performed while repairing the machine.

"Don't let my wife know how well you did this or she'll get jealous," he told her.

Morgan smiled and said. "I figured I'd be talented in any reality."

"Oh," Richard said with a chuckle. "You are. She's just, you know, different."

Richard picked up the control helmet and put it on.

"We're ready," he said. "Time to bring it up."

Morgan began the startup sequence at the control panel and the machine sprang to life. Richard felt the energy waves slowly roll into his mind and was surprised by how strong they were. He was impressed that Chris had been able to withstand the shock from the primitive machine.

Eventually, Richard was able to make the viewing chamber show an image of the real world's lab. The lab's power had clearly been restored, with lights and equipment turned back on. A dozen men dressed in black stood throughout the room.

"Who are they?" Morgan yelled.

Behind her, Ben spoke up. "They're Jai's men. They'll take the machine."

Everyone listened to the discussion taking place in the real world. Richard noticed the real Chris speaking softly to the real Morgan and zoomed in on the pair.

"I know that Dad will be waiting," Chris insisted. "We just need to get the portal open again."

The other Ben was nearby as Morgan asked him. "Just like before, right?"

Ben nodded and stepped over to examine the control helmet. Jai had been observing nearby and came over to speak with Ben.

"All they need is to be sure that it works and then this will all be over," Jai said. "Maybe we can still work out a deal Ben."

Ben played along, smiling, and then stepped over to rejoin Morgan at the control panel.

Still watching closely, Richard knew that the men weren't simply going to leave everyone alive once the demonstration was done. He fixated on Chris and Morgan for a split-second and then abruptly took off the control helmet. The viewing chamber's image blinked out.

"We don't have very long," Richard said.

Morgan wasn't immediately sure what Richard meant, but she still initiated the machine's power down sequence.

"They're going to open the portal," Richard continued. "Is there a car that we can use? We need to go to where the portal dropped me here."

"Of course," Morgan said

"I have my car," Jessica said, trying to help.

Morgan noticed that Richard had begun searching hurriedly around the lab.

"What are you looking for?" Morgan asked.

Richard paused to think through his plans.

"I'm going to need something that I can use to try to distract them," he said.

"I might have something that would work," Morgan said, reaching for the flasher device.

"What's that?" Richard asked. "A weapon?"

"It's something that Ben and I have been working on," Morgan said.

She motioned to the red button that sat atop the device.

"It overwhelms the visual senses and puts anyone looking at it into an immediate state of shock."

"Sounds perfect," Richard said, excitedly.

"Well," Morgan said. "The one thing is that you'll need everyone's attention, at least the attention of those you want knocked out."

"That shouldn't be a problem." Richard said.

"The other thing is that we haven't really tested it."

Richard was concerned and asked "What?"

"We tested it, just not very thoroughly. If you take it through the portal, who knows."

"I'll take my chances." Richard said, turning to the other Chris. "Can you give me a hand moving him?"

Richard motioned to the still-bound Ben.

"Sure thing," Chris said.

The drive in Jessica's car only lasted a couple of minutes. Richard led them to where the portal had dropped him into the other world. The location was a couple of miles away lab, in a residential neighborhood.

While they waited for the portal to be re-opened, Richard and the other Morgan stood outside the car on a sidewalk.

The other Chris and Jessica stayed next to the car, keeping their eyes on Ben.

Morgan knew that the portal might open up again at any moment. She felt sick at the thought of Richard leaving. She loved Ben, but it was confusing for her to suddenly have a man around who looked and acted like her late husband. Seeing Richard again, it was hard for her not to think about the many difficult decisions that she'd made since Richard's death.

"I never got to say goodbye to my Richard," Morgan said. "It feels like now I won't get to say good-bye all over again."

Richard could tell that Morgan was still feeling deep pain from the loss of her husband and worried that his presence would bring those feelings to the surface again. He chose his words to her carefully.

"I wish that I'd gotten to meet your Richard," Richard said. "But I think that I understand him well enough to say that he would have supported your decisions after his death."

Morgan got choked up. She knew what he was trying to do and she appreciated it.

"Thank you," she said. "Chris is a terrific kid. I can tell that he looks up to you. I'm glad that you've had all this success Richard, but don't forget about him."

Richard took the words to heart and hugged Morgan. He held her until he noticed the portal open up behind them on the sidewalk.

"Come on Ben," Richard said. "We're going home."

Chris helped roughly push Ben toward the portal opening. Ben didn't resist and walked through though it under his own power.

"I want to help Richard," Ben said while a step away from the portal. "This is all my fault and I want to make it right again."

"I have it under control Ben," Richard said, sadly. "We don't need your help."

"I have a plan too," Ben replied as he then passed through the portal, disappearing.

Richard, worried by Ben's potentially-misguided plan, followed through the portal and also disappeared.

Day 5 {8:00pm}

♣

The real Ben arrived back in the real world to blank looks and confusion from Jai's men. All had their weapons pointed at him, but no one made any moves.

"What is this?" Jai yelled, clearly confused that another Ben had suddenly appeared in the lab.

Despite his hands still being bound, the real Ben ran at Jai, intending to attack him. Ben managed to get close to Jai, but one of the armed men blocked his way him before he could finish his attack.

The situation in the lab was on the verge of chaos when Richard appeared through the portal. His appearance only further confounded the armed men and Richard knew that he only had a split-second in which to act.

Still at the control panel, Chris immediately noticed that Richard had the flasher box in his hand and pushed Morgan away from Richard's direction. Jai noticed the device too, but didn't understand what was about to happen.

Everyone else in the room watched Richard as he pressed the activator button on the flasher. Then…

Nothing happened.

Jai was about to take advantage of the miscue while Richard struggled with the flasher's activation button. Jai's men focused on Richard, readying their fire.

They would be too late though, as Richard's persistence paid off. The flasher sprang to life, with its core mechanism sending out high powered blasts of light. It draped the entire lab in blinding light. Jai and his men collapsed, stunned by the intense light.

As soon as the men were down, Richard let off the activator button. The other Ben, who had also been astute enough to look away, took off the control helmet as Morgan powered down the machine. The portal immediately ceased behind Richard.

"Tie them up!" Richard yelled to his family and the other Ben.

Chris, along with the other Ben, Morgan and Richard all raced throughout the lab. After they found makeshift bindings, they systematically bound each man, simultaneously confiscating their guns.

When everyone had been restrained, Richard hugged Chris and whispered into Chris's ear. "Good work."

"What about me?" Morgan said as she pushed up to Richard for a hug of her own.

"I told you that I'd be okay," Richard said, pulling her in for a tight embrace.

"And what about me?" Rachel said, standing up groggily in the back of the lab. She'd caught part of the flasher's light and had been partially knocked unconscious.

While everyone was distracted by Rachel, the real Ben made a break out of the lab, trying to escape down the hallway. Chris was the first to notice.

"Hey!" Chris yelled as he started after Ben.

Ben didn't get far though. A group of footsteps rumbled from the opposite direction, coming toward him down the hallway.

Those inside the lab heard shouts of "Get him!"

A moment later, a group of men in dark fatigues burst into the lab. Ben was in tow, having been apprehended by them. One of the men looked to Richard.

"You Richard Jennings?" the man asked.

"Yes," Richard replied.

"Major Cohagen," the man said, his tone military hard. "We had a report of some trouble?"

Cohagen and his men looked around the lab at the bound, still-unconscious bodies of Jai and his men. They noticed that the other Ben was similar in appearance to Ben, doing a double-take in the process. Richard realized how ridiculous the scene probably looked to the soldiers.

"What's going on here?" Cohagen asked.

Day 5 {9:00pm}

♣

It was some time before Richard was able to explain everything to the soldiers. They'd responded to Morgan's earlier call for help; the junior officer who'd skeptically taken her call had proved more efficient than she'd suspected. Talking at a high level, Richard had left out a few key details about the event, such as his son and himself traveling to a parallel universe and back.

By this point, Jai and his men had already been taken into custody and cleared out of the room. Cohagen came by for what would be a final bit of business. Richard knew that there would be more significant rounds of questioning in the coming days and that they'd need to get their stories straight. For now, the government men were collecting the basics of what had occurred.

"So," Cohagen said to Richard, referring to Mr. Chu. "You didn't know anything about that guy?"

"No," Richard said. Morgan and the other Ben both nodded behind him in agreement.

"Well," Cohagen said. "You may have helped us scratch the surface of the most-wanted ring of industrial espionage crooks in the world."

Richard tried to look impressed, his mind already back to thinking about the recent breakthroughs in their work.

"Glad we could help," he said.

Cohagen pointed to Ben, who was still being held in a corner of the room.

"He said that he was their mole," Cohagen said. "Awfully talkative guy."

"He feels guilty," Richard said. "This all got a lot more complicated than he'd expected."

Richard noticed that the real Ben was being led away in handcuffs. He knew that he needed a final conversation with his now-former partner.

"May I speak with him?" Richard asked.

Cohagen seemed hesitant, but decided to allow the request.

"Bring him over!" he called out to the soldiers who were leading Ben away.

"Thanks," Richard said.

Cohagen simply replied. "Keep it short."

The soldiers continued to stand guard nearby. Ben looked at Richard with the same ashamed expression that had marked his demeanor over the past several hours. As difficult as he'd felt his life had become, Ben knew that it was about to get worse. The gravity of his situation had only further become clear to Ben while he was being interrogated by the soldiers. He was considered a traitor.

"How did it ever come to this?" Richard asked, hoping somehow for a different answer than he'd been given before from Ben.

Ben could barely get his reply out without breaking down.

"I don't know Richard," Ben said. "It all got out of hand. I didn't mean for this to happen."

As tears rolled down Ben's cheeks, Richard kept his distance. Richard felt pity and loss toward Ben, but he also carried inside the sting of betrayal. Richard knew that, given the chance, Ben would have harmed Chris and those facts were hard to overlook.

Ben finally added. "Don't give it all away Richard."

"Give what away?" Richard asked.

"You know," Ben said. "Everything that we worked for and everything that has happened. No one is ready. Certainly not them."

Cohagen gave Richard a quizzical look over the remark and decided to end the conversation. He prodded Ben to get moving again. Richard was speechless as Ben was led away. He had still not been able to understand why Ben had betrayed him. Ben's last remarks weren't as difficult to decode.

Morgan walked up to Richard. Together, the pair watched as Ben exited the building with the guard. With Ben arrested,

Morgan held any biting remarks. As much as she'd disliked Ben, she knew that Richard was taking it hard. She hoped that time would heal some of those wounds.

"I was thinking that maybe I'd start helping you out more," Morgan said. "You're going to need an assistant, right?"

Morgan's question broke Richard's concentration. He looked to Morgan and then over at the other Ben and Chris. In many ways, the other Ben represented the Ben whom Richard had wished the real Ben still was.

Not to be overlooked though, Chris had grown up a great deal in Richard's eyes over the past few days.

"I have some ideas about that," Richard said. "Help here at the lab, I mean."

Morgan noticed Richard's gaze. It didn't take her long to figure out his intent.

"He'll need to go back you know," Morgan said, indicating the other Ben. "He has a family there."

"I know," Richard said. "Maybe we can work something out. An arrangement."

"And I still don't want Chris around the lab," Morgan said. "I mean, look what happened."

"Yes," Richard said, with playful sarcasm, his eyes excited with the possibilities of what might lay ahead. "Look what happened."

Morgan sighed.

Richard continued. "You know that we're not going to be able to lock him up forever. He's not a little boy anymore Morgan."

"He's still learning," Morgan said.

"He is," Richard smiled and said. "We'll help him to learn even more."

Morgan knew that Richard was right, even if her overprotective nature clashed with the logic. They'd have to work something out. Still pressing on Morgan's mind was wondering how they'd handle the project's government sponsors. They'd given some statements to Cohagen, but she knew that there would be even more explaining to do.

"When do you plan on telling them what's really going on with the machine?" she asked.

Richard took a long pause before answering. He'd just begun formulating that part of the plan himself.

"We're on to something massive here," Richard said. "I feel like we just won the lottery."

"You're not worried that Ben or one of those guys might have told the military all about what really happened here?"

"I don't think so," Richard said. "Jai and those men didn't seem to know what was truly happening. And Ben didn't tell them. In fact, I don't think that he wanted to."

"Why not?" Morgan asked.

"Something he said," Richard said. "The world isn't ready for this."

Morgan felt as though Richard might be acting impulsively based on recent events, but she also trusted his judgment.

"I don't know that we're ready for this either Richard," Morgan said.

"Probably not," Richard admitted. "We won't be able to keep this a secret forever, but we'll figure it out and enjoy it for now."

Morgan knew that this discovery had already changed their lives. It opened up cans of worms that they didn't want to face. She wondered if they could still maintain the kind of life that they'd lead before. It was doubtful. Chris would be affected and maybe even Rachel too. People couldn't invent a gateway to another dimension and not have their lives drastically change.

"So what's next?" Morgan asked Richard.

"We shouldn't have any problem getting funding." Richard said. "We'll hint at some things when we give our presentation. When we're ready, we'll let the sponsors in on it."

The other Ben approached them.

"So," he asked. "Any ideas on how we are going to get me home?"

"What do you think about working with us a little longer?" Richard suggested.

The other Ben chuckled. The idea both excited and overwhelmed him.

"You're holding me hostage?" he mused

"I'm going to need help," Richard said, more seriously. "And it isn't as though many people know this work. There's a lot about the machine that we don't understand."

Ben smiled at the suggestion. Given his earlier taste of working with Richard, he knew that it would be the ideal plan going forward.

"I'd love to," Ben said, then hesitating. "But my wife would kill me."

"I'm sure she would." Morgan interjected.

"Let's get that portal open," Ben said. "So that I can get back and find out."

Across the room, Rachel had been sharing stories with Chris about what had occurred in the real world during his absence. He'd largely let her do the talking.

"So then," Rachel said. "You crashed the pep rally."

Chris was skeptical. "That didn't strike you as odd?"

"Actually," Rachel replied. "It seemed like something that you might do. It was odd, but still…. Oh and you tried to cheat on our science test."

"I know."

Rachel was confused. "How?"

"Because I got away with it over there," Chris said, indicating the other world."

"Anyway," Rachel said, switching gears. "Stop avoiding my questions. What was I like?"

"I'm not really sure," Chris said. "We weren't friends."

Rachel wasn't surprised by the remarks, given her earlier discussions with the other Chris.

"That's what I found out," she said. "I'm sorry to hear that he wasn't exaggerating."

"It's okay," Chris said. "It sounded like I was a real jerk over there."

"Oh," Rachel said, smiling to herself. "Their Chris wasn't that bad."

Chris didn't notice Rachel's tone shift when she mentioned the other Chris. She missed him a little bit. He was Chris, but without some of the rough edges.

"I'm just glad that I don't act like that," Chris said.

Rachel took a moment to respond, finally saying. "You do."

"No I don't," Chris said, reflexively, almost without thinking.

"Chris," Rachel said. "You don't have any friends."

"I have friends," Chris said, annoyed

He knew that she was right, even if he didn't want to admit it. Rachel let him sit in silence for a second before she continued.

"I have you," Chris continued.

Rachel was touched, but she wasn't letting him off the hook that easily.

"Glad you noticed," she said. "Haven't you ever wondered why it's just me?"

"Maybe," Chris admitted. He hadn't thought about it overly-hard, but he had sometimes wondered why his antics never seemed to win him any new friends. "Why didn't you tell me that before?"

"I didn't want to hurt you," Rachel said. "I figured you'd freak out and just get rid of me."

Chris looked sadly at Rachel, knowing that she might have been right, at least in the past.

"I'm sorry that I made you feel that way," Chris said. "So, everyone at school just thinks that I'm a big jerk?"

Rachel gave Chris a half-smile. "Most think that you're just annoying."

"Huh," Chris replied, still processing the revelation. "And why do you put up with me?"

"Well," Rachel said, softly. "After someone gets past all the other stuff with you, you're a pretty good guy."

"I'd like to think so," Chris quipped.

"And," Rachel added. "It's never boring with you. But after all this, I don't know that I need any more excitement for a while."

"Me either," Chris said.

"Oh," Rachel said, remembering something more. "One more thing."

"What now?" Chris asked, groaning.

"You might want to steer clear of Jessica at school."

Chris immediately assumed that he knew why.

"The other Chris thought that I was dating her here?" he guessed.

"For a little while," Rachel said. "Don't worry though, Tyler already beat you up."

Day 5 {11:00pm}

♣

Two hours later, Richard, Morgan, Chris, and the other Ben had gotten the machine running again. They powered it up with Richard wearing the control helmet and the others managing the control panel.

The other Morgan and other Chris were glimpsed in the viewing chamber. They were still in their lab, still trying to make sense of what to do next.

Chris walked up to take a spot at the control panel. Ben shook Chris's hand and pulled him in for a hug.

"Thanks for everything," he said. "You have no idea what all of this has meant to me."

Chris thought back on his own adventures and agreed.

"Actually," Chris said. "I think I do. Say hello to everyone for me."

"Maybe I'll see you soon?" Ben suggested.

Chris smiled, knowing that it wasn't truly goodbye, at least not for long.

Richard yelled to Morgan. "I'm ready!"

Morgan and Chris inputted the commands to generate the portal. The portal flashed opened with a flicker, stabilizing after a few seconds. Ben tentatively approached it at first, but then confidently walked through it, disappearing.

Through the viewing chamber, they watched for Ben's reemergence into the parallel universe. After a few minutes, they witnessed him stride into the lab. The other Morgan and the other Chris were overjoyed to see him suddenly reappear.

Soon after the reunion, Morgan eased the machine's power levels down and disabled the portal. Richard was exhausted and removed the control helmet from his head, setting it on top of the control panel.

"You didn't tell me that I was prettier over there," Morgan said playfully to Richard.

"I didn't have to," Richard said, not taking her bait.

Morgan gave Richard a quick peck of a kiss and said to Chris and Rachel, "Let's go home."

Chris was still too excited to want to call it a night though.

"What are you talking about?" Chris said. "We're just getting started."

Epilogue:
In The Shadows

♣

Several rooftops away from the real world's lab, a small team of Mr. Chu's men retreated into the night. They had served as backup for the raid, but they had never had a chance to take part in the operation. Rather, from their vantage point, they had seen Jai being led outside, along with Mr. Chu after it was too late.

Their orders, under such circumstances, had been to abort the mission. As they pulled out though, each of the men knew that there were contingency plans waiting for them.

As it was for those inside the lab, the men in the shadows recognized that it was only the beginning.

Acknowledgements

▼

This book would not have been possible without the narrative and editorial support of:

JoAnn Jacobusse

Ian Dickenson

Judy Thofson

35307003R00195

Made in the USA
Charleston, SC
04 November 2014